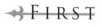

FIRST

MW00639524

USA TODAY BESTSELLING AUTHOR

KRISTEN
PAINTER

SUCKS TO BE ME:
A Paranormal Women's Fiction Novel
First Fangs Club, Book One

Copyright © 2020 Kristen Painter

Published in the United States of America

Huge thanks to Shalene Schmidt for coming up with this title!

CHAPTER 1

Twenty-seven years of being married to the mob had taught Belladonna Barrone a lot of things. Firstly, she hated the life. That one had come first and fast.

Secondly, getting out meant being willing to risk your life. And possibly the life of a loved one.

Thirdly, the police at your door was never a good thing, unless they were there to finally arrest your low-life, criminal husband.

She opened the door, praying that was the case. She was bleary-eyed but awake from the knocking and the shock of seeing a couple of uniforms standing there. She rubbed at her eyes. "Evening, Officers."

"Evening, ma'am. Are you Mrs. Barrone?"

"I am, and if you're looking for Joe, he's not here. Unfortunately, I have no idea where he is."

His arrest had been bound to happen sooner or later. She just wished it had been sooner. A lot sooner. In fact, she'd prayed for it.

The officer closest to her, his solemn expression unchanging, was young and earnest. "Mrs. Barrone?"

"Please, Donna is fine." Unlike the rest of the Villachi family, she had no problem with police.

1

"Yes, ma'am. Your husband was in a car accident this evening."

She hadn't thought much about him not being home, even at one in the morning. Joe did what he wanted, when he wanted, and nothing she could ever say would change that. "Is he hurt? What hospital is he in?"

The officer's gaze looked past her just a little bit, and she knew what he was going to say before he said it. "I'm sorry, ma'am. He didn't make it."

She stared at the officers, the words rattling around in her head but failing to process. "He didn't make what?"

"He didn't survive the crash."

A numbness came over her. "You mean…he's dead."

The officer at the back nodded. "We're very sorry for your loss."

She nodded, reaching out for the support of the doorframe. She'd imagined this, imagined how simple it would make things, but it had also seemed so cut and dried in her fantasies. The easy way out of this life. But now that it had actually happened, none of that felt true.

Only a monster could be happy about a thing like this. And at worst, she considered herself a desperate woman. Or maybe she was a monster, because she wasn't instantly overcome with grief. She wasn't joyous either, though. Joe had been a good man once. Hadn't he? At least she liked to think that.

She took a breath. "Do you need me to…identify the body?"

"No, ma'am. There was…" He cleared his throat and seemed to be searching for words.

The second officer stepped up. "The vehicle was engulfed in flames for quite some time before we arrived on scene. We won't have dental confirmation for a few days, but—"

Her knees buckled at the awful image. The closest officer caught her elbow. "Can we call someone to come stay with you?"

She shook her head. "No. I'll…I'll be fine. Thank you."

They nodded and left.

She closed the door, then turned and pressed her back to it. Joe was gone. It was terrible. But it also wasn't. She leaned against the door for a long while, waiting for tears, but they never came. Not for the man she'd been trying to escape for most of her married life.

* Five days later *

One funeral mass down, one graveside interment ceremony to go. Donna was just watching the clock now, counting down the seconds until she was completely and finally free, and really hoping she didn't have a hot flash before the funeral ended.

"Joseph Barrone was a good man…"

She barely managed not to roll her eyes at that opening line. The priest had to know that wasn't true, didn't he? But then, she understood that Father Leonardo couldn't very well tell the truth. Just like she couldn't very well leave.

This *was* her husband's funeral, after all. Even if a man-sized lump of charcoal was the only thing in that box. Dental records had confirmed it was him.

So until she could leave, she retreated into her head until it was over. In this crowd, it was the only truly safe place to be.

She put her hands flat against her stomach, against the soft knit of her dress, and took a breath. She looked as good as could be expected today. That was something, she supposed. But then, it was hard to go wrong with classic black from Dolce & Gabbana. And she'd always looked great in black. But retaining this figure at age forty-nine? That took work, as any woman knew. Maintaining a size four was a full-time job. At least she imagined it was.

After two kids, the best she could manage was an eight, and that was with Pilates, Saturday yoga at the park, jogging, some free weights, and general carb avoidance, which was hellaciously hard to do with the amount of pasta and bread consumed in this community. Because of that, she also had to fast occasionally on top of the rest of the standard stuff. Beauty meant sacrifice and pain.

And she wasn't even including the other things. The more invasive things. The *med spa* things.

She glanced at the other women in attendance at her husband's funeral. They were all going through the same routine she was to stay in shape and hold on to their looks. Some with better results than others. It was expected of the wives. After all, none of them had jobs outside the home. And the assumption was that the

SUCKS TO BE ME

better a woman looked, the better her husband must be doing.

The Mafia was old-fashioned like that.

So the women worked hard at being their best selves and looking as close to a million dollars as they could. Because, really, that was part of the job of a mob wife.

All except for Lucinda Villachi, Joe's sister. Donna was pretty sure Lucinda had never seen the inside of a Pilates studio and never would. At best, she'd had a few units of Botox. But not lately, that was for sure. Not with those major-league elevens furrowed like two freshly dug ditches between her under-groomed brows.

But Lucinda wasn't just Donna's sister-in-law. She was also the wife of Big Tony, aka Anthony Villachi, the boss, and she lorded that over the rest of the wives with the kind of head-tilted, nose-in-the-air arrogance that spoke volumes about how she perceived herself. And where the other wives rated on her status scale.

Whatever. Donna almost rolled her eyes again. She was done with this life, these people, this family-by-marriage. Done with these manufactured levels of respect. Done with these criminal men and their shady business. Done with all of it.

And not just because her husband had died in a car accident. She'd already been planning to divorce him. His being burned beyond all recognition just saved her the paperwork.

FBI agent Rico Medina wasn't as pleased as she was about Joe's demise, however, seeing as how she'd also been planning on turning state's evidence and nailing this whole crew to the wall. But with Joe dead...she had second thoughts about becoming a key witness for the prosecution.

Christina, her college junior daughter, sniffed and wrapped her arm around Donna's. Donna patted Christina's hand. Christina knew what was what. She'd flat out told her father it was time to go straight the last time they'd argued, which had barely been a month ago.

On Donna's left, Joe Jr. looked straight ahead with military precision, stoic and unblinking in the face of all this mortality. He'd gone into the Air Force because it was as far away from his father and the family as he could get. At least that's what he'd told Donna, and she believed him.

The kids were going to be fine. They'd figured out a long time ago their father was not a good man.

But their presence underlined why she was reconsidering her agreement with the FBI.

They were phenomenal kids. Christina was about to enter her last year of college, and Joe Jr. had just pinned on first lieutenant. Now that Joe was gone, Donna wasn't about to go into WITSEC and leave them behind, which meant that if she still went through with providing the FBI with the kind of testimony necessary to take the Villachi family down, she would put herself—and the kids—in serious danger.

Big Tony hadn't gotten where he'd been by being the forgiving sort.

Then again, if the main players of the Villachi

syndicate were all behind bars, she figured her life expectancy would be better. She hoped, anyway. Plus, she planned to move out of Jersey and relocate to the Florida Panhandle.

Joe Jr. was stationed at Eglin Air Force Base, and she knew Christina wouldn't have a problem visiting her mom at a beachfront condo. Donna would bleach her hair, change her name, and blend in. She'd also make sure her building had good security. With the life insurance money, she'd be able to afford it. Good thing, too, because her marketable skills were pretty minimal. But that wasn't about to stop her.

Like for everything else in life, she had a plan.

What she hadn't planned on was standing graveside for quite so long. Her Louboutins were killing her. Granted, they were beautiful shoes, and good shoes were part of the mob-wife uniform, but forty-nine-year-old feet had only so many hours of stiletto time in them.

The priest droned on about what a loss Joe's death was to the community, and she went back to checking out the other wives.

Maria Zapatti was the only other woman besides Donna in a veil. It was a nice touch, and she appreciated it. But then, Maria tried harder. Her husband had only just been made, and she wanted to be liked. She looked up to Donna too. Or had. Now that Joe was gone, Maria might not care what Donna thought.

Donna didn't blame her. Joe could have helped Maria's husband's mobility in the family. Donna, not so much. Joe had been the second-in-command, after all.

Teresa DePalma's forehead looked especially smooth. And the crow's-feet around her eyes were gone. A recent peel? Or she was upping her injectables. Good for her. Donna was doing only a little Botox between the brows at the moment, but she was fully prepared to go broader when it became necessary.

Which was going to be very soon. Time was no friend to any of them.

Just like she was no friend to any of these women. Sure, she was chummy on the surface, doing all the required things. Lunches, spin class, family dinners, shopping trips, the occasional girls' weekend in Atlantic City, but she wasn't that close to any of the wives on purpose. She wanted distance. Thankfully, after twenty-seven years, she was about to get some.

Why had it taken so long?

Lots of reasons. But why not start with the big one? Fear.

She'd been six years into this marriage before she realized what was really going on. Call her naïve, but she'd actually believed her husband was in the construction business. Yes, she'd thought her brother-in-law was shady, but not her husband.

Once she figured out that Joe was in as deep as Big Tony, fear set in. Especially when she started putting two and two together and understood that some of the people who moved away over the years didn't really move away so much as they were done away with.

These guys her husband associated with were real-life, flesh-and-blood bad guys. Gangsters. Mafioso. Killers when necessary. So was her husband. Now, she wasn't sure he'd killed anyone. But her eyes had been opened a long time ago. Joe was an ambitious man. She had no problem believing he'd do whatever Big Tony told him to. Including murder.

In those early days of revelation, the knowledge of who her husband really was made her skin crawl when she lay in bed next to him at night.

Over time, she learned to compartmentalize some of that as a way of coping. But that didn't mean she was any less disgusted by him. Or the entire Villachi crew.

She swallowed and lifted her chin as the memories swamped her with old emotions. She was glad for her veil and the little bit of separation it gave her from those around her.

Anyone who thought the mob was romantic was an idiot.

So that was the answer. Fear. That was why she stayed with Joe. Not because she was afraid for her own life, but because she was afraid for her kids. What would happen to them? If she left with them, there was no way Joe wouldn't hunt her down, hurt her, and take them back. Maybe he'd let her go with Christina, but Joe Jr.? Not a chance.

And what if something happened to her? Accidentally or otherwise. Who would raise her kids? Some chirpy little trophy wife who thought life as a Soprano was super cool?

Donna wasn't going to lie. On the surface, things looked good because they were good. They had more money than they could spend. The kids wanted for nothing. Still didn't. Her closet looked like a Neiman's pop-up event. They had the big house, the flashy cars, and a weird kind of respect from the rest of the community, which treated them like benevolent dictators. For example, they never waited for a table at a local restaurant. She called for a hair or nail or spa appointment and always got one at the exact time she wanted it.

And they got a lot of stuff gratis. Gifts for no reason other than to curry favor with Joe. Flowers sometimes. But food, mostly. Turkeys and hams at Christmas and Easter, always. But then all throughout the year, things arrived. Imported sausages. Boxes of Italian cookies and pastries. Cases of wine. Once, a six-month lease on a Land Rover, which Joe sent back because he thought the car might be bugged. Another time, handblown wineglasses with the initial B etched on them. Even a basket of toys, treats, and catnip for Lucky, their cat.

But none of the reverence and graft erased the dirty underbelly of who her husband was or what he was involved with. If anything, it just made the depths of his involvement that much clearer.

At first, she didn't ask questions. She didn't want to know more than she'd already figured out. Not knowing felt safer somehow. Head-in-the-sand syndrome, she guessed.

Then she'd shaken the sand out of her ears and decided she needed some kind of protection.

Some kind of exit strategy.

She didn't want to be married to the mob. Her hand went to the crucifix she always wore, a gift from her sister's trip to the Vatican. Donna was a good Catholic girl who knew the difference between right and wrong.

Heaven and hell.

More than anything, she wanted a way out before the option was taken from her.

So she started listening. Taking notes. Collecting evidence. Anything she could safely do to get dirt on Joe and the whole crew. For future use.

But when was that future going to be the present? She asked herself that so many times it became a mantra that played on repeat like a soundtrack to everything she did.

Then the answer to that question finally arrived three months ago, and she knew the time to get out was coming.

The priest was saying his final words. Rosanella Gambisto was at a right angle from Donna, standing with her husband, Bobbie the Bull. Rosie had tried very hard to become Donna's BFF, but Donna had kept her at arm's length. Bobbie was the Villachis' cleaner. A hit man.

Donna didn't need a close connection to someone like that. Too bad, because Rosie seemed genuine, whereas these other women would probably stab her in the back for a new Gucci clutch if the opportunity presented itself.

Mafia wives were an interesting lot. They liked to say they were tough cookies. And they were. They had to be. This life had a way of chewing a person up if they didn't grow a thick skin. Donna had seen it happen. Wives who couldn't handle the family *situation* got divorced out of it, then they lost custody of their kids, and sometimes they disappeared.

It was like something out of a movie. Except it was real life. *Her* life.

Rosie looked over at her, her smile not reaching her eyes. Donna offered the same kind of smile right back. Appearances had to be kept up. At least for a little while longer.

No matter how much she'd wanted to be rid of Joe, this was still a sad day. Her kids had lost their father, after all. She'd lost a man she had truly loved once upon a time.

She had loved him, hadn't she? She must have. She wouldn't have married him otherwise.

As people paid their last respects, offering her their condolences, she went a little numb to it all. She still had to deal with people at the house. She didn't want that, but there was nothing she could do about it.

That's just how things were done.

Thankfully, her sister, Sister Mary Lazarus Immaculata, aka Camille, would be there to help keep people in order. The effect of the presence of a nun on a predominately Catholic crowd was astonishing.

Cammie, as Donna always called her sister regardless of the name she'd chosen when she'd joined the convent, knew all about Joe and the Villachis too. It was why she hadn't come to the funeral, opting instead to stay at the house and get things ready for the crowd that would be pouring in.

Cammie had never liked Joe. Not since day one. But she was older and wiser, and Donna had been young and dumb and swept off her feet by Joe's kind words and sweet, generous gestures that had made her feel like a princess.

She'd never imagined he'd turn into a cold, calculating man who carried a gun and broke the law for a living. She suspected he'd even had a couple girlfriends too. That was pretty common among these men. She'd never been able to prove it. And she'd tried, mostly because that was the kind of thing that would really help in a divorce but following a member of the family was a good way to get into deep trouble.

She hadn't been ready to go that far. Not yet. Although she'd been getting close. And Rico had promised her protection.

Didn't matter now. Not with Joe being lowered six feet into Jersey soil.

She and the kids dropped white roses on the casket, then made their way to the car. It took forever. So many people wanted to offer their condolences.

Finally they were in the car, and the driver took them back to the house. It sat back from the road on an estate lot, giving them a little more privacy and a much longer driveway. Cars were already lined up along the length of the horseshoe drive.

She sighed at the sight of so many vehicles.

"It'll be over soon, Mom," Joe Jr. said.

She nodded. "I wish it was over now."

"Me too," Christina added. "These people are all so phony."

She put her hand on her daughter's leg and shot her a look. They didn't know the driver, didn't know his loyalties, and Donna always erred on the side of caution. The Villachi family had eyes and ears everywhere. "Honey, that's just your grief talking. These people all loved your father very much."

Christina seemed to get her mother's drift and looked out the window instead of saying anything else.

That small gesture, the need to silence her daughter for her own good, refueled Donna's hatred for this life. It was a suffocating way to live.

But not for much longer.

They headed inside, and while the kids went into the living room where people were already gathered, Donna veered into the kitchen.

Cammie was there in her black and white habit, directing the catering service and handling everything like a pro. But then, who was going to back-talk a nun?

Donna smiled. "Hi, Sis."

"Hi, Sis," Cammie said back. She opened her arms and welcomed Donna in. "How was it?"

"It was…a nice ceremony. And it's thankfully over." Donna closed her eyes for the briefest of moments and leaned into her sister before pulling out of the hug. "How are things here?"

"Fine." Cammie slanted her eyes toward the front of the house. "There's quite a crowd out there already."

Donna nodded. "The cars are on both sides of the driveway. I'm glad I hired a valet service." It was what everyone did for big gatherings. Then she leaned in. "But I really don't want them here past five."

"I don't think Lucky does either. Poor cat. Pretty

sure he's hiding upstairs in Christina's room." Cammie smiled. "But you leave that to me."

"Poor Lucky. I'm sure the noise is freaking him out. Although I'd like to be up there hiding with him. Thank you so much for being here today. I know you don't want to be."

Cammie put her hands lightly on her sister's cheeks. "Belladonna, I love you. I would do anything for you."

"I know. I feel the same about you."

Cammie let her go. "Now, you should do some mingling and let people tell you their favorite Joe stories so they can feel like they did their part."

"I will. But not without a—"

Cammie handed her a glass of merlot.

Donna smiled. "You're going to make saint in no time."

CHAPTER 2

D onna did what she had to do. Mingled, drank a measured amount of wine (too much, and she worried the things she really wanted to say would slip out), and made copious mental notes about all the things she wanted to discuss with her therapist, Dr. Ursula Goldberg, at their next session.

Yes, being a Mafia wife had driven her to therapy. Part of it was because of the doctor-patient confidentiality. She needed someone she could unburden herself to, and La Goldberg had become that person. Plus, there was something balancing about spending her husband's ill-gotten gains to tell someone else about what a terrible person he was.

Rosie walked up to her with the same sympathetic smile that she'd been getting from everyone today. "How are you doing?"

Same question everyone was asking too. Donna made herself smile, but not too much. "I'm hanging in there." She'd said that more times than she could count in the last two hours.

"You need anything, you just call me or Bobbie. Anytime, night or day. We're here for you."

"Thanks, Rosie." Donna appreciated Rosie's desire

to be friends, but Donna just couldn't get past her husband. Bobbie the Bull made Joe look like a choirboy. "I should check in with the caterers in the kitchen. Thanks for coming."

"Of course." Rosie flashed a familiar compassionate smile.

She was halfway to the kitchen when Vinnie Positano blocked her path. He was one of Big Tony's lunks. Nice enough guy, but not enough brain cells to be much more than hired muscle, that was for sure.

"Mrs. Barrone, my sympathies. Joseph was a good man." He shrugged, spreading his hands. He spoke with his whole body. Like a marionette dancing on strings.

"Thank you, Vinnie."

"Yeah, so, uh, Big Tony would like to see you."

Donna looked around. "I'm right here. Where is he?"

Vinnie jerked his thumb over his shoulder. The movement sent a ripple of motion down his body. "In Joe's office."

She stiffened. That was Joe's private space. Her space now. Big Tony had no right to be in there, but of course he didn't think that way. "Oh?"

"Yeah, he'd like to talk to you in private like."

"I see." She had no desire to talk to Big Tony anywhere, but especially not alone. She considered asking Vinnie what this was about, but the chances of him knowing were slim. No doubt this had something to do with Joe's death. What else could it be? She nodded, doing her best to hide her reluctance. "Okay."

Vinnie gestured for her to go ahead of him. Like

this wasn't her house and she didn't already have the right-of-way. She plastered an appropriate grieving-widow expression on her face and walked back to Joe's office. Her heels clicked on the inlaid marble floors.

She found Big Tony sitting behind Joe's desk with one of Joe's Cuban cigars tucked in the corner of his mouth. The nerve. He smiled at her and put the cigar in the ashtray. "Belladonna. I am so sorry for your loss. For all of our loss. Joe was a good man. A strong soldier. A trusted friend and brother-in-law. He will be deeply missed."

She nodded and swallowed, words escaping her in the moment. Appropriate words, anyway. Two more of his lunks flanked him, Nick and Franco. She wasn't sure why they were necessary, but it sure made things seem very official.

A cold trickle went down her spine. Nothing about this felt good.

He pointed to the seat on the other side of the desk. "Please. Sit. We have things to discuss."

She sat. "We do?"

He nodded, his thick, sausage fingers steepled under his chin. "What are your plans?"

She hadn't expected that question, not so soon. But she was prepared for it. She liked to think she was prepared for anything. That was how she survived. She shook her head and stared at her lap like she was trying not to cry. "Joe was my world."

She heard Big Tony snap his fingers. A few seconds later, a box of tissues appeared under her nose. She took one, to be polite, then dabbed at her eyes before glancing up. "Right now, I'm just going to concentrate on getting through this very difficult time."

The great concern on his face was proof he was as good an actor as she was. "I understand."

"I might go away for a while. With Christina in college and Joe Jr. in the Air Force, there's no one here for me to take care of anymore. A little trip, maybe." She paused like that was a brand-new idea. "A little trip might do me good." A little trip she'd never come back from.

He held up one hand. "That's a wonderful idea. Maybe back to the old country? You could take some of the girls with you."

Not a chance in hell was she going anywhere with those women. She sniffed and nodded, adding a small smile for effect. "That would be nice."

He picked up the cigar and used it to punctuate his next sentence. "But here's the thing."

She just barely hung on to her smile.

"Joe left some unfinished business."

"He did?" That was news to her. She'd been trying to keep tabs on Joe's comings and goings so she could tell Rico what was happening.

Big Tony pursed his lips. "He did."

She shrugged. "I wouldn't know anything about that. I never asked about his work, and frankly, he never shared any of it with me."

"Good." Big Tony nodded. "A wife that knows the importance of her husband's privacy, that's commendable. But you don't need to know details to do what I need you to do."

"You need me to do something?"

"I do." His pinkie ring flashed in the light of the desk lamp. It was a two-carat diamond in the mouth of a lion.

She couldn't say no. Well, she could, but that wouldn't be the healthiest thing to do. "I probably need to know a *few* details if I'm going to do whatever it is you need me to do."

Big Tony was stone-faced for a moment, then he grinned and let out a big honk of a laugh. "Yeah, I guess you do."

The lunks laughed, too, right on cue. It was like being on the worst reality show ever. Which was saying a lot, considering how bad most reality shows were.

Big Tony tucked the cigar back into his mouth, then flattened his hands on the desk. "You're a beautiful woman, Belladonna. I understand that you will eventually want to remarry and—"

That was never going to happen again. Her face responded before she could stop it.

But Big Tony just nodded, reading it differently. "I know the idea seems impossible right now, even unsavory, but beautiful women don't stay single long. Do this job for me, and your future is your own. Do you understand what I'm saying?"

He was offering her a way out. A clean break. That was what he was saying, wasn't it? Hope unlike anything she'd felt before spilled through her. She nodded. "This would be a kindness between us," she said. "A way of…saying goodbye."

His nod was slow and methodical. "A kindness. I like that. And that's exactly what this would be. Unless you marry back into the family. Capisce?"

"Capisce." That would not be happening, ever. "When do you need me to do this job?"

"Tomorrow night." He chomped down on the cigar. "Will that work for your schedule?"

He was so considerate. "Sure. The kids are both leaving in the morning because of school and duty, so that's fine."

"Perfect. One of the boys will drop off a package by noon, along with the place and time to deliver it. That's all." He got up from the desk chair, making it creak as the hydraulics relaxed. There was a reason they called him Big Tony.

A package to deliver. That didn't sound so bad. Especially if she didn't think about what might be in it. Regardless, running this errand would be a small price to pay for freedom. She rose to leave. "Okay."

He came around the desk and took her hands, holding them both together in his giant mitts. "Words aren't enough to express how much we all feel Joe's loss. Know that you are always family to us. If you need anything, you have only to ask."

He was so full of it she was surprised flies weren't buzzing over his head. "That's so kind of you. Thank you for all you've done for us."

"God bless." He gestured at Vinnie, who'd stayed by the door.

Vinnie opened the door, and Big Tony left, then Nick and Franco followed. She stood there for a moment, contemplating what had happened. But only for a moment. She had a house full of people, and she could contemplate later.

She walked out of the office and straight into Lucinda.

Her sneer smelled like garlic and Chianti. "I know you were in there with my husband."

She had to be kidding.

Donna tried to tamp down her irritation. She just had to maintain this façade a little longer. "Yes, I was. And with Vinnie too. And Nick and Franco. Tony was offering his condolences and letting me know how much you are all here for me if I need something."

Lucinda's eyes narrowed, accentuating her already impressive crow's-feet. "You think you're going to make a play for him, you got another think coming. I will cut you. Do you understand?"

She was a real barrel of monkeys. The rabid kind that flung poop at people. "Lucinda, I would never disrespect you like that. And I promise you, I have no designs on any man, but especially not my brother-in-law. And for the love of Saint Francis, Joe's not even cold. Why don't you let me mourn him in peace before making accusations like that? Or if you want, we can go get Big Tony, and you can ask him what we were talking about. If you don't believe me."

Donna was completely fed up. She'd definitely let some of that irritation slip into her tone, but the threat of getting Big Tony involved was all it took to get Lucinda to back up. If there was one person she was afraid of, it was her husband.

Lucinda lifted her chin. Donna took some satisfaction in spotting one long black hair jutting out from underneath it. "Just know I'm watching you."

"Keep a book handy, because you're going to get very bored, very fast." Donna turned and walked away before she said anything more. To think that Lucinda would confront her like that at her husband's funeral in her house…the woman was made of nerves and brass.

Donna made it through another hour or so of small talk and rambling condolences, then hit a wall. She couldn't take another moment of pretending to care about these people or appearances or acting appropriately.

She wanted to drink wine with her sister and her children, then fall into bed and worry about tomorrow…tomorrow.

Cammie appeared at her elbow. "You have that look."

"What look?" Donna asked.

"Like you're about to tell everyone to go copulate themselves."

Donna snorted. Her sister had such an interesting way with words since becoming a nun. "The thought crossed my mind."

"Go upstairs and chill. Use the back steps so no one sees you. I'll get rid of everyone."

Donna gave Cammie an incredulous look.

"Trust me."

"I do. But there's a little bit of holy fear thrown in."

"Probably smart." Cammie grinned, then pointed toward the back steps. "Go."

"Going." With that, Donna went through the kitchen, pulling her shoes off as she went, and straight up to her bedroom.

She walked through the double doors and stood there looking around. Joe's aftershave lingered. There was so much of him in this room. In this house. She tossed the shoes toward her closet to deal with later.

She had to sell the house. There was no part of her that wanted to live with all these memories. Too many of them weren't good.

"Mom?"

At her daughter's voice, she turned. Christina and Joe Jr. stood in the doorway. Christina had Lucky in her arms. "Hey, guys."

Joe Jr. glanced toward the downstairs. "Aunt Cammie told us to come up here. She's getting rid of everyone."

"Should I even ask how?"

Christina smiled. "She announced she'd be leading everyone in a half hour of the Holy Rosary, followed by another half hour of Our Fathers. The place is clearing out like Edison's is giving away free cannolis."

Donna laughed. "I couldn't love her more if I tried."

Joe Jr. stepped into the room. "Are you okay?"

She nodded. "Yes. Just thinking about how much I have to do." She was not going to tell them about the deal she'd made with Big Tony. At least not until it was done and over with. And even then maybe not. "You know I'm probably going to sell the house. Eventually."

Christina shrugged and put Lucky down. He went straight for the bed. "It's a lot of house for one person."

Joe Jr. nodded. "Yeah. It's too much. Plus…there's a lot of Dad here."

"I was just thinking the same thing." These kids were so smart. So capable. She got weepy then, not because of Joe, but because of how wonderful the kids were. "I love you two so much."

Christina sniffled, and they ended up in a group hug.

Donna hesitated, wondering if maybe she should tell them about Big Tony's promise of freedom, but then Cammie walked in.

"Everyone's gone except for the caterers, who are finishing the cleanup. They've been cleaning as they go, so they should be gone in twenty minutes or less."

Donna wiped away an errant tear and smiled. "You're a miracle worker."

Cammie put her hands together and glanced upward. "I'm just a conduit for miracles."

The kids laughed, and the tearfulness was forgotten.

Donna flexed her toes against the thick rug. The ache was finally leaving her arches. "What do you kids want to do tonight, seeing as how you both have to leave in the morning? Go out to eat somewhere?"

Cammie put her hands on her hips. "Do you know how much food is downstairs?"

Christina shook her head. "But none of it is Tressler's ice cream."

"No, it is not," Joe Jr. added. "And I could maul some rocky road."

"Tressler's it is." Donna would have to go for an

extra-long run in the morning to burn off all those delicious carbs, but it would be worth it to spend this quality time with her kids. She was well aware of how rare an evening out with her two children was getting to be. "Cammie, you in?"

"I wouldn't miss it."

If Joe were alive, she would have had to ask if it was all right that they go to Tressler's. Now, she could go anywhere and do anything she liked. No permission needed. An odd lightness filled Donna's spirit. Was this what freedom felt like? It had been so long, she couldn't be sure. But it was a feeling she could very easily get used to.

All that was keeping her from it was one little package delivery.

CHAPTER 3

The package wasn't that little, but it wasn't that big either. It was a medium-sized duffel bag. Black with black straps. Nothing special. From the weight of the bag and the angles that showed through the nylon sides, she guessed drugs or money. Whichever it was, it was most likely wrapped in smaller bundles.

That was as far as her interest in the package went. This was a means to an end. A very worthwhile end. Freedom.

She'd left the bag by the door to the garage, put it out of her mind, and went for her run to work off the pistachio fudge ice cream from last night.

Upon her return, she noticed that Vinnie's cologne, which he apparently bought and applied in ample quantities, still lingered in the air.

He had arrived about five minutes after the kids and Cammie had gone. Almost like he'd been watching the house, waiting for them to leave.

Donna tried not to dwell on that possibility.

He'd handed her the duffel, given her the address of the drop-off and told her at least three times that she wasn't supposed to look inside. "We'll know if that lock has been tampered with," he'd said, pointing at the small brass padlock holding the zippers together.

She'd just nodded and assured him she wasn't about to touch anything. That finally seemed enough to satisfy Vinnie, and he'd left.

That cologne, though. Whuff.

She'd grabbed a bottle of water and gone up to take a well-earned hot shower. Lucky was still asleep on the bed where she'd left him, curled up like a house tiger.

After her shower, however, she wasn't left with much to do. The kitchen had already been cleaned after the breakfast she'd made for Cammie and the kids. There wasn't much laundry to speak of either. Sheets, maybe.

But that wasn't going to fill her day.

She supposed she could call her therapist, but her regular appointment wasn't today, and La was pretty busy. The only way Donna was likely to get in earlier was if La had a cancellation.

Which was unlikely. So that was out.

And the drop-off wasn't until nine tonight. What was she going to do until then? Not that she wanted to work out after her run, but she couldn't exactly go to the gym or show up at the yoga studio, since she was supposed to be the grieving widow. Same with getting her hair or nails done, neither of which she needed anyway. Going out would just invite questions and more condolences, and she didn't want to deal with more of that after yesterday.

If one more person asked her how she was doing or gave her that sad smile...she shook her head. She was doing great. Truth was, Joe's death was the best thing that had happened to her since her kids were born.

But she couldn't say that.

She stood in the living room, staring out the big windows that overlooked the expanse of front yard. Being in the house alone was odd now that the reason for being alone was her newly acquired widowhood.

The alone part wasn't new. She'd been alone in the house for a few hours almost every day since she and Joe had gotten married. Joe went out a lot.

But since the kids had gone off to live their own lives, those spans of time were always punctuated by Joe's return. Or preparing for Joe's return. Or something that had to do with him. There were always meals to fix for him, functions to get ready for because of who he was, events she was required to show her face. And then there was her personal schedule of appointments necessary to maintain herself at the level Joe expected.

None of that existed anymore. The family no longer influenced her day-to-day activities.

If she wanted to stop working out and watching what she ate and coloring her hair and having her eyebrows done and getting things waxed and injected and do nothing but sit in front of the television in sweatpants and eating cheese puffs out of a Costco-sized vat, she could.

If she wanted to get a tattoo and streak her hair pink and go out dancing every night, she could do that too.

She could join the convent and keep Cammie company. Would they let her keep Lucky, though?

Didn't matter. The convent was not for her. Point was, nothing was off-limits.

What an odd feeling. It was heady, having charge of her own life after twenty-seven years, but it also made her feel a little at sea. The urge to go off the deep end and do something crazy was there, for sure.

She wouldn't, of course. That wasn't her nature. Sticking to the plan was what worked for her. But if she wanted to veer from that, she could. Her life was her own.

Okay, except for the drop-off. That wasn't something she could veer from. But that was one evening. It would take her forty-five minutes to drive out to the old industrial park where she was supposed to leave the duffel, which would take all of five minutes, then forty-five minutes to drive home. Two hours, tops, and she was done with this business.

All that remained was to figure out the appropriate timing of her plan for the rest of her life. How soon could she resume some of her usual routine? How soon could she put the house up for sale? Get rid of Joe's stuff? Go to Florida to condo-shop?

And when would the insurance check arrive?

Actually, she knew that one. About thirty days after she sent them the certificate of death, which she'd put in the mail this morning, the insurance company should pay out.

Thirty days. She could do that standing on her head. Well, not literally. She hadn't quite mastered that move in yoga. But figuratively? She'd done twenty-seven years with Joe. For a month, she would wear dark clothes and lie low and be every inch the woman in mourning. She would catch up on her reading, get the house ready for sale, and daydream about her new life.

A month was cake.

She glanced toward the kitchen. Speaking of cake, there was half of a cannoli cake from Edison's Bakery on the counter. She'd tried to get the kids to take food with them, but they hadn't wanted to, saying it didn't travel well. Donna understood. It was funeral food. A reminder that their father was gone.

At least Cammie had taken two boxes of Italian cookies back to the convent with her. The sisters would enjoy those.

But that cake.

Donna wandered toward the kitchen. Her morning run had taken care of last night's ice cream but eating this cake would mean another run tomorrow.

She opened the cake box and stared at the seven layers of golden vanilla sponge filled with cannoli buttercream, the whole thing drenched in chocolate ganache.

Would it really mean another run? Or could she just this once say *screw it* and eat what she wanted without immediately scheduling herself for the workout that would erase the calories she'd consumed?

She smiled. She could. This was her life now. Plus, she was grieving. And a lot of people ate their way through grief. Why should she be any different?

She took a fork from the utensil drawer, but her phone rang before she could get a plate.

The screen showed the call was from Martin's Cleaners. There was no Martin's Cleaners. That was the name she'd typed into the contacts for Rico Medina. She let the call go to voicemail. She wasn't in the mood to talk to the FBI right now. Even if Rico was awfully pretty and she was newly single.

Nope, nope, nope. She had to stop thinking like that. Rico wasn't going to happen. Not even in a one-night stand, how-Belladonna-got-her-groove-back kind of way. It would be fun. But she was pretty sure the FBI had rules about their agents getting horizontal with their mob-connected informants.

She lifted the cake out of the box and set it on the counter. Was that what she was? An informant? She hadn't actually informed the FBI about anything yet. Just told them she would. She stuck the fork into the cake and came away with a nice chunk.

As soon as the cake was in her mouth, she wanted a tall glass of cold milk. Not something she usually drank, but Joe always had, and she had some in the house because Joe Jr. liked it too.

She poured a glass, then went back to the cake, which apparently, she was not going to slice and put on a plate.

Her phone rang again. Martin's Cleaners.

Hmm. Rico really wanted to talk to her. That could be good or bad. Obviously. She ate another bite of cake. But she was afraid if she talked to him, she'd let slip about the drop-off. That couldn't happen. She couldn't have FBI agents swarm the place and ruin her perfect out.

Turning informant would get her free, too, but finishing this last job for Big Tony was cleaner and faster. And didn't require her to disappear into WITSEC for her own protection.

Once the house was sold and she had her place in Florida, she could still give Rico enough information to make Big Tony's life miserable. But Big Tony didn't need to know it was coming from her.

She downed another forkful of cannoli cake, expanding the growing crater on the side of it. She did need to talk to Rico and tell him that things had changed. Although she suspected he already knew, and that's why he was calling.

Rico wasn't stupid. With Joe's death, Rico understood she had all kinds of options now. And when the insurance came, the money to do whatever she liked.

But she liked Rico. He was a good man. The kind of guy she should have married. He was full of heroic ideals. A protector. A righter of wrongs. And he'd given her hope and a way out when she'd had neither.

For all of that, she owed him the truth. One last bite of cake, and back into the box it went. She tossed the fork into the sink. Tomorrow morning, first thing, she'd go to his office and tell him everything.

But tonight, she had to take care of her own business. This wasn't just about her. It was about safety for her family. It was about freedom for all of them. And no one was going to get in the way of that.

She downed the last of the milk, put the glass in the

sink too, then groaned and patted her stomach. That had been a lot of carbs for the middle of the day. She smiled. It was fun doing whatever she wanted. It might end up costing her a whole new wardrobe one size bigger, but it was fun.

There were hours left to kill. Maybe she should try to be productive. But where to start?

Her mind went to the one room of the house that had always been off-limits to her.

Joe's office.

She went down the hall and stood in the doorway, reaching around to flip the light switch. The room reeked of his cigars and aftershave. Spotlights on the walnut bookshelves behind his desk lit up all kinds of signed sports memorabilia. Baseballs, footballs, a couple helmets, a bat, a hockey puck, a basketball, and some very rare baseball cards in their own glass cases.

There were books, too, but those were just for looks. Joe had been more caveman than scholar, but then that was part of what had made him so adept at his chosen profession. Thugs and criminals didn't need to be well read, just willing to do what others weren't.

Joe certainly had been willing.

She stepped into the office. No expense had been spared in this room. It was even soundproof, something Joe had personally overseen during the building of the house. That had made eavesdropping on his meetings impossible.

Her fingers coasted across the top of his desk. Much of his time at home had been spent in this space. There was a large television mounted on the wall opposite the desk. He'd usually have a game on while he was in here.

She walked around the desk and sat in his leather chair. She'd never done that before, and for some reason, it was both empowering and a little sad.

Joe, for all his crimes and misdemeanors, had started out a decent man. She'd thought so, anyway. And even after any pretense of decency was gone, he'd made sure none of them wanted for a single thing. She'd had a new car every year. The children went to excellent schools. His parents, now deceased, had spent their golden years with the best care money could buy.

He'd been a generous man in that way.

A lying, cheating, corrupt, vicious, generous man.

She flattened her hands on the desk. Maybe his generosity was his way of trying to balance all the bad he did. Or maybe he was just showing the world how well he was doing. Making his position in the family clear. He was an earner. Big Tony had often said that about Joe with a kind of sly smile that made other members of the crew jealous.

And now Joe was gone. Fat lot of good his status and money had done him. She took a deep breath, struggling with a sudden wave of sadness. How odd.

She would not cry for that man. Not after everything he'd done. Not after how coldly he'd treated her after she once dared to hint that maybe he should go straight. Why did she care at all that he was dead? She'd wanted out. Wanted to be free of him and this life and these criminal people who flaunted their illicit lifestyle like it was something to be proud of. As if it was enviable.

Fools. All of them.

She had spent more than half her life with the man. They'd had some good times in the early days. Made two beautiful children.

She'd never thought of herself as sentimental, but maybe she was a little. Maybe being a widow did that to a person. It was easy to romanticize a person when they were gone. She needed to be careful about that. To remember who Joe really was.

On a lark, she opened the top desk drawer.

All the usual stuff was in there. Pens, a pair of scissors, a roll of stamps, tape, a couple legal pads, some paper clips and rubber bands. Odds and ends accumulated over the years.

Plus two small silver keys on a simple wire loop.

CHAPTER 4

The keys looked like the kind that might go to a safe-deposit box. Or maybe a safe.

They had a safe. It was no secret. It was upstairs in Joe's walk-in closet. It held the handgun Joe had bought her for home protection, a couple thousand dollars for emergencies, some important paperwork, a good strand of pearls inherited from her grandmother that were going to Christina at graduation, and some pictures.

She knew how to open it. Her birthday, then Christina's, then Joe Jr.'s. That was the combination.

It didn't take keys.

That meant there was another safe somewhere, or a safe-deposit box. She doubted it was the second one. Joe, like most of the family, including Big Tony, had no love for banks. Accounts could be frozen all too easily. Records subpoenaed.

She stood up, staring at the four walls around her with new eyes, trying to find something she'd missed.

Joe had personally supervised the construction of this room, but maybe soundproofing wasn't the only extra he'd added.

She started with the wall across from the desk. There wasn't much to it, just the big-screen television mounted at eye level. She peeked behind it. Nothing but the mount and cables going through the wall. A closet on the other side stored a lot of the home's electronics. That space was accessible from the hall.

The walls on either side of the desk couldn't really hide anything either. One held the door from the hall into the office, and the other joined up to the kitchen. Some framed sports jerseys adorned those walls.

In the center of the wall shared with the kitchen was a bar cart. She opened the doors. Liquor. Glasses. A cocktail shaker.

Then, just to be sure, she looked behind all of the framed jerseys. No hidden locks. No secret panels. No wall safe.

That left the bookshelves behind his desk. They were custom-made walnut and went all the way to the ceiling. The bottom half was cabinets. She opened those first.

The right side was all shelves of stuff. Some office supplies, a couple baseball hats, a poker set, a box of cheap cigars he'd probably gotten as a gift.

On the left side, the shelves were stacked with nudie magazines. She rolled her eyes. Those were going straight into recycling.

She shut the doors and fixed her gaze on the shelves above. There was no lock visible anywhere, so if one existed, it had to be hidden.

Then her eye caught on one of the books. They

were all hardbacks, all mostly best sellers. This one started the middle row. *The Godfather* by Mario Puzo. The top of the spine was a little shinier than the rest of it. Like it had been touched a lot.

Could it be that easy? She reached up and pulled the book out of its spot.

Behind it was a lock. "Are you freakin' kidding me?" She tossed the book on the desk. "*The Godfather*. Honestly, Joe. So unoriginal."

She grabbed the keys out of the drawer and tried one. It fit. She turned it and was rewarded with a soft snick.

The entire bookcase gave way, easing out from the wall about a half inch.

"Un-freakin'-believable."

She grabbed the edge of the bookshelf and pulled. It swung wide easily, just clearing the back of Joe's desk chair.

Her jaw went south as lights flickered on, and the space behind it was revealed.

All these years he'd told her the kitchen pantry wasn't bigger because all the major ductwork and trunk lines in the house ran behind it. "That lying dog."

The room was as big as her walk-in closet. Maybe bigger. The side walls had built-in shelves. On the right side, the top five shelves were filled end to end with wrapped bundles of currency. The bills were hundreds, at first glance. More than she'd ever seen in one place. She couldn't even estimate how much money there might be.

A million? Two? More, maybe. If anything was going to give her a hot flash, this was it. She braced for the onslaught of her own personal summer as she investigated further.

The wall across from that one held some more boxes. One was a box of condoms. Lovely. The rest of the boxes were larger and plain cardboard, but there were also some metal ones she recognized as ammunition boxes. Her father had had a few of those when she was a kid.

There were maybe a dozen of those and only three of the larger cardboard ones. Another shelf held a bulletproof vest, a couple sets of handcuffs, a riot baton, a Taser, some kind of tool set in a bound leather pouch. The shelf below that held a years' worth of notebooks, which she guessed were filled with the kind of information Rico Medina would love to get his hands on.

But the back wall was where her attention was drawn and stayed.

Guns. Handguns, shotguns, rifles, all kinds. Guns she didn't know the names of or want to know the names of. Each in its own niche. It wasn't a collection so much as an arsenal.

"Mary and Joseph," Donna breathed out. The discovery had her trembling. A little bit from fear, but mostly with anger. She wasn't afraid of guns. Most Mafia wives knew better. They learned how to shoot, how to handle a weapon with respect.

What made her mad was the extent of this secret. How dare he keep this from her? How dare he bring all of this into a house where they'd raised two children? What if the house had been raided? She'd seen it happen. Not to anyone in the Villachi family, but she'd seen it.

This was the kind of thing that put people away.

She put her hand to her heart, took a deep breath, and reminded herself that nothing had happened. And Joe was already dead unfortunately, so she couldn't act on the sudden desire to strangle him.

The deep breath helped put rational thought back into her head. She could handle this. She'd handled everything else. The money was easy to deal with. She'd donate some to the church. Cammie would like that. Although she wasn't about to tell Cammie where it had come from or even that she'd donated it.

There was no doubt in Donna's mind that this was blood money. Ill-gotten gains. And she wanted nothing to do with the rest of it. Sure, the possibility existed that Joe had earned this money in some completely above-board kind of way.

But that possibility was so slim it was laughable.

She took a moment to think about what she should do. She'd like to put a nice bit into the kids' trust accounts, but she didn't think they'd be happy about the money's origins either.

Right now, it was probably best if she put it all in a safe-deposit box somewhere just to get it out of the house. That felt like the right move. Maybe not all of it, though. She'd probably borrow a little bit, just until the insurance check came.

Then she'd repay whatever she'd spent and be done with it. Done with all of this.

The guns...she narrowed her eyes, staring at them. She had no idea what those guns had been used for. If anything. Maybe they were just for show, but she doubted he'd opened this room for anyone. Either way, they ought to go to Rico. He could do the forensics on them. Maybe link them to some cases that would help put the Villachis away. She was good with that.

Actually, Rico could have all of it. She certainly didn't need the ammunition. Assuming that's what was in those canisters. She checked. Yep, ammunition. So that could go to Rico. Just like the bulletproof vest and the rest of it. Maybe she'd keep the Taser for protection.

Her gaze shifted to the cardboard boxes. More ammunition? She grabbed the closest one and pulled it off the shelf. It was heavy, but not filled-with-bullets heavy. She put it on the floor and opened it up.

Boxes and boxes of playing cards. Instinct and experience told her they were probably marked. The crew was heavily into illicit gambling. They ran games all over town.

She took the second box down and opened it.

A new curse slipped from her lips. The box was filled with bundles of plastic-wrapped white powder. Cocaine, she guessed. The third box held the same thing. Red edged her vision. How. Dare. He. In her house. Where her children had grown up.

Now she was really mad. The kind of mad that wasn't going to go away for a while. He'd thought she was an oblivious fool, evidently, to keep such things in this house right under her nose. Probably laughed about it to the rest of the crew.

But then, she had been oblivious, hadn't she? The thought was utterly disheartening.

Did all the families have rooms like this? She might ask Rosie, because Rosie would say if she knew. But then, Rosie still had to live with Bobbie. Maybe not saying anything would be better. Of course, Rosie was a little more streetwise. Maybe she already knew and was happy to look the other way.

Donna shook her head in disgust. She'd seen enough for now. She closed the secret room, then stomped upstairs. Still seething, she changed out of her leggings and T-shirt and into skinny black jeans, a black silk blouse, and knee-high boots. "What do you think, Lucky?"

The cat had no comment.

She wanted to look tough and capable. Not like Joe's oblivious widow. Not like someone easily taken advantage of. She was no one's patsy, not anymore.

Her mood being what it was, she went to the safe in Joe's closet, opened it, and took out her handgun. It was loaded. She tucked it into the waistband of her jeans at her back. She was done being the fool. Joe had undoubtedly never gone to a meeting without protection, why should she?

She went downstairs, put her red trench coat on, mostly because it made her feel powerful, grabbed her purse and her keys, and headed for the garage.

On the way, she picked up the duffel bag. She

scowled at it. Putting gloves on probably would have been wise to keep her prints off it, but it was too late for that now. Besides, her patience was nearly gone. She took a breath, reminding herself she just had to keep it together a little while longer.

Very soon, she would spill her guts to Rico and watch the Villachis swing while she soaked up the sun on the warm, white sands of Pensacola Beach.

She threw the bag in the trunk of her Mercedes, then climbed behind the wheel and tapped the button to raise the garage door. It was too early to leave for the drop-off, but she had a stop to make first.

The cemetery.

Joe might be dead, but that wasn't about to stop her from giving him a piece of her mind. And when she was done, he'd be glad he was already deceased.

Holy Cross Cemetery was twenty minutes out of her way to the industrial park, but the time flew by. She practiced her words in her head, revising and editing as she drove, perfecting each cutting line until it was razor-edged and dagger sharp.

The clouds that had been muting the twilight glow of the setting sun parted and gave way to the rise of a fat, full moon.

She slowed and turned into the cemetery. It looked different at night, but she watched for the markers and found Joe's site. She parked and got out after storing the gun in the glove box. She stayed by the side of the car for a moment.

It was a little creepy being here alone at night, but

she focused on how mad she was. A few weird shadows and a couple bare trees weren't going to spook her off her mission.

She locked the car and made the trek to his graveside. His stone wasn't there yet. It would take a few weeks for that to be completed. In the meantime, there was a flat marker with a number on it. Hard to find in the dark. Even harder to read. She looked closer to be sure she was at the right spot.

Eleven forty-seven. That was Joe. Temporarily reduced to a number. How low the mighty had fallen.

She stared at the marker, all the words she'd worked up in the car on the verge of spilling out. "How could you?" she whispered. "I never really thought I hated you, but *that* room. With all that…contraband in it. Drugs, Joe? In the house with the kids?"

Her hands clenched into tight fists. "I'm not even going to discuss the condoms, you cheating son of a—"

A noise off in the distance pulled her attention. It sounded almost like someone laughing. Had to be an animal. A crow, maybe. They could make sounds like that. Right?

"Do you know how much trouble we could have been in? How much—"

The noise repeated, farther away this time.

She looked at the marker again, but she couldn't quite remember where she'd been. "I'm furious with you, Joseph Barrone. Furious that you thought so little of me and the kids to keep all that garbage in our house. Furious you didn't love us more. Furious that you'd willingly put us all in danger. Furious at myself for actually being sad you're gone."

She barked out a bitter laugh. "I'm not sad anymore. I want you to know that. I'm fine with you being gone. It's the best thing you ever did for me, outside of Christina and Joe Jr., you know that?"

She shook her head. "What would your mother say if she was alive?"

Donna's jaw clenched. She forced herself to take a breath. "I'm glad you're dead, Joe. You're scum. You and Big Tony and the whole gang. Criminals. You all deserve to go to jail for a long, long time."

The sound of odd laughter rang through the cemetery a third time. Closer now. A small trickle of unease went down her back. Maybe she should have brought the gun. The noise was just from an animal, she told herself. But it didn't sound like an animal at all.

She stared into the distance, toward where the sound had come from, but even in the moonlight, the landscape was all shapes and shadows.

The clouds drifted across the moon, deepening the shadows into pure darkness. Shapes disappeared. She tried to will herself to see into the blackness, but nothing was discernable. The wind picked up, whistling softly past.

She pulled her coat closer and wrapped her arms around herself, unable to take her gaze off the landscape around her.

Something formed in the darkness. A shape. Moving. Speeding toward her. *Laughing.* She opened her mouth to scream. The form struck her like a bullet, knocking her down and taking the air from her lungs.

The thing was on top of her, pinning her to the ground. Pain erupted like fire in her neck. She fought, but blackness closed in. All she heard was laughter.

Then nothing.

CHAPTER 5

The earth beneath Donna hummed. Insects, she thought in a kind of hazy, foggy, out-of-body way. The realization that she could hear the movement of such small creatures deep in the ground beneath her did nothing to anchor her to whatever was actually going on.

For the briefest of moments, she wondered hopefully if some of those bugs were feasting on Joe. He deserved it.

The pain in her neck was gone. Or she'd stopped feeling it. Her sight hadn't returned. Nor had the feeling in any part of her body. She wasn't even sure she was in her body.

Was she floating? Or flying? Or maybe none of those things. She would have said she was numb, but when you went numb, you were still aware of yourself in a physical way.

That awareness didn't exist. All that she could identify was the creeping, crawling, tunneling sounds of the insects in the dirt beneath her.

Was she dead?

If she was dead, she was going to hunt down Joe's ghost and beat the boo out of him.

Then a bitter, metallic taste swirled through her senses, coating her tongue. She gagged as her throat tried to close. That didn't feel like something that would happen after death.

Next the shapes and shadows returned with vague, indiscernible lines. Her vision was back, but with the clarity of peering through murky water. At least the laughter was gone. Just the buzzing beneath her. And the whistling breeze.

The metallic taste filled her mouth. Perfume tickled her nose. The scent was complex and curious and smelled expensive. She swallowed. A shape looming over her took on a female form.

Donna became aware of flesh pressed to her mouth. That was where the blood was coming from that was spilling down her throat. She tried to pull away, but she didn't have enough strength to make much of an effort.

Then she no longer wanted to pull away. She wanted the blood. Craved it. She opened her mouth wider, trying to get more.

"Ah," a voice said. "There you are. Back from the brink, I see."

Donna blinked, her vision clearing and sharpening as if lights had been turned on. Nothing made sense and she didn't care. She reached for the wrist pressed to her mouth, and the woman laughed. Not the same sound as before.

"That will do." A few of her words had the slightest hint of a French accent. She pulled her arm away, and a second later, the puncture wounds on her wrist closed up. "I am very sorry about my rogue protégé. And I am also sorry that I must leave you now, but I have to catch him before he strikes again. Not to worry. I will find you soon and explain everything. Until then, follow your instincts and you should be fine, but keep your head. Try to remember that, okay? You will probably drift off again and forget all of this, but at some point, it should come back to you. Go easy now. Everything is—"

The cackling laughter echoed from somewhere behind them.

The woman's gaze snapped toward the sound. She frowned and muttered something in French.

"Who…are…you?" Donna managed.

The woman looked at her again. "I'm Claudette. Don't be alarmed if you sleep a lot. Now I must go. Don't feed until we speak again. Remember that."

Then she disappeared so quickly it was almost as if she'd been erased from the air. Donna lay there, staring into the blank space Claudette had just occupied. Don't feed? What did that mean? The stars in the night sky were brilliant pinpoints of light.

They mesmerized Donna. She couldn't look away. Then the sudden weight of lethargy pressed down on her. She closed her eyes, and everything went dark a second time.

When Donna opened her eyes again, she had no idea why she was on the ground. She felt fine, but a little foggy. She sat up. What had happened? She'd come to tell Joe off, and something had knocked her down. A dog? She could only remember pieces at first. Yes, maybe a dog. A big one. Her hand went to her throat. It had bitten her. But the skin on her neck felt fine. A little sticky.

A new thought pushed through all the foggy uncertainty. The drop-off. Oh no. What time was it? She checked her watch. Crap. She was twenty-three minutes away, and she had thirty-two minutes to make it there on time.

There'd better not be an accident on the interstate.

She got to her feet. Not wobbly like she expected. The moon had gotten oddly bright too. She looked back at Joe's marker, which was surprisingly easy to read all of a sudden. It was almost like daylight out here.

But she didn't have time to dwell. She needed to be in the car, driving, now.

Five minutes later, she was on the highway and headed toward the industrial park. So long as she didn't hit a snag, she'd be there with a few minutes to spare. Being late to this drop-off would not be good. She didn't need Big Tony thinking she'd backed out. Or was a no-show. Or worse, had taken off with whatever was in the bag.

But now that she was on track to get there on time, she could take a moment to think about what had happened to her at the cemetery.

She hadn't been knocked down by a dog. She knew that now. It had been a man. A young man. And he *had* bitten her. She was sure of that.

The sign for her exit was up ahead. *Way* up ahead. How was it possible that she could read it from here?

Must be the clear night air. That would also explain how bright the stars had been after Claudette had left.

Claudette.

Donna could see the woman's face as clearly as if she was looking at her now. Claudette was stunningly beautiful. Dark-skinned and bright-eyed with high cheekbones and...fangs.

Donna let that word sit in her thoughts for a long moment. The word that went with it, the V-word... She wasn't going there. Because that way led to crazy.

She took the exit for the industrial park, passing the old Heidelman's Costume Shop on the way. Her gaze stayed on the sign a second longer than necessary, and she laughed. Wow. Being in the cemetery had really played with her head. Costumes. Of course.

That's all she'd stumbled into. A couple of weirdos playing vampire in the cemetery. The word had no bite now, pun intended. What did the kids call that whole dressing-up thing? Cosplay?

Freaks. She shook her head. If it didn't go against everything the family had drilled into her, she'd have dialed 911 and turned them in right then. Biting people was not cool. Neither was smearing them with fake blood. Or making them think they were drinking blood!

She couldn't imagine what kind of sickos got off on that. All she wanted to do now was go home and take a shower.

Just as soon as this drop-off was over, that's exactly what she would do. Then she would eat some more of that cannoli cake. Possibly while watching *The Bachelor*. In bed.

There were no limits on her newfound freedom, apparently. Although she might need to set the bar higher than indulging in carbs and reality TV. Baby steps.

She slowed down and checked her GPS, but it was showing she'd arrived, and she knew this wasn't the right spot yet. This wasn't the building number Vinnie had given her. She leaned forward to see more of the building.

She turned into the next section of buildings and saw a car. This had to be it. The lights weren't on, but she was pretty sure someone was in there. She could just make out a shape. Amazing, considering how dark it was back here. She'd wanted to be the first one to arrive, but the creepos at the cemetery had ruined that.

Should she drive closer? She wasn't sure. She'd never done this before.

Almost like the other driver knew what she was thinking, he flashed the car's lights. Okay, maybe that meant closer. She inched forward until about ten yards separated them, then the other car's lights came on. That seemed like a signal that she'd gone far enough. She parked but left the engine on. That put her in a canyon between two buildings with the other car directly in front of her.

Her nerves were itching, but she chalked that up to two things. The night she'd already had and the desire to get this over with.

She glanced at the glove box, but if she went for the

gun now, it might be obvious what she was doing. That might look bad. She didn't need to tick off whoever she was handing this bag off to.

With a frown, she left the handgun where it was and said a little prayer that she wouldn't regret that decision. Then she touched her crucifix and said another prayer that Big Tony had informed whoever she was meeting that Joe wasn't the one showing up here today.

They had to know that, right?

Because if they didn't, they were in for a big surprise. She put her hand on the door latch and eased it open. No sudden movements seemed like the best possible plan. She grabbed her key fob out of the console. If nothing else, she could hit the panic button and hope for a small distraction, but she needed the fob to open the trunk anyway.

Then she stepped out. With the car lights shining in her eyes, she couldn't see much of what was going on in the other car.

Did they have a window down? Could they hear her? She hoped so. She jerked a thumb over her shoulder. "I have to get the bag out of the trunk."

She stood there for a moment, waiting for some response, but there was none.

This was nerve-racking. She left the door open as she backed toward the trunk. She tapped the button on the fob to open it. The little *thunk* that sounded when the lock released sounded like a distant gunshot.

Her heart was racing, but she was doing some of this to herself. Nothing had happened yet that she needed to be worried about. Sure, it would be nice if someone would get out of the other car, but then, maybe that's not how these things went. Maybe you just left the duffel and never saw the other person.

Big Tony hadn't said anything about an exchange. Just a package delivery. She didn't really need to see anyone else for that to happen.

She pushed the trunk all the way up, blocking her view of the other vehicle.

Footsteps. Running. Behind her. She turned in time to see a big man in a ski mask barreling toward her.

Before she could open her mouth to scream, another one came around the side of the car. He grabbed her, looped his arm around her neck, and pulled her back against his chest.

She gasped for air. Her heart pounded in her ears, drowning out all thought but the immediate choices of fight or flight. Fight won. As the first man approached, she grabbed the second man's arm around her neck and used it to swing her feet up and shove them into the first man's gut.

With a whoosh of breath, he hinged forward as he flew back. Then she dug her nails into her attacker's arm and opened her mouth to scream. His hand clapped over her face, covering her mouth.

She bit him as hard as she could.

He cried out and let go with a snarled curse, giving her a chance to break free. She spun away from him and punched him in the face with everything she had.

His head snapped back, and he went down hard.

The pain she'd expected in her hand never came.

Good old adrenaline. That had to be what was giving her such strength too.

A grunt turned her around. The man she'd kicked was getting to his feet. At the same time, a door on the other car opened and closed. Before the first guy could get up, she kicked him in the crotch, thankful she'd worn boots. They weren't steel-toed, but they were hard.

He made a soft, sharp inhale as he bowed inward, then collapsed, a rerun of their first encounter.

A gunshot cracked the stillness, the bullet whistling past her so close that she swore she could feel it. A second shot rang out right behind it.

Pain lanced through her shoulder, and she knew she'd been hit this time.

Red, fiery rage exploded within her, pushing rational thought and natural reaction out of the way. More adrenaline coursed through her. Where this was coming from, she had no idea. She shook with the energy that demanded to be spent. There was no stopping what had already begun. And she was not going down like this. With an animalistic growl, she launched toward the third man.

The shooter.

She was at him instantly. She plowed her good shoulder into his chest and was rewarded with the sound of cracking ribs and his cry of pain. Surprised by her sudden attack, he dropped the gun.

She kicked it into the darkness.

He staggered for a moment, then righted himself and drew a fist back.

In a move that defied her capabilities, she let out a grunt and shoved him with both hands, sending him flying into the side of his car.

The driver's window shattered, and he crumpled to the ground, out cold.

She looked at her hands. Was this really just adrenaline? Or was this one of those things where women could move cars when their children were trapped underneath? A moment of superhuman strength brought on by a life-or-death situation? She had no idea, but she was thankful.

Whatever it was, it had saved her.

Trembling with the remnants of the energy that had propelled her, she stumbled back to her car. All that mattered now was getting home, but she had to close the trunk before she could leave. That purpose kept her moving, because she was afraid if she stopped, she'd fall apart. She stepped over the second man to get to the back of her car.

The first man was still down too. She hoped they all stayed like that long enough for her to get away. None of them seemed to be making any attempts to move, though, so maybe she was good.

Except she wasn't good. Any minute, the reality of what had just happened would set in, and she'd probably pass out as the adrenaline's surge faded.

Did she have any hope of making the drive home like this? She'd been shot, after all. She felt her shoulder, but it was hard to tell how bad the wound was through her trench coat. Grazed, maybe? But still. She should probably go to a hospital.

But that would mean questions. A lot of questions, given who she was. She wasn't up for that. Home would have to do. She could patch herself up. She was a mom. She'd handled more than her share of minor medical emergencies in her time.

She took hold of the trunk, about to shut it, when she changed her mind and reached for the duffel bag instead. She had a few questions of her own.

With her last bit of adrenaline, which was probably also keeping her from feeling any pain, she ripped the zipper open, popping off the small brass padlock.

No drugs. No money. Just bundles of cut newspaper taped together like wads of cash.

"Mary and Joseph." Her whole body went cold. She'd been set up.

CHAPTER 6

S et up.

The words raked down her spine like nails on a chalkboard. Anger helped erase some of her exhaustion. Anger at whoever had done this, but also anger at herself for being so gullible that she hadn't anticipated this might happen.

Had her years of marriage to Joe taught her nothing? She stopped short of berating herself. Big Tony's promise of freedom had been all she'd focused on, so it was no wonder she'd gone after it with such blind confidence.

And she wasn't a soldier. She didn't have the years of experience that Joe'd had. Didn't know what to expect like he had. She cut herself a break for that.

Despite all that, she'd still managed to survive. Another point for her.

A few seconds ticked by as she got her head wrapped around this new betrayal and tried to make sense of it as best she could. Freaking out wasn't going to help. She had to be analytical. Figure out where the threat was coming from. There were two possibilities. Either Vinnie was behind this—he was the one who'd stressed how critical it was that she not look in the bag—or this was Big Tony's doing. After all, he'd felt this drop-off was important enough to talk to her about it at the funeral reception.

The memory of that caused a third possibility to kick in.

Lucinda.

Donna slammed the trunk closed, picked her key fob off the ground where she'd dropped it earlier, then got in the car. She started the engine and put it in reverse, careful not to also back over any of the men, not that the thought didn't occur to her. But she wasn't looking to finish them off. She wasn't a killer. Besides, better to leave them alive so they could take a message back to their boss that she wasn't to be messed with.

At least she hoped it worked like that.

Her mind quickly returned to Lucinda. Could she actually be behind this? Donna had no idea how much Lucinda knew about Big Tony's operations, but Donna was pretty sure the woman knew enough to pull off something like this. She had the nerve too. She'd demonstrated that at the funeral.

As for motive, the incident at the funeral might be enough. Especially if she'd been listening at the door of Joe's office. Lucinda would have heard all about the drop-off.

But if she hadn't, if she'd only known that Big Tony was talking to Donna, would that really be enough for Lucinda to try to have Donna killed for talking to Big Tony? Was she that crazy? Or maybe she hadn't thought it would go that far. Maybe she'd just thought she'd get Donna in trouble. Or give her a good scare.

No. Wait. Donna growled in frustration as she shifted into drive and pulled out of the industrial park. She wasn't thinking straight. Those men had attacked her *before* they knew the duffel was full of paper. So if Lucinda had done that, her plan hadn't even had a chance to work.

Think, Donna, think. Those men weren't even Big Tony's guys. They were working for whoever Big Tony had wanted that package delivered to.

So those lunks belonged to some other mob boss. Which meant they'd been about to use her to send a message to Big Tony. Or declare war.

Holy Francis, she'd really gotten into the middle of it this time. She drove on, letting all the details percolate in her head.

If Joe had been the one making that drop, he might have been the one killed. Or taken prisoner. Or whatever those men had intended to do. Instead, it had been her.

Where did that leave her, then?

She really wasn't sure. She just knew she needed to think this through when she wasn't still buzzing from the chaos of it all. And when her shoulder wasn't bleeding from a gunshot wound.

What a night. Thankfully, whatever buzz remained in her system was keeping her pain level to a minimum.

Forty-five minutes later, she made it home and into the garage. She took the handgun out of the glove box so she could put it away but left the duffel bag in the trunk until she figured out what to do with it. And what to do about this whole mess.

At some point, she'd have to tell Big Tony what had happened. Wouldn't she? She tucked the gun into her waistband. Wasn't he going to wonder why his delivery hadn't been made?

Or maybe he wasn't going to wonder, because he was the one who'd filled the bag with worthless paper.

Her head hurt from so much thinking and so few solutions. She locked the garage door behind her, then turned on the house alarm before going into the kitchen. There, she dropped her purse on the counter and fed Lucky, then went straight for the cabinet where she kept the wineglasses. With no appetite for cannoli cake, she poured herself a big glass of red and took it upstairs. The glass went on her nightstand. The gun went into her nightstand drawer.

After tonight, keeping it close felt like a better idea.

She put a home shopping channel on for company. Something about the background chatter made her feel safer. Like she wasn't home alone.

Which was crazy, but considering what she'd just been through, nothing was that crazy.

She cranked on the shower, then went back for a sip of wine. Lucky was on the bed, cleaning himself. "Hey, baby."

He kept cleaning himself.

With a little smile, she shucked her clothing into a pile on the bedroom floor. She'd figure out tomorrow if any of it had to be tossed.

Then she knotted her hair on top of her head and

climbed under the spray. It stung her skin with delicious heat. She inhaled the steam, letting it warm her and calm her down.

She started to soap up, then ran her hand over her shoulder. The bullet had grazed her, she was sure of it. She'd felt the pain of it. But there was nothing on her skin. No mark that she could find. She glanced through the glass shower wall at the mirror opposite to see if she could find the spot, but the steam had fogged everything.

Was there no wound? She swore she'd been hit. Grazed, sure, but what about the pain? That had been real. She looked down at her body. No bruises that she could see either. But then as she replayed the evening in her head, she'd done most of the hitting.

How was that possible?

No idea. Nothing about tonight made sense. In fact, she was ready to stop thinking. She soaped up, spent a few more indulgent minutes under the hot water, then got out, wrapping herself in a towel.

She padded to the mirror and wiped away a circle of steam so she could do a closer inspection. Her shoulder was unblemished. So was her neck where she'd thought she'd been bitten.

With a sigh, she shook her head. Enough. Whatever had happened—or hadn't happened—she'd spend more energy on it tomorrow. For tonight, she was done. The Pinot Noir was calling her name. So was some mindless television.

She put on a tank top and a pair of boyshort underwear and slipped under the covers. She drank her wine while watching an old Cary Grant movie, then turned the TV off and fell asleep dreaming about simpler times and men in fedoras. Lucky curled up on the pillow next to hers, his soft snoring a sweet reminder that she wasn't alone.

When she woke up, she had a moment of uncertainty. She blinked at the fog that clung to her. What time was it? What day? Had she been asleep for an hour or ten?

The room was dark, so maybe it was still night.

She sat up, a little more awake suddenly. Despite the dark, everything was easily visible. Like the little decorative crystal clock on her dresser, which was usually unreadable even with the lights on.

But she could see it plainly. It said nine seventeen. Nine? As in the morning? That didn't make sense. There was no light glowing at the edges of the drapes. And it couldn't be nine p.m. because it had been almost eleven by the time she'd gotten home last night and close to midnight when she'd finally turned off the television.

The clock battery must have died.

So what time was it? She reached for her phone, remembering a second later that she'd left her purse on the kitchen counter.

She turned the television on, the guide coming to life on the screen.

Nine eighteen.

She stared at the numbers. Had time gone backward? What was going on? She didn't feel like she'd been in bed for almost twenty-four hours, but that was the only explanation.

After last night, she didn't know what to think about anything anymore. Things were making less sense. That wasn't a great direction for her life to take. Not when she was on the verge of reclaiming her freedom after all these years.

"Okay, Donna, get a grip. There has to be a reason for all this." Was this what being premenopausal felt like? She hoped not. But then she hadn't had a hot flash all night. She hadn't sweated through the sheets, either, and that was even more unusual. "Maybe last night just really wore you out. Get up, get a shower, and catch up."

She slipped her feet to the floor, expecting to be sore all over after the fight she'd put up, but not a single muscle complained. "I guess the Pilates are really paying off."

Lucky ran into the room, meowing his head off.

"Hey, big man. You must be starving, huh? I guess that's proof I really have been asleep for a day. Just hold on for another minute or two, okay? I need to pull myself together."

She went into the bathroom and flipped on the light, catching her reflection in the mirror. It stopped her cold. "Holy—is that me? I should always sleep that much."

The woman in the mirror *was* her. But…better. And not just med spa better. Turn-back-the-clock better. She poked and prodded at her face. Everything bounced back with the kind of elasticity she'd taken for granted in her twenties.

Her eyes were the same. Well, the baby crow's-feet that had been forming at the corners were gone, but the color was the same. That seemed proof enough that this was really her.

How were those wrinkles gone? How was everything so taut and lifted? And glowing? None of it made sense. That was the theme of this new life apparently.

Could this be what freedom looked like on her? Or did widowhood just really agree with her?

She stripped off her tank top, eager to see if the transformation had hit her below the neck too. "Holy Francis."

It had. Her boobs were higher, her stomach flatter, and her boyshort underwear was almost falling off her. She turned sideways. She had definitely lost weight and toned up. Overnight. "How is this possible?"

She rubbed her eyes. Was this some kind of stress response? If it was, she'd never heard of anything like it. One more look in the mirror, one more shake of her head. "Please let this be permanent."

She pulled her tank top back on, then put on a pair of sweatpants and some fuzzy socks. She gathered up the clothes she'd left on the floor last night and tossed most of them in the hamper. The trench coat she took a closer look at.

There was a hole across the top of the shoulder. A scorched tear that could have been made only by a bullet. She'd definitely been grazed.

She shook her head. She couldn't make sense of how she hadn't been hurt more.

Lucky meowed at her.

"Okay, I know." She took the coat downstairs with her, laying it over the dryer in the laundry room to deal with later. Lucky scampered past, sliding into the kitchen ahead of her.

She stuck a K-Cup in the machine and hit brew, then fed Lucky. The coffee was finishing up as she dug her phone out of her purse to see what she'd missed by sleeping a day away. Wow. A couple new texts. One from Rico, one from Rosie. Both essentially checking to see if she was okay. That was nice. But there were twelve new voicemails. She looked at her missed calls. Actually, two of those were from Rico from yesterday.

Three were from him today. Three were from Big Tony. Then one each from Rosie, Christina, Joe Jr., and Cammie.

None from Lucinda. Good.

Donna added stevia and creamer to her coffee, then took a sip as she dialed her voicemail and tapped in her code.

The automated voicemail began. "First message. *Donna, this is Rico. We need to talk.* Second message. *Donna, it's Rico. Please call me. Soon.* Third message. *Donna, are you okay? I know yesterday was Joe's funeral, but not hearing from you worries me. Please check in.*"

"Aw, Rico's worried." She drank a little more coffee. "That's sweet."

"Fourth message. *Donna. It's Tony. Everything go all right?*"

She squinted at the phone, trying to figure out if he'd sounded sincere or not.

"Fifth message. *Donna, call me.*"

She shook her head. She was not calling Big Tony now. Not at this hour. Not because he wouldn't be up, but because it was too late to start with him.

Although she was going to have to deal with him at some point. She was a little surprised he hadn't sent Vinnie out to check on her. Or maybe he had, and she'd slept through the visit. That was more likely. So maybe Big Tony didn't even think she was home.

She hoped that was the case and it would buy her some time.

The sixth message was a hang-up from Big Tony. The seventh was Rosie repeating what her text had said. *"Wanted to make sure you're all right. Don't be a stranger."* Then the eighth message was from Christina. *"Hey, Mom. Just wondering how you're doing. Love ya."*

"Love you too, baby." She held the warm mug in her hand, still smiling from the sound of her daughter's voice.

"Ninth message." This one was from Joe Jr. *"Hey, Mom. Just checking in. Love you."*

"Love you too, Son."

"Tenth message. *Hi, Donna. The sisters loved the cookies. They wanted me to let you know they're praying for you. Talk soon.*"

Donna nodded. "Those prayers worked." She glanced down at her body. "Maybe better than expected."

She disconnected from voicemail, then stared at her

screen. She needed to talk to Rico. Which meant she had to tell him what she was doing about the whole state's evidence thing. Also, she was definitely giving him the guns from the safe room. And the drugs.

The money, however... She sighed and bit her bottom lip. That was tainted money. She knew that. But it also represented security for herself and her kids until she got her insurance money. And she really wanted to donate some to the church as a way of balancing out all the bad that had probably been done to earn it.

So right now, she couldn't just give that money to the FBI.

But she also couldn't call Rico and tell him about the contents of the stash room until she dealt with that money. With everything else facing her, taking care of the cash seemed like the easiest thing to check off her to-do list.

She drained the last of her coffee. "I guess I know what I'm doing tonight."

CHAPTER 7

There was too much money to count it all bill by bill. That would take too long, and she wanted this room dealt with tonight. Instead, she counted the bundled stacks. First, she counted one stack to find out how much it was. Each bank-band-wrapped stack held a hundred bills. Each bill was a hundred. Which meant each banded bundle was worth ten thousand dollars.

A hundred of those made a million.

And all of it tainted. Such a freakin' shame.

She used a pencil and scratch pad from Joe's desk to keep things straight. This wasn't any kind of accounting she'd ever done before, and she wanted to get it right.

When she finished, she looked at the numbers written on the scratch pad. Then back at the stacks of bills. Then at the scratch pad again.

Was that right? It had to be. She'd been careful and thorough. But she didn't really believe the number she was looking at, so she counted it again.

Same number.

Five million, four hundred twenty thousand dollars.

She stood there for an undetermined amount of

time, hands on her hips, just looking at it, taking it all in. "Wow."

As soon as the bank opened, she was going to get herself a safe-deposit box and put the money in there. She couldn't deposit it. That would create a record, and she knew better. But she refused to have that money in the house a second longer, either. After her insurance check came, she'd probably turn this stash over to Rico. Let him figure it out.

Until then, it was going to the bank. As soon as possible. Once that was done, she was going to the church to make her anonymous donation. She'd see Cammie, too.

She needed to see Rico, too. She'd put him off long enough. Staring at all this money helped convince her that talking to him next was what made sense. So did giving Rico whatever he needed to shut down the Villachi syndicate.

That was her best path forward. Maybe her only path forward, considering what had gone down last night.

The Villachis had to be stopped. And her family needed to be safe from them.

With that decision made, she picked up one of the ledgers. The latest one. She flipped through it. Names, numbers, amounts. A few notes in Italian. This had to be about Big Tony's business. She wasn't sure what, exactly. People paid off? People who owed money? Who'd bought drugs? Whatever it meant, the information had to be incriminating since Joe had kept the ledgers in this room.

Rico would figure it out. He'd probably get a promotion for this. She was good with that. Maybe he'd think of her kindly then, because she was pretty sure right now he just thought of her as one more mobbed-up informant.

That's not who she wanted to be. Never again. Not the mobbed-up part, anyway. She hated having that taint attached to her name.

She wanted to do something good with what was left of her life. Like help take down the Villachis. Like right some of the wrongs they'd done. She could, too, with all this money. Now there was a thought. She could do a lot of good with this kind of bankroll. Donate to charities. Help those in need.

Maybe even start a scholarship for kids to go to Quantico. Wasn't that where the FBI trainees went to school?

She laughed. Mob money helping to make more FBI agents. Now that was rich. If she decided to use the money for charitable purposes, she'd talk to Rico about setting up an FBI scholarship once the Villachis were behind her.

She went out to the garage, remembering just in time to turn off the alarm, and found a duffel bag big enough to hold the cash among Joe's sports equipment. Surprisingly, five and a half million dollars wasn't as bulky as you might think.

She'd hold a million back. That was for the convent. The rest would go into the safe-deposit box until she needed it.

Of course, getting that duffel bag out made her think about the one still in the trunk.

But she wasn't making any other moves until she talked to Rico. No calls to Big Tony. No messages. Nothing. She was not getting pulled into any more schemes with him. And there was definitely a chance of that. With Big Tony, you never knew what to expect.

And saying no wasn't really an option. So, better not to talk to him.

She hesitated at the garage door, her gaze returning to the trunk of her Mercedes. Big Tony knew where she lived. And there was nothing stopping him from coming here whenever he wanted.

Suddenly, she didn't feel so safe in her home. She ground her teeth together. That was unacceptable. She was *not* going to be intimidated by him. If Big Tony showed up here, Donna would call Lucinda and let her know where her husband was.

Let Big Tony deal with that.

Donna lifted her chin, marched back into the house, and turned the alarm on.

So what if Big Tony showed up here? Nothing said she had to let him in. Or even acknowledge his presence. She wouldn't either. In fact, if he got ugly, she'd not only call his wife, she'd call the cops. She was a free woman. She owed him nothing. Least of all loyalty. He was a criminal.

She went back to Joe's office, more determined than ever to extricate herself from this mess. The sooner she could talk to Rico, the better.

She bagged the money, grabbed the Taser and a pair

of handcuffs just because, and locked up the secret room. She put the million for the convent into a boot box, which just about filled it, and put that in a shopping bag. That and the duffel went into the coat closet by the garage door for tomorrow morning.

Having that done made her happy. Right now, however, she needed to eat. She didn't feel weak, exactly, but for some reason, she was dying for a steak. There wasn't any in the house, though. Some frozen ones, but she wasn't waiting for them to defrost.

Blue Bell's Diner was open twenty-four hours, and she was pretty sure she could get a steak there. Maybe not the same quality as at Lorenzo's Chophouse, but at this hour Lorenzo's wasn't an option. Reluctantly, she went upstairs to get dressed.

It took digging into her skinny clothes to find a pair of jeans that didn't hang off her. And the ones she found still weren't snug. She checked herself out in the mirror. The last time she'd fit into these jeans, she'd had the flu for a week and had been living on sugar-free Jell-O and wonton soup broth from her favorite Chinese place.

To the jeans, she added a slouchy sweater and flats. She scraped her hair into a ponytail and didn't bother with makeup. She looked nothing like herself. She figured that was a good thing, even if the odds of running into someone she knew at Blue Bell's at this time of night were slim. Also good.

She drove carefully, well aware of the duffel bag in the trunk. If she got pulled over for anything, the name on her license would trigger a search of the vehicle. It had happened before.

She made it to the diner without incident. Even at this hour, the parking lot at Blue Bell's had a handful of cars in it, which surprised her. Maybe it was the pie. Blue Bell's was known for great pie.

She went in and took an end booth so she could see the whole restaurant and had her back to no one. None of the other patrons paid attention to her. She liked that.

The waitress came over with a glass of water and a menu. Her name tag said Nell. "I'll give you a minute, hon." Her voice had a Jamaican lilt that made Donna smile.

Donna liked her instantly. "No, that's okay. I know what I want. What's your biggest steak?"

The waitress gave her a smile. "That'd be the porterhouse. Comes with two sides and a roll. Big meal for a little woman like you."

"I haven't eaten in a while." Donna handed the menu back to her. Little. Hah. She couldn't remember the last time anyone had called her that. "The porterhouse sounds great. Rare. Can I get a baked potato as one of the sides?"

"Sure thing. Loaded?"

"Yes. And for the second one..." Donna realized she'd given the menu back too quickly.

"Mac and cheese, green beans, coleslaw, french fries, corn casserole."

"Mac and cheese." Donna suddenly felt the need to carbo-load.

The woman's demeanor changed ever so slightly into admiration. "You got it. Anything to drink?"

"Water's fine."

"All right." The waitress took the menu and went back behind the counter to put the order in.

Donna stared out the window into the night. Something about being here in this diner made her happy. It felt like an adventure, as sad as that sounded. Maybe because she'd never done anything like this before? Her life had been a prison before Joe had died. Now that she was free, it was still chaotic, but it was hers. Hopefully, her meeting with Rico would straighten a lot of it out.

She pulled her phone from her purse and decided to send him a quick text. *Just wanted to let you know I'm all right. Would like to talk tomorrow.*

She didn't expect him to answer. It was late, and she imagined she was texting his work phone. He might not answer that unless he was in his office for some kind of FBI emergency.

But an answer pinged back almost immediately. *Good to hear from you. Was a little worried. What time tomorrow?*

The bank opened at eight. She figured an hour there, max, then fifteen minutes to get to him. As soon as she was done there, she'd go to her standing appointment with Dr. Goldberg, then finish the day with a visit to the convent to see Cammie. That way she wouldn't be rushed while visiting her sister, and she could fill Cammie in on whatever Rico said. She tapped out her response. *Nine fifteen okay?*

Great. See you then.

She smiled. "It's a date." Would Rico notice her new figure? If she still had it, that was. Maybe she'd imagined it. She glanced down. Nope, she hadn't imagined it.

This meal might put an end to it, though.

The waitress returned with a plate the size of a family serving platter and set it down in front of Donna. "There you go, hon. You want any steak sauce with that?"

"No, I'm good." The steak was enormous and smelled like everything that was right in the world. Who knew Blue Bell's could turn out a porterhouse like this? The baked potato was dripping with butter, sour cream, cheese, bacon bits, and chives. *Loaded* really meant loaded. The mac and cheese had a crumb topping, and the yeast roll was the size of a softball. Donna's stomach rumbled. She couldn't remember when she'd eaten a meal like this. Probably because she never had.

"Yell if you need something."

"Thank you." Donna picked up her fork and knife and dug in. Juice oozed out of the meat as she cut into it, and her mouth watered.

She was so hungry her gums started to ache. Okay, that had never happened before. Suddenly, sharp pain jolted through her upper jaw. She let out a little noise and pressed her hand to her mouth.

"What the—" Her tongue collided with teeth that hadn't been there before. Longer, sharper teeth.

She kept her mouth closed while she ran her tongue

over these two new canines. Discreetly, she turned on her phone's camera and put it in selfie mode so she could look at what was going on.

With her head down, she parted her lips. "Mary and Joseph."

She had fangs. There was no other word for them. That wasn't possible. Or normal. Or—

"Here you go."

Donna clamped her mouth shut and looked up at Nell.

She put a little dish on the table. "Forgot your butter for your roll."

"Thanks," Donna mumbled. It came out a little lispy.

"Practicing for Halloween?" Nell asked.

Donna nodded. Sure, that was as good an excuse as any.

"Don't go trying to eat your steak with those things in, or you might choke," Nell said. "I know the Heimlich maneuver, but I'd be afraid I'd snap you in half."

Donna nodded. "Right."

The waitress walked away, but Donna sat there, paralyzed. Why *did* she have fangs? What in the name of Mary was going on with her?

She closed her eyes for a moment. *Please go away.* She took a few deep breaths, hoping to calm down whatever response had caused this.

They didn't seem to be budging. She sipped her water, wondering if something cold would make them shrink. It didn't, and she dribbled a little down her chin.

Her stomach rumbled again.

Finally, she finished cutting a bite of steak and ate it. She chewed carefully. She didn't want to stab her own lip with these crazy teeth.

Little by little, she got the hang of it. About a third of a way through the meal, the fangs retracted as quickly as they'd shown up.

She wasn't sure why they'd disappeared, but she ate faster, trying to get through the rest of her food before they returned. *If* they returned. Which she hoped they didn't.

Somehow, she finished everything on her plate, the roll included, but what really surprised her was that she didn't feel the need to unbutton her jeans. She wasn't uncomfortably full, didn't feel bloated or even remotely stuffed.

Nell returned. "Well now, you did a good job. Don't suppose you saved any room for pie?"

Out of habit, Donna started to say no. Then she stopped herself. "What kind of pie do you have?"

Nell picked up the empty plate. "Blueberry, apple-cranberry crumb, chocolate silk, coconut cream, pumpkin, and a bourbon pecan. We also have cheesecake. It's from Junior's, brought in from the city."

Donna was slightly stunned by the selection. "What's your favorite?"

"Apple-cranberry crumb a la mode. Or the bourbon pecan, but that's a sweet one. You'd better like sugar if you order a slice of that."

"I like sweets," Donna said. "But the apple-cranberry sounds really good too."

"Get both. I'll box them to go, and you can have a

bite of each. What you don't finish, you can have for breakfast." Nell glanced at the empty plate. "You clearly have the metabolism to burn it off."

Donna smiled. Someone was getting a big tip. "I love that idea."

"You want a cup of coffee to go with it?"

"Yes. Probably should make it decaf."

Nell nodded. "Be right back."

Donna sighed and leaned back. This was all so surreal. And she wasn't even talking about the fangs. Although what was *that* about? Should she call her dentist? Maybe. But really, just being here on her own, that was something.

She'd do more of it too. Just as soon as she put everything with the Villachi crew behind her. Then she could move on with her life.

Except for this business with the overnight makeover and the new set of choppers. That couldn't just be a stress reaction, could it?

Or was it time to stop pretending that what had happened in the cemetery hadn't been just some freaks in cosplay?

If that's what she was going with, it was so far-out it made the mob seem like the least of her problems.

CHAPTER 8

Donna thought she'd go home and crash after everything she'd eaten (neither slice of pie ended up making it home), but she wasn't the least bit tired. Because of that, she decided to get to work on the house.

Namely, Joe's closet.

By six a.m., she had bagged up almost everything. She had two piles: donate and discard. Most of it was in the donate pile. Joe loved suits, and almost all of his were custom-made and very expensive. She already knew Joe Jr. wouldn't want them. Not only was he three inches taller and fifty pounds lighter than his father, he wore a uniform every day. Hopefully, the charity shop would make some decent money off of them.

There were fifteen bags altogether, including the suits, shirts, ties, and shoes. She'd included some of his casual stuff and his big collection of team jerseys, but most of his around-the-house clothing had gone into the discard pile.

For a man who liked designer goods outside the house, inside he'd worn a lot of holey T-shirts and basketball shorts.

She'd held back a few things in case Joe Jr. wanted something to remember his dad by, but Donna doubted it. The kid had done his best to distance himself from his father. Still, things sometimes changed after a loved one passed.

Funny term to use for Joe. *Loved one.* She had loved him. And she was sure the kids loved him, because he was their father, but they certainly didn't *like* him.

Lucky meowed and rubbed against her legs.

She looked at him. "You hungry?"

He meowed again and pawed at her.

"Okay, come on. I should get a cup of coffee too. Then I have to get ready. Big day today." She was off to see Rico. Going to see the FBI agent who had the power to put most of the people she knew in prison shouldn't fill her stomach with butterflies. But it did.

She also had an appointment with her therapist this afternoon. Maybe talking about how Rico gave her butterflies would be a good topic.

In the kitchen, she fixed Lucky a dish of food, gave him fresh water, then got herself some coffee and took it back upstairs.

She wasn't hungry, not surprising after the enormous meal she'd eaten only a few hours ago, but if that changed, she could get something while she was out. She needed to grocery shop anyway.

Her fridge was filled with funeral food, but there wasn't much chance she'd eat any of that. For one thing, she didn't trust other people's cooking.

For another, all of that stuff was filled with so many carbs. Which didn't seem to be affecting her like they used to, but old habits died hard. And if she was going to indulge in carbs, it was going to be more pie from Blue Bell's Diner and not Betty Francesco's cream of chicken and asparagus casserole.

Donna showered, washed her hair, did her makeup with a lighter hand than usual, then picked out something appropriate. What did one wear to visit an FBI agent? Especially when one had to choose from a limited wardrobe of clothes that still fit.

She went with a black and red patterned wrap dress because it could be adjusted, but after she had it on, she realized it was the kind of dress that needed heels. There was no way she wanted to be in heels all day, even if she'd be sitting down for a good portion of the time.

Even so, she tried on her black studded Valentino pumps. She sighed longingly as she turned to and fro in the mirror. They were definitely the way to go. But her feet would be crying after an hour. It would be the funeral all over again.

Maybe she'd take a pair of flats to change into. She really wanted this look for when she saw Rico. It showed off her new figure. Which was a vain reason to wear them, but at least she could admit that truth.

She grabbed a pair of black flats and set them on the bed to take with her, then found the perfect structured blazer to wear instead of a coat. Late October weather was definitely getting chilly, but she'd been out last night in just a sweater, and the temperature hadn't bothered her. Plus, the sun would probably be out. That would help.

Her engagement ring stayed in her jewelry box. She opted just to wear her diamond wedding band instead. That felt like a good compromise since she didn't really want to wear either one. If she ran into someone she knew, someone who would judge her, this wouldn't raise any eyebrows.

Some diamond hoops, a gold bracelet, and she was done. Pretty understated, considering she owned enough bling to open up her own shop.

Joe had always thought jewelry was the way to keep her happy. To keep her quiet. It wasn't, but he'd never taken the time to dig deeper. She'd let it go, too, because if nothing else, it was inventory that could be sold for escape money.

Or for money to live on, like she still might have to do someday. But she'd cross that bridge when she came to it.

Lastly, she found a big pair of sunglasses perfect for hiding behind. Anyone who recognized her would expect her to be red-eyed from crying. With these glasses on, it was impossible to tell what her eyes looked like.

She took the flats and her now-empty coffee cup and went downstairs. She put her cup in the sink. Lucky's dish was empty, but he was nowhere to be found. Probably napping somewhere. He had dry food if he got hungry. "Bye, Lucky. See you later, baby."

Then she headed to the garage, stopping at the coat closet to retrieve the duffel bag and the boot box. She also set the house alarm. No one was getting in while she was away.

Both packages were going into the trunk, then she thought better of it. The duffel with the cash went on the rear seat behind the driver's seat, the boot box in its shopping bag went on the floor in front of the duffel. That way, if she showed Rico the duffel bag from the drop-off, there wouldn't be a million dollars just sitting there.

There was almost no chance that anything would have come of the money being in the trunk, but with the way things had been going lately, those weren't favorable odds.

Money secured, she opened the garage door and left for Westbrook Credit Union. The day was gray. Not what she'd expected, but even with the cloud cover, it seemed oddly bright. She kept the sunglasses on.

The bank errand took thirty minutes. She listed Cammie as a co-owner of the safe-deposit box, just in case something went horribly, horribly wrong. She also realized, based on the curious looks from the tellers, that bringing a duffel bag into the bank had probably not been her best move.

She should have brought the money in gradually. As much as she could carry in her purse. No more. It would have taken longer to get the money out of the house that way, but it didn't matter now. What was done was done.

At the last minute, she kept two bundles of hundreds. If her feet held up, she might do some shopping after her appointment with La. She'd have to pay the money back from the insurance when she got it, but she really needed a few things that fit. Besides, if a little mental and emotional therapy was good for her, so was a little retail therapy.

Not that she was going to spend all of that. But having some cash on hand was probably a good idea.

She was going to be early to Rico's office, so she got coffees for both of them. The good stuff. She knew he'd appreciate that. The coffee at his office wasn't worth drinking. She knew. She'd tasted it. And if she was going to tell him what had gone down the other night, she wanted a hot, comforting drink to keep her company while she did it.

Before parking at his office, however, she drove around the block twice, watching the cars behind her, making sure she wasn't being tailed. That was the last thing she needed.

The coast seemed clear. She parked but sat in the car a few minutes longer making sure no one pulled in behind her. Finally satisfied, she grabbed her purse and the coffees and walked in. She took her sunglasses off. Seeing the FBI insignia etched into the glass door always filled her with courage.

This was the right thing to do and the right place to do it.

She went straight to the front desk and the receptionist battle-ax, Marlene, who was always there. "Hi. Agent Medina, please. He's expecting me."

Marlene looked up with hard eyes and an unforgiving jawline. "Name?"

"Donna Barrone." This was the third time Donna had been here in two months, but Marlene must not have a memory for faces or names. Odd for someone who worked at the FBI. Especially at the office of one of the FBI's Organized Crime Units. Or did Donna look that different? Either way, Donna decided to give the woman a big hint. "The wife of the late Joseph Barrone."

The older woman's eyes widened momentarily, then she regained her composure. It happened so fast, Donna wasn't sure she'd have noticed it if she wasn't paying attention. "I'll call Agent Medina for you."

"Thanks." Donna backed away as the woman picked up the phone. She walked over to the bulletin board showing pictures of the FBI's most wanted. Had Joe been up there before his death?

"Agent Medina, your appointment is here," Marlene said into the phone. "You're welcome." She hung up and looked at Donna. "He'll be right out."

"Thanks."

He was right out too. Less than a minute later, the door on the right opened, and Rico appeared in navy pants and a light blue dress shirt with the sleeves rolled up. His navy tie was patterned with gold handcuffs, and she instantly wondered if it had been a gift. His gaze raked her, but he snapped his head up as if he'd forgotten himself. "Donna. Good to see you."

"You too." She smiled at him. What wasn't to smile at? He was a few years her junior, fit in that lean, rangy way of the ex-military, and ruggedly handsome. There was something the slightest bit feral about him too. Like he wasn't the kind of man you wanted to make angry. "I brought you coffee."

There was concern in his eyes. She hadn't expected that, only because their relationship had always been very businesslike. Probably how the agency wanted it. Although, he'd also left those messages for her. Something had changed. "That was kind of you. Are you okay?"

She nodded, a little confused. Did he mean because of Joe's death? He knew how she felt about Joe, though, so that didn't seem like what he was referring to. Based on everything that had been happening, her inability to follow Rico's comments seemed on track. "Sure. I'm good." She shrugged one shoulder. "You know."

He gave a quick nod to the woman behind the counter. "Thanks, Marlene." Then he held his arm out toward the door he'd just come through. "Let's go to my office and talk."

"Great," Donna said. She preferred the privacy of that space, even though she knew everything she said became part of her record.

She walked with him through the bullpen into his office. A few heads turned, but mostly she got side glances. Joseph Barrone's widow was in the building. That didn't happen every day. She waited to sit until he'd shut the door.

She held out his coffee, which he took. "Black, right?"

He nodded. "Yes, good memory."

Black coffee wasn't hard to remember. She sipped hers. She'd had the barista add a shot of mocha. "Sorry I was out of touch for a bit there."

He drank a little of the coffee, then set it on his

desk. "I understand. But you had me worried. Especially after what happened two nights ago."

"Oh?" She sat up a little straighter. "What happened?"

He glanced toward a file on his desk. "You haven't heard? I guess you wouldn't have. With Joe gone, you're probably not as keyed into the Villachis' goings-on."

"No, I'm not." She wasn't sure it had as much to do with Joe being gone as her being busy fighting off an ambush. "What happened?"

"We don't know all the details yet, but a deal went bad. Very bad. Two of Tony's boys ended up dead."

"Oh no. Who? Frankie? Vinnie?" They might all be part of the problem, but she'd rather see them locked up than taken out.

Rico flipped open the file on his desk. "Turo Sanudo and Sam Doria."

She shook her head. "Those aren't names I recognize, and I'm not *that* out of the loop. Everyone—and I mean everyone—was at the funeral and the reception that followed at the house. I'd remember if I'd been introduced to new people. Are you sure they're Big Tony's guys?"

His gaze stayed on the file. "Pretty sure. He was seen with them at the Starlight Lounge last week. And they all golfed together two weeks ago at the Westbrook Country Club."

All the wiseguys golfed. Didn't matter if you were a boss or a lunk, you had a set of sticks and knew enough not to get kicked off the course. It was a way to get together, smoke cigars, drink beer, and talk shop without fear of being bugged. "Yeah, well, I still don't know them. They must be new. I didn't realize Tony was expanding his crew."

"These guys might have been a one-off for this particular job. We're not sure." Rico closed the file. "Anyway, how are things going with Joe gone? I'd ask you how you're doing, but you look like you're doing fine."

She smiled. "I'm doing well. I keep having to remind myself that I'm supposed to be the grieving widow. I just can't bring myself to be all broken up about a man who did such terrible things and made me fear for my children's safety and my own."

"I understand." His smile went from jovial to tentative. "Are you still going to testify for us?"

"About that." She sighed. "Not exactly. *But* I am happy to give you all the information I can. And I have a lot that you haven't seen yet. I don't want to do anything that would put myself or my kids in danger. Joe's gone. I'm free."

Rico frowned. "You really believe that?"

"Yes. Mostly. But I know it won't be complete freedom until the Villachis are put away. I want that. That's why I'm here."

"Good. Anything new going on that you know about?"

"Sort of. Big Tony approached me after the funeral. He told me if I finished Joe's last job, a package drop-off, that I would be free to live my life."

Rico's brow furrowed, and he laughed bitterly. "You

don't really believe that, do you? I mean, you're not going to do this drop-off, are you?"

She sat back with a little attitude. "It's already been done."

His brows lifted.

She shrugged. "It was too good an opportunity to pass up. But here's the thing. It wasn't so simple."

"Of course it wasn't. Nothing with Big Tony ever is."

She held up her hands. "I was stupid to think it would be. I know that. Wishful thinking, I guess."

"What happened?"

"Someone set me up. The bag I was supposed to deliver? Full of wrapped newspaper. And the guys I was supposed to deliver to? They tried to kidnap me. Or maybe they were going to do worse. I'm not sure. I managed to get free."

His eyes narrowed. "How many guys?"

"Three. Why?"

"Because that's how many new guys Big Tony hired. And that's how many were involved in the deal that went bad."

CHAPTER 9

"No." Alarms started ringing in Donna's head, but she tried to shut them down. "These weren't Tony's guys. These guys were there to take delivery of the package. They had to be working for whoever Tony was doing business with."

"Are you sure?"

She hesitated, not wanting to think Big Tony was behind this, even though she knew he had to be the prime suspect. Besides Vinnie, he'd had the most access to the bag, after all. It just would really complicate her life if he was to blame. "No, I'm not."

"I know that's hard to swallow. It means your brother-in-law was behind this."

She shook her head. "It's not that hard to think about. This is Tony Villachi we're talking about. He's ruthless. But why would he want to hurt me?"

"Maybe he knows you want out?"

"Maybe." She suddenly realized what he'd said earlier. "Wait. So two of these guys are dead?"

Rico nodded. "Yes, but the third, Albert Moran, survived."

Two men dead. So sad. But it was no surprise that

Big Tony had taken his revenge for the failed mission. "Do you have this Albert in custody?"

"No, he's at Mercy General. But we're being kept in the loop. We'll speak to him when he comes to. More importantly…" Rico's expression hardened a little. "You need to tell me who went with you."

"No one. Just me."

Incredulous, he raised his brows. "Could someone have followed you?"

"Didn't seem like it. What are you getting at?"

"Two men are dead, Donna."

"Right, you said that. Wait. Are you saying you think I did it? I didn't kill anyone. I just fought my way free." The memory was blurry in places as she tried to piece it together. She needed to change the subject until she could gather her thoughts. "You think Tony hired these three new guys to handle this one specific job?"

Rico's gaze was piercing. He wasn't letting up. "Where did this drop-off of yours take place?"

She stared at her coffee cup. There was no way to go except forward. "An old industrial park near Midden."

"And you're sure you weren't followed? And that no one went with you?"

"I'm not completely sure I wasn't followed, but I promise on my children's lives that I went alone." She picked her gaze up. "H-how did the men die?"

"Blunt force trauma."

Those three words were chilling. Was it possible? Had she really done that? She knew she'd been high on

93

the adrenaline of the situation, but there was no way she was physically capable of that kind of damage.

Was she? "Do you think I did that?"

"Honestly, no. But this job has taught me to expect the unexpected."

There were other possibilities. She pointed them out. "Maybe Big Tony followed me. Or showed up after I left. Or sent a couple more of his guys to see how things were going."

"Maybe. What time was the meeting?"

"Nine."

"Fits time of death."

She shook her head, out of words. The idea that she might have killed two men left her numb with grief and disappointment, even if they had been trying to hurt her.

Rico seemed to sense she was closing down and changed the subject. "We found a few shell casings, but they matched the guns recovered at the scene. Also, none of the men were shot."

She had been, though. Her trench coat was proof of that. "Blood?"

"A good bit. All but one sample matched the three men. The lab is still trying to find a match for that one."

That had to be hers. Which wasn't on file, that she knew of. Or was it? She didn't know. Couldn't think clearly enough to figure it out. Funny that she'd never had a panic attack before, but sitting here in Rico's office, she felt like she might be about to have her first one. Holy smokes, she was going to have a lot to talk to La about this afternoon.

But right now, she needed fresh air.

"I should go." She clutched the strap of her purse. "I just remembered a thing I have to do."

She didn't wait for Rico's response, just got up and left the office, walking as quickly toward the door as her stupid high heels would let her.

"Donna?" Rico called after her.

She kept going.

He didn't catch up with her until the parking lot. "Hey, hold up. Wow, you can move. When did you get so fast?"

Key fob in hand, she turned, squinting even in the overcast light. "I need to go."

"What aren't you telling me? I know you're holding back, and it's clear you're freaking out about something. I don't think you killed those men, okay?"

"But you think I'm capable of it."

"We're all capable of it if the situation is right. But I like to think I know you well enough that killing someone is the last thing you'd want to do."

"It is." Ending a life, or two lives, would make her as bad as the Villachis. At least Rico understood that. "Then how did those men end up dead?"

"Most likely, the person who killed them was already there, waiting to see how things went down. When the guys failed to do whatever they were supposed to do, they paid the price."

That didn't explain why one man had been left alive. Or why none of the men had been shot. The Mafia did things a certain way. Bullets were a big part of that. But she let it go, because it felt like Rico was

95

doing his best to find another explanation, and she appreciated that.

He leaned against her car. "So what's going on? Did Tony threaten you? Someone else? You know we can protect you. I need to know everything that happened the other night so I can piece this together."

She shook her head, so upset she couldn't think straight. She wanted to tell him everything. If only just to tell someone. "That's the problem. I…don't really know what happened."

"Come back inside. You can tell me what you do know, and maybe we can make sense of it together."

She glanced toward the office. What if Tony had tried to have her kidnapped, or worse, killed because he figured out she was about to rat them all out? "I'm afraid."

"I know." He reached out and took her hand, surprising her. "But I also know how brave you are. And how much you want to put all of this behind you."

She thought about her kids and what they would want her to do. The right thing. It's what she'd always taught them. She nodded and took a breath. His hand was warm and strong and a little calloused. "Okay."

They walked back in together. Donna prayed Rico didn't laugh when she told him the whole story. Well, maybe not the whole story. There were a few parts she planned on leaving out. She couldn't afford to have him think she'd lost it.

In his office, she sat in the same chair. He closed the blinds so that no one could see in. Not like they didn't know she was already in there, but it gave her a little sense of privacy all the same.

"Can I get you anything? Warm up your coffee?"

"No." Her taste for it was gone now. She put her purse on the other chair, then looked him straight in the eyes as he sat behind his desk. "Are you going to record this?"

"Do you want me to?"

"No. I would prefer you didn't. Not this first part, anyway."

"Okay." He sat back and folded his hands over his belt buckle, the curiosity in his gaze undeniable. "I'm listening."

She couldn't look at him all of a sudden, so she focused on the file on his desk. The tab read Villachi #301. Was that how many files they had on Big Tony's organization?

She took a breath and began. "The drop-off was at nine, but I didn't go straight there. I found some things at the house, things I want to turn over to you. We'll talk about it more later but suffice it to say that what I found made me very angry. So I left early and went to the cemetery to have it out with Joe one last time."

She looked up at him. He was nodding like he understood. "I had a whole speech planned, but before I could really get into it, I was knocked down and attacked by some idiot playing at being a vampire."

Rico's smile disappeared. "What?"

She nodded. "He bit me and everything. Knocked me out. When I came to, a woman was crouched over me. Checking that I was all right. She apologized for her friend and said she had to go after him. And then she was gone. Just like that."

His eyes widened slightly, then immediately narrowed as he pushed forward in his chair. "Did you have a doctor look you over?"

"No, but I'm fine." The fact that he even asked such a thing made him more caring than Joe had ever been. "I checked myself out when I got home. I didn't find any marks. Not even a bruise."

That seemed to relax him. "You're sure you shouldn't still see a doctor?"

"Positive." She turned her head and pulled her hair back on the side where she'd been bitten. "See? Nothing."

He exhaled. "Okay. Then what happened?"

"I realized I was in danger of being late for the drop-off, so I jumped in the car and hit the gas." She wasn't telling him everything but leaving out the craziest parts seemed like the best decision. Explaining that she'd woken up to find herself drinking blood from the wrist of a woman named Claudette just wasn't something Donna wanted in her file, because even if this wasn't being recorded, Rico would undoubtedly add his own notes.

"Did you make it in time?"

"I did, although I'd really wanted to be early. There was another car there, which I expected. I didn't really know what to do next, though, so I got out and opened my trunk to get the duffel bag I was given to deliver. That's when the first guy rushed me."

"Did you get a look at his face?"

Was this a test? "No. They had ski masks on."

He nodded. "Yes, that matches how we found them. It also supports the kidnapping idea. If they'd intended to kill you, hiding their faces wouldn't have mattered. What then?"

"He was coming toward me, and I thought he was going to shove me into the trunk. Not sure why, but that's what I thought. Anyway, as I turned I realized there was a second guy coming at me from the other side of the car. He grabbed me with his arm around my throat."

Rico's gaze went very serious.

She kept talking, miming the moves she'd made by reaching her hands toward her throat. "I used his arm for leverage to pull myself up and kick the first guy away."

"Smart," Rico said.

"I bit the second guy and got him to release me, then punched him as hard as I could." She faded back into the moment. "That's when I heard the car door open and the first shot went off."

He let her talk, not saying anything.

"It grazed me. My shoulder. Or maybe it just grazed my coat, now that I think about it." Although she'd been sure she'd felt pain. "The blood sample that hasn't been matched could be mine. Not sure if I actually bled or not."

"I'll tell the lab."

"Thanks. Where was I? Oh, yes, something about being shot at flipped a switch in me. I got crazy-angry."

She smiled. "I'm half Sicilian on my mother's side, you know."

He grinned. "We know."

"Makes for a long, slow fuse that burns white-hot. Anyway, I turned toward the third man, the one shooting at me, and charged him." She shook her head. "All I can tell you is that something came over me that I can't explain. I shoved him into his car. I don't know how I had the kind of strength I had. I've never experienced anything like it before. Adrenaline, I guess."

"The driver's side window was shattered."

"That happened when he hit it." She pulled her bottom lip between her teeth for a moment. "Is he the one who survived?"

Rico shook his head. "From your telling, the man who survived would be the one you punched."

"Oh."

"I highly doubt you'll be charged with anything. It's up to the DA, but we have some influence. In case that's worrying you. For one thing, it was self-defense. For another, you're cooperating in an ongoing case. We make allowances for such things. For a third, I'm still not convinced you had anything to do with these deaths."

"Good to know." She stared at her hands. "But if I did kill them, I didn't mean to. I was terrified. And trying not to end up dead myself."

"The bureau knows. And considering the circumstances, you did exceptionally well."

"Thanks." But there was no real gratitude in her

SUCKS TO BE ME

voice. She was pretty convinced she'd ended two lives. That made her no better than Joe.

That was a lot to take in. A lot to process. La was going to earn her $275 an hour today.

If Donna went. She was starting to think she should just pack up and move while she still could.

CHAPTER 10

"Hey," Rico said.

She looked up.

"Don't torture yourself over those goons. They weren't saints. And they would have killed you. I'm sure of it."

She shrugged. "I'm sure you're right. Doesn't make me feel all that much better at the moment."

"Time helps." His chair squeaked as he shifted. "You said the bag you were given to deliver was filled with newspaper. Did you know that before you went to the drop?"

"No. Vinnie was adamant that I not look in the bag, so I didn't. It had a padlock on it anyway. But after the third man was knocked out, I got curious. That's when I realized something bad had been about to happen one way or the other."

"Who do you think did it?"

"The way I figure, it has to be one of three people. Vinnie, who dropped off the bag to me and stressed over and over that I'd better keep out of it. Big Tony, because the bag had to have come from him. Or Lucinda, his wife."

Rico made a face. "Why would your sister-in-law do that?"

"Because she's got some wild idea that I'm after Big Tony. Can you imagine?" Donna made a gagging sound. "Please."

Rico laughed. "He's so out of your league. I mean—" He blinked a few times. "It's just that—I've seen Big Tony. He's not exactly a male model, and you..."

For the first time since she'd returned to his office, she grinned. "Yeah?"

He flushed a little. "I shouldn't have said anything."

"But you did."

He took a breath. "You could have any man you wanted. That's all I'm saying. So Lucinda Villachi is crazy. Except, if she thinks you want to stay in the family, then she might imagine you'd come after Big Tony."

"I suppose. I've never given her any indication that's true, though." Her insides were warm and toasty from Rico's kind words. Also, the butterflies were back. Rico thought she could have any man she wanted.

Little did he know his was the only name on her list.

"Do you still have that duffel bag?"

"I do. It's in the trunk. Do you want me to go get it?"

"No, I can send one of my guys out to grab it."

What if he saw the boot box behind the driver's seat? He'd have keys to her car. He could do some snooping. "Why don't you just walk out with me when I leave? I'll give it to you then."

"That's fine. What's this stuff you found in your

house? The stuff that made you mad? Where did you find it?"

She sighed hard. "I found a secret room in Joe's office. A stash room. You can have everything in it. Or I'll find a way to dispose of it, but I'm guessing you might consider some of it evidence. Lots of guns, some body armor, boxes of ammunition, and a few more boxes of what looks like cocaine and marked playing cards."

His brows went up. "I'll take all of that. The guns could be especially important once ballistics tests them."

"That's what I thought too. But what I think you'll find the most interesting are the ledgers. There's one for every year that Joe worked for Tony."

Rico's eyes rounded a little, and his excitement was undeniable. "Ledgers?"

She nodded. "I looked at one of them. Didn't make much sense to me, but there's a whole lot of names, numbers, dates, information like that. I figure you guys will make sense of it."

"When can I have them?"

"The sooner that stuff is out of my house, the better. But first, do we have a deal?"

His eyes tapered down like he was thinking. "About?"

"I want your word that I won't have to testify and that you'll still protect me, since I'm providing you with all kinds of new evidence."

"You have it, Donna. I promise."

"Good. Now, we have to figure out a way for you to

get that stuff out of my house without making it plain that the FBI is paying me a visit. Any ideas?"

He smiled. "We can handle that. And we can be there tomorrow."

"We?"

"I'd like to bring another agent with me. Agent Kowalski. Good man. He's been working organized crime almost as long as I have, and with this case getting hot, the help would be welcome." Rico's phone buzzed. He looked at the screen and nodded.

She waited until he made eye contact with her again. "Okay. Tomorrow. What time?"

"Three all right? I should be able to coordinate everything by then."

"Yes. Text me if that changes."

"I will."

She looked at her watch. "I should go. I have another appointment I need to get to. Are we good?"

"We're good." He stood. "I'll walk you out and get that bag."

She got to her feet and started for the door. "I'll be happy to have it out of my trunk." Then she stopped and looked at him. "Regardless of whether Big Tony's the one who set me up or not, won't he expect me to give the bag back to him? He's texted and left me a voicemail, wanting to know how things went."

He came around from behind the desk. "So he's either playing dumb, or truly out of the loop. But I think playing dumb. Covering his bases so he looks innocent. Tell him the guys took the bag."

"But he'll know that's not true if he talks to the one who survived. What's that one's name again?"

"Albert Moran." Rico was so close she could smell his aftershave. It was clean and a little woodsy. "And Big Tony won't have that opportunity. We plan on taking Moran into custody this afternoon. The message I got earlier was to let me know ballistics matched the handgun found on him to a murder committed last year in Staten Island."

"Wow." Her brows lifted. "I can't wait to see what you find after you test all those guns of Joe's."

Rico's smile was sly and telling. "Me too. Now let's go get that duffel bag."

After she gave him the bag, she left. Her mood was good from talking to Rico, and she wanted to browse the little boutique that was next door to La's office.

My Closet was one of Donna's favorite places to look. She'd never done much shopping there, because even getting into their size eights had sometimes been impossible. She had a feeling things would be different today.

She parked, grabbed her purse, and headed in.

A soft chime announced her entrance. The store's interior looked like it was designed to cater to the mob wife. And maybe it was. Shades of pink adorned the walls, leopard carpet covered the floor, and three crystal chandeliers hung from the ceiling. Touches of gold completed the look.

Donna couldn't lie. It was appealing, but that was because it was somehow still done tastefully and with a touch of whimsy.

If Lucinda attempted that combination, she'd look like a reject from the *Jersey Shore* reality show. And not one of the cute ones.

"Hi there, welcome to My Closet," a salesgirl said.

"Hello," Donna answered. The store's name was meant to be cheeky, a way for women to truthfully answer their husbands when asked where their new outfit had come from.

"Anything I can help you find?"

"Just browsing at the moment. I'll let you know."

"Absolutely. Great shoes, by the way."

"Thanks." They were great shoes. So great Donna had forgotten she had them on. And usually by now, her feet would be aching for something comfier with a lower heel.

How odd. But the shoes were soon forgotten again, and a few minutes later Donna had an armful of things to try on in a swath of sizes. She had no idea what she'd shrunk down to, so trying a few was her only way to find out.

My Closet was known for its spendy, embellished jeans. Donna wasn't crazy about looking like she'd been the victim of someone's weekend bedazzling project, but she found a few pairs that weren't as disco fabulous as the rest.

She picked out some black pants too. And some leggings, a couple tops, a little black dress, and a black jumpsuit. Okay, and one pair of leopard pants. That should get her started. Once she figured out her size, she'd get serious.

The salesgirl put her things in a dressing room

while Donna did one more sweep of the store, but she stopped herself from getting too crazy until she knew her size. Plus, she had about half an hour before her appointment with La.

She started with the jeans, working her way through the largest size, an eight, and ending up in a four.

Time ticked by as she stared at the number on the tag in disbelief. A four? How was that possible? You didn't just go to bed and wake up a four. You just didn't.

She stared at her reflection in the mirror. The jeans not only fit, they looked phenomenal. These were a must-buy.

She got busy trying on the rest of her haul and found a few more things to add to her purchase pile. Two pairs of jeans, black leggings, some tunic-length T-shirts in small, the little black dress, and a slouchy sweater that hung off one shoulder in that sexy, nonchalant way she'd never quite pulled off before. It was a good mix. Enough to give her some options.

And as much as she would have loved to scoop up a few more *fours*, time was getting short. Running late to her therapist appointment would eat into her hour, and she had too much to discuss to do that.

Back in her wrap dress, she headed for the counter, arms full. "Found a few things."

The salesgirl smiled. "Wonderful. Is this your first time shopping with us?"

"No. But it's the first time I've been able to fit into anything comfortably."

The salesgirl's smile faltered, then she regained it. "Well...welcome back. And just so you know, new merchandise comes in every Thursday."

"Oh, I'll be back." While the girl rang up Donna's purchases, she slipped her hand into her purse and eased a few hundreds out of the bundle.

Then the girl gave her the total, and Donna eased out a few more. Whatever. This wasn't clean money, but it *was* Joe's money, and it would probably scorch him to know she was spending it on clothes.

She put the shopping bag into her trunk, then went straight into Dr. Goldberg's waiting room with five minutes to spare. She stood in front of the fish tank, watching the angelfish glide through the water like supermodels with fins.

Dr. Goldberg came out shortly. "Hello, Donna. How are you?"

Donna smiled. If there was anyplace she could be herself, outside of Rico's office, it was here. "I'm doing well."

"That's good to hear." Dr. Goldberg gestured toward her office. "Come on in, and let's talk about it."

Ursula Goldberg was some kind of hippie-chick, intellectual, earth-mother hybrid. Her curly gray and white hair hung past her shoulder blades, setting off her green eyes beautifully. She was curvy and played it up with long skirts, tunic tops, and hip belts. Thick silver cuffs embraced both wrists. Her round glasses were the same shade of blue as her turquoise stud earrings.

In the warmer months, she wore Birkenstocks. In the winter, cowboy boots.

She was cool without trying, and Donna liked her immensely. There was nothing remotely Mafia about her. Except that she knew how connected Donna was, but therein lay the beauty of the doctor-patient confidentiality privilege.

Donna could tell La anything. And had.

Today would be no different.

La pulled out her scuffed leather portfolio that she filled with white legal pads and picked up her pen, then looked at Donna and said the same thing she said at the start of every session. "What's new in your life?"

Donna took a breath. "I may have killed two men."

CHAPTER 11

In her usual unflappable style, La put her pen to the legal pad and started writing. "What makes you think this?"

"Well…" Donna gave her the short version of the long story, leaving out the part about the cemetery and focusing on what had gone down at the industrial park. And then what Rico had told her today.

When she was all done, La nodded. "I see. It does sound like you could be responsible. And you seem to think you are. How does that make you feel?"

"Terrible." Donna kicked off her heels and tucked her feet up under her. "Like if I'm capable of that, how am I any different than Joe?"

"You know how. What you did was in self-defense. The most basic act of self-preservation. The same can't be said for what Joe did."

Donna adjusted the drape of her dress. "I understand that, I do. And Rico said pretty much the same thing. But I can't help the way I feel."

"No, you can't, and those feelings are valid. Do you value Rico's opinion?"

"Absolutely. He's one of the few people I trust."

La jotted something down. "Has your opinion of him changed since Joe's death?"

"No. I still feel the same way about him."

La's eyes narrowed ever so slightly. "You don't find yourself more attracted to him now that you're no longer bound by the confines of your marriage?"

Donna snorted softly. "Yeah, maybe. I mean, he's a handsome man. Very handsome. And he's one of the good guys. How am I not supposed to be attracted to that?"

"It's a natural thing to feel. Especially at this point in your life."

"You mean because Joe's out of the picture?"

"In part, but there's more to it than that. You're truly alone for the first time in many, many years. Yes, Joe is gone, but your children have started their adult lives. And you've spent the entirety of your marriage protecting those children, struggling with the hard truth of your husband's life, and now that weight has been lifted. It would be understandable if everything you've been suppressing these last couple of decades suddenly came to the forefront, and you acted out in a manner that seems out of character."

Donna's mouth fell open. "Are you saying that it would be perfectly reasonable if I had a one-night stand?"

La laughed. "What I am saying is that you may feel like doing things that you never even considered when Joe was alive. Those feelings are to be expected. Welcomed, even, because they're the part of you that's been silenced coming to life again."

"Some of that's definitely been happening. But I'm not sure I like all of it. Some, yes. Some...not so much."

"Remember that just because you feel something, you don't have to act on it. But don't feel bad about those feelings either."

Donna took a breath. "Good to know. I have been going through a lot of changes recently."

"Like the weight loss?"

"You noticed."

"Hard not to," La said. "You look wonderful, but losing so much weight in such a short period of time hints at some underlying issues. You say you're not really grieving, but I'm not so sure that's true. On a subconscious level, you may be mourning Joe's loss more than you realize."

"This isn't because I'm not eating, I promise. And I am grieving in a way, I guess. But this is just..." Donna shook her head while La wrote on the legal pad. Funny that she'd been able to tell Rico about the incident in the cemetery, but couldn't bring herself to share that with La. Maybe Donna feared La would tell her it had all been a grief-induced hallucination? "Losing weight isn't anything I set out to do, I can assure you. It was more of a surprise, really."

"Well, listen. I know you have a doctor, but if you'd like a referral to a nutritionist, I can give you one. He might be able to help you sort this all out. Get you on a plan to keep you from becoming underweight."

"That's kind of you, but I don't think it's my diet. Not only have I had some cake recently, but last night I had a porterhouse, a loaded baked potato, a side of mac and cheese, and a buttered roll at Blue Bell's Diner. Plus two pieces of pie, one with ice cream. I am definitely eating."

La nodded and made some notes. "And there's nothing else going on that you haven't told me about?"

Donna frowned. Sometimes La keyed into things that gave Donna pause, like now. But Donna wasn't talking about what had happened in the cemetery. "Nope, nothing."

"All right. But your health should never be ignored. Especially as you approach menopause. Don't you think losing so much weight so quickly is concerning?"

"To some extent, yes. But I think it's just stress." Donna shifted to cross one leg over the other. This really wasn't what she wanted to talk about. "Speaking of stress, I found a secret stash room in Joe's office. He had drugs and guns in the house. Can you imagine? With our kids there. So yeah, with that and thinking I was going to turn state's evidence and then Joe's death and the funeral preparations and the whole drop-off gone wrong, my stress levels have been up lately. Really up."

"Those are all valid, high-stress events, so that does seem to track. But stress, as hard as it is, can bring about great things in our life. A Zen master once said, 'No mud, no lotus.' Does that make sense?"

"Yes. Sometimes the ugly brings about the beautiful. I need to go through this to get to the good stuff."

La smiled as she nodded. "Essentially, yes. Did you feel any relief at the funeral, or was it just stress?"

"Some relief. Having the kids and Cammie there

helped because I didn't have to deal with it alone, you know?"

"Do you feel like you have to be strong for the kids?"

"I do," Donna said. "But I also realized that they are going to be just fine. They're smart, capable adults. You know they knew what their father was really about. It's not like I have to pretend around them."

"Mm-hmm. That has to be freeing."

"It is." Donna smiled for a moment. "But as you know, because we've talked about this before, I struggle with the harsh reality they've had to face."

"Do they seem to be struggling with it?"

"Not really."

"What do you make of that?"

She let out a hard exhale. "I guess they're more resilient than I give them credit for?"

"I'd say that's true. Where do you think they learned that?"

Donna laughed. "Me? Well, it would have to be. They didn't learn much from Joe."

"You are a much stronger woman than I think you realize. I want you to work on recognizing and embracing that this week."

"I will." Donna tipped her head, thinking about that. She did need to give herself credit for surviving her life.

"What's next? I know you like to make plans."

"I do. I want to move to Florida when this is all over. Start fresh. Really leave this whole world behind. I'll miss you. And Cammie. But I'm never going to fully shake the shadow of the syndicate until I get some distance."

"I think that's a great idea. And I'm happy to recommend a few therapists in that state if you like. If you want to continue with therapy, of course."

"I think I will. It's incredibly liberating to be able to talk to someone with no judgment, no strings, and complete privacy. Not sure I'm ready to give that up." Then Donna realized there was one other person she'd miss besides La and Cammie.

Rico.

Maybe a one-night stand wasn't such a crazy idea after all. The image that suddenly filled her mind caused her cheeks to warm and a sudden smile to bend her mouth. She tipped her head, causing her hair to fall around her face.

"What's the little smile about?" La asked. "What just came into your head?"

Donna laughed softly and brushed a strand of hair back. "If I'm being honest, and I have no reason not to be…Rico."

La smiled. "Because if you're going to move anyway, you might as well test those waters. Am I right?"

Donna laughed a little louder this time. "You know me too well, I think."

"You're a woman in the prime of her life, undergoing great emotional upheaval. My only advice is don't do anything if you think you'll regret it."

"I don't think I'd regret Rico." Donna stared at the oval table between them and the iridescent blue bowl filled with clear and white marbles. "But it would hurt to get rejected by him, that's for sure. And I'm pretty sure there's an FBI policy about not sleeping with informants, so it's probably best I don't knock on that door. Better to just admire him from afar and keep my fantasies to myself."

"Whatever you think is best." La glanced at the clock on the bookcase. "Our time is almost up. Anything else you'd like to discuss before our session ends?"

Donna kicked her legs out and slipped her feet back into her shoes, sitting up straight. "Yes. One thing. If Joe left me money, and I know it's essentially blood money…" She tried to put her tangled thoughts into words.

"Should you feel guilty about spending it?"

"Yes."

"You already do, or you wouldn't be asking me this. Find a way to do something good with that money. Something you feel balances the bad. Or get rid of it. Maybe even a little of both."

"That's exactly what I was going to do. Thank you." She pulled the straps of her purse over her shoulder and stood. "Great session."

La got to her feet, her long skirt swishing. "Same time next week?"

"Absolutely. See you then. Have a great day."

"You too."

Donna went out to her car feeling like things were on the right path. Complicated, for sure, but nothing was so off the rails she couldn't handle it. After all, she'd managed her crazy life for this long and done a good job of it. There was no reason she couldn't keep managing it.

She started the engine and got onto the highway headed for the convent. Giving some of Joe's money to the convent would help a lot. She was excited about and looking forward to seeing her sister.

Maybe she could talk Cammie into transferring to a convent in Florida. Could nuns do that? Donna had no idea, but she was going to ask. Or at least bring up the subject. It would be great to have Cammie in Florida with her.

If Donna went to Florida. She wasn't having doubts, exactly, but if the FBI sewed up the Villachi crew, was there really a need for her to move? She'd still sell the house. It was too big and held too many memories she was ready to forget.

But maybe she'd just buy a nice condo somewhere. She could still buy a little place in Florida. Be one of those snowbirds.

She suddenly realized she had more options than she'd considered. Now she just had to figure out which ones made the most sense.

She took the exit for the convent and fifteen minutes later pulled into the parking lot of the Sisters of the Holy Rosary. She grabbed the boot box filled with cash and headed into the chapel.

After this donation, they ought to let Cammie do whatever she wanted.

Although, Donna had already decided the donation would be anonymous. There was no other option. Not if she wanted to distance this money from how it had been earned. If *earned* was even the right word, which it probably wasn't.

She genuflected at the back of the chapel and crossed herself, lifting her crucifix to her mouth. There was such peace here. She could see why this life held appeal. The chapel was empty except for a sister kneeling at the front. Her head was bowed in prayer.

Donna went straight to the donation box. The slot wasn't meant for large things, so she had to take the money bundles out of the box and put them in one by one. She kept an eye on the praying sister, but the woman stayed kneeling the entire time.

When the last bundle was through, Donna left the chapel and dropped the box in a trash receptacle as she walked around the building to the entrance of the convent.

Her being felt lighter for having made the donation. Part of her wished she could tell Cammie about it, but part of her was thrilled to have gotten rid of some of Joe's blood money in such a positive way.

But the real thrill came from knowing that Joe would have lost his mind over such an enormous donation.

And if that made Donna petty, then so be it. Because petty felt amazing.

CHAPTER 12

She followed the flagstone path around the side of the building. Crispy fall leaves littered the trail, crunching underfoot. The scent of woodsmoke filled the air. It was a perfect autumn afternoon, really.

It would probably turn into the perfect night to use the fireplace. That might be nice. Lucky would certainly enjoy it.

She lifted her hand to knock on the convent door, but it opened before her knuckles touched wood.

Sister Agnes Magdalena stood there. Donna recognized her only because she wore a particular blue ceramic-bead rosary that she'd gotten while serving in Guatemala or Nicaragua, something Donna knew because of Cammie. "Can I help you?"

"I'm here to see Camm—I mean, Sister Mary Lazarus Immaculata."

Sister Agnes frowned, perhaps because Donna had started to use Cammie's given name instead of her converted one. "Just a moment."

Sister Agnes shut the door, leaving Donna to stand outside.

"Not very charitable," Donna muttered with amusement. But it was fine. The weather was perfect. The only thing that bothered her was the light. Odd, because the sky was still overcast. But the sun was already headed down, and it would be dusk soon.

Her stomach rumbled. Maybe she'd pop into Blue Bell's on the way home for another steak. Her mouth watered. Definitely easier than cooking for herself. Cooking for one wasn't in her wheelhouse.

The door opened. "Donna!"

"Hi, Cammie. I mean, Sister Mary Lazarus."

Cammie snorted. "Thanks. Come in." Then her eyes went wide. "What on earth happened to you?"

"What do you mean?" But Donna realized instantly. "You mean the way I look."

"Of course I mean the way you look. Have you been starving yourself?"

"No, I promise."

Donna stepped inside. The foyer was wood paneled and opened onto a hall that led back to the private quarters, while dividing the common areas of the convent. A sitting room with a television for news was on one side, a dining room with a kitchen beyond on the other. "I think it's stress."

"Stress doesn't make you half the size you used to be and give you glowing skin."

Donna grinned. "You think I'm glowing?"

Cammie made a face. "What's going on?"

"Can we sit?"

"Sure, come on. But you're telling me everything."

Donna wasn't so sure about that.

Cammie led her into the sitting room and took a spot on the outdated couch. Donna took the matching mustard-yellow armchair. The living room furniture looked like it had been donated after someone's remodel in the late seventies. Which it probably had been.

Cammie crossed her ankles. "Is this why you came by? To explain why you're wasting away?"

"No, silly. I was just coming from Dr. Goldberg's and thought I'd see how my favorite sister is doing."

"I'm your only sister."

"True. But you *are* my favorite nun." There were no frills anywhere, something Donna had struggled with the first time she'd visited, but she'd grown to appreciate this simple life more and more.

"I'll give you that one. What did Dr. Goldberg have to say about all this?"

"That I am definitely under a lot of stress and that it's just something I have to get through, but that there is light on the other side."

"I still don't like it. But you look fabulous." Cammie leaned in. "Now what else is going on?"

Donna looked toward the hall. "Is this a safe place to talk?"

"Sure," Cammie said. Her brows bent. "Is this Villachi business?"

"I think you could call it that. Big Tony approached me at the funeral. Well, he called me into Joe's office to talk, actually. Like he had a right to that space."

"The nerve."

"That's what I said. Anyway, he basically told me that if I wanted out of the family, I had to finish Joe's last job."

"You said no, right?"

Donna shook her head. "No. I agreed to do it."

Cammie's mouth dropped open. "What the hell, Donna?"

Donna snorted. "Are you allowed to talk like that?"

"'Hell' is a Bible curse. And don't change the subject. I'm a little mad at you right now."

"Are nuns allowed to be mad at churchgoers? Especially widowed ones?"

Cammie glared at Donna. "Stop that already. How could you do something like that for Big Tony? He's a criminal."

"So was Joe. And I did it because he offered me a clean break. Plus, it was only a drop-off." She hesitated.

Cammie sighed. "Why do I feel a 'but' coming?"

"Because the drop-off didn't go so well."

Cammie threw her hands into the air. "Who would have predicted?"

"I'm fine, thanks for asking, but two of the three guys involved...not so much."

That got Cammie's attention. "What does that mean?"

"I should back up a little. I went to see Rico this morning."

"And?"

"The third man from the drop-off is in the hospital." Donna took a breath. "The other two are in the morgue."

Cammie's lips parted, but she didn't say anything, just sat there for a few long seconds. Finally, she spoke. "Did Big Tony go with you? Or some of his lunks?"

"No." Donna glanced at her lap. "I went alone."

Cammie shook her head. "So who killed those guys? Did you see anyone?"

"No. I didn't see another soul."

Cammie was silent a moment. "Wait a minute. Rico doesn't think that you—I mean, that's not possible." She gasped. "Did you take a gun?" Her voice dropped to a whisper. "Did you shoot those men, Belladonna?"

"No, yes, and no. And the gun never left the glove box."

"So Rico doesn't think you did it?"

"Right. Like you, he thinks there must have been someone else there. But I don't think that's the case. I think...I really don't know what to think. But I'm struggling with this, that's for sure."

"I'll pray for you. And pray that the feds find the real killer."

Donna nodded. Her sister was such a good person. "That's not even the whole of it. The bag I was supposed to deliver was filled with bundles of newspaper. Nothing worth actually delivering. So it was a setup from the get-go." She held her hands up. "Which means you were right in thinking I shouldn't do it. I was just so eager for the out, you know?"

"I know. And who could blame you? After all those years with Joe, this had to look like a gift. A chance to make the break you've been wanting. Without having to put yourself in the kind of position testifying would." Cammie took her sister's hand. "I can't imagine the courage it took to do something like that, but I know you did it with the kids in mind."

"I did. For all of us, really. I don't think Tony would dare come after you, but I wouldn't put anything past him."

Cammie's eyes narrowed. "He'd face eternal damnation if he came after me, especially here. This is sacred ground."

A younger nun came running in. "Sister Mary Lazarus, you'll never guess what just—oh, I'm sorry. I didn't know you had company."

"That's all right, Sister Grace." Cammie turned toward the young woman. "This is my sister, Belladonna."

Sister Grace's smile got a little bigger. "Nice to meet you, Belladonna. You've come on the most amazing day."

"Why is that?" Cammie asked.

"A miracle has occurred." Sister Grace was beaming now, her hands clasped before her in a state of prayer. "We have truly been blessed with God's abundance this day."

Donna had a sneaking suspicion what Sister Grace was talking about.

Cammie didn't, of course. "What is it? What's happened?"

Sister Grace pressed the tips of her fingers to her chin. "An anonymous gift in the donation box." Her voice went a little quivery. "Of a *million* dollars."

Cammie's mouth opened, but it took a moment for words to come out. "That is truly a miracle. God is good, and we are indeed blessed."

"God is good." Sister Grace nodded. "I have to go

tell the others." She waved at Donna. "Nice to meet you."

"You too," Donna said, waving back.

Sister Grace disappeared down the hall.

Cammie turned to face her sister with a curious but knowing expression. "Isn't that interesting?"

"It sure is." Donna looked at her watch. "I should probably let you get back to whatever nun business you need to do."

"Funny that the same day you decide to visit me out of the blue, an enormous anonymous donation shows up."

"It is funny. I'm glad I got to be here for it."

"Belladonna." Cammie's brows were arched so high they almost disappeared under the edge of her wimple.

"What?"

"Where did that money come from?"

"How would I know? I've been in here talking to you."

Cammie's mouth was a hard, bent line of no-nonsense skepticism. "Don't make me check the security cameras in the chapel."

Donna rolled her eyes. "You would do that? So much for donations being anonymous."

"Was it the insurance money? If it was, that was very generous, but don't you need that to live off of?"

"It wasn't the insurance money. It was money Joe had stashed away."

"Dirty money?"

"I don't know exactly how it was earned, but yes,

maybe." Donna glared at her sister. "And I can't believe you have security cameras in the chapel."

"Only on the altar. Did you really put a million dollars of Mafia cash in the donation box?"

Donna sighed. "Are all nuns as wily as you? Yes. But I wanted it to be anonymous."

Cammie put a hand to her head. "It will be. I won't say a word. Trust me. The last thing I want is for the Mother Superior to find out the origin of that donation. But that's a big number. Are you going to be okay giving away that much?"

"Yes. I'll be fine. So will the kids. There was more." She glanced toward the hall. "I'm only using what I need until the insurance money comes in, then I'm going to replace it. But I had to do some good with some of it right now. Something to balance out how it was probably earned."

Cammie nodded knowingly. "It will be put to good use here. But for the record, we are *not* God's money-laundering service. The church actually has a policy against accepting tainted donations."

Donna swallowed. "Are you going to turn me in?"

"No. I should. But the orphanage we support in Nicaragua is desperate for a second building."

"Thank you. That's what I was hoping for. That it would be used for good purposes." She picked up her purse. "Now I really should go. But I'll come see you again, I promise."

"I'd like that. Just no more dirty donations, okay?"

"Okay." Donna stood, and Cammie got up too. They hugged, then Cammie walked her out.

"Take care of yourself, Donna. Don't get any thinner. I mean it."

"It's not the plan. See you soon. Love you."

"Love you too."

Donna walked back to her car, happy that she'd accomplished most of what she'd come to do, but she wished she'd been able to confess to Cammie more of what had really happened. What would she think about Donna being attacked in the cemetery?

Or suddenly growing fangs?

Although those hadn't come back, so…had that actually happened? Or had those been a weird stress hallucination? Honestly, she wasn't sure about anything anymore.

Except that she really wanted a steak from Blue Bell's Diner, and she didn't care if it came with a baked potato or not.

Actually, she didn't even care if the steak was cooked. She was so hungry that raw sounded just fine.

Apparently, *weird* was her new normal.

CHAPTER 13

Donna ordered her porterhouse rare, which got her a look from the waitress, but being a Mafia wife meant Donna was used to looks. Most of them she wasn't meant to see, but she did.

Hard not to notice people staring and talking behind their hands. Or worse, trying to slyly snap a pic with their phones, which was never that sly given the size of people's phones these days.

Thankfully, Joe hadn't been as well-known as Big Tony. The Villachis had had a small bout with infamy ten years ago when one of Big Tony's crew had gotten popped for tax evasion, but the guy had kept his mouth shut, done his time, and after a while, the heat had died out a little. The incident was enough to put them all on the map, though.

Because of that, there were times when that small taste of notoriety made her sympathize with celebrities. Thankfully, most locals left them alone. Probably out of fear.

It wasn't ideal, but Donna was okay with it.

The waitress, unfortunately not Nell from the other night, brought Donna's plate. "You sure you don't want the sides? I could box them up for you."

129

"No, I'm good." Donna smiled as politely as possible. "Watching my carbs."

The waitress put the plate down, shrugged, and walked off.

Donna wasn't watching her carbs. Not lately, anyway. It was just that the thought of eating something that wasn't this steak turned her stomach. But the smell of the steak was making saliva pool in her mouth. In fact, if the diner hadn't been packed with people, she might have picked it up and bitten directly into it. She was that starved all of a sudden.

But the diner was full, as it was approaching dinnertime, so she remained civilized and used her knife and fork, cutting a good-sized piece.

Once again, at the sight of the juices running out of the steak, fangs shot through her gums.

Which confirmed that the first time hadn't been a fluke or a hallucination or some other weird, one-time thing.

She carefully navigated past the jutting canines to put the bite of steak into her mouth. As she chewed, she hoped they'd disappear like they had the other night.

They didn't.

There was no way to pretend this was normal. No excuse or explanation that she could come up with.

No human had fangs like this. Wolves, big cats. Honey badgers, maybe. Bears. Snakes had smaller versions.

But not people. Not unless they were…

She closed her eyes, unable to process the word that

would explain what had happened in the cemetery and why she was craving raw meat and why the sunlight bothered her eyes today.

She wasn't going to say it or think it or accept it, because it wasn't possible. Only people who'd lost their hold on reality would think a thing like that was even conceivable. Or genuine creepos, like those two in the cemetery.

The idea of those two still roaming around in the dark...

She ate the rest of her steak as quickly as possible, threw money down on the table, and left.

To her dismay, she was still hungry. Still craving meat. Preferably raw. Against her better judgment, she made a quick trip to her favorite grocery store, Wegmans, hitting the meat department for about ten pounds of steaks.

Hiding her fangs, she kept her mouth shut and her head down and made it back to her car without scaring anyone. Once she was behind the wheel, she exhaled and relaxed her clenched jaw. She was going to eat another steak or two as soon as she got home.

Home. With a glass of wine in front of the fire. That's where she needed to be. Maybe she'd even have a good cry about what a mess her life was.

Although, even with her life being a mess, she didn't really feel like crying. Besides being hungry and confused, she felt pretty good, actually. Like she could run a marathon. Or take on Big Tony. Not that she was going to do either of those things. But a run might not be a bad idea. A couple miles around the neighborhood.

A good sweat could cure a lot of things. Not fangs, probably. But maybe it would help her shake off some of this stress.

Then she could have her glass of wine in front of the fire. And then she'd have more steak, maybe some cake, just to counteract the calories burned on her run. After all, she'd told Cammie she wouldn't lose any more weight. She almost smiled as she headed for home.

That was the plan. And having a plan made her happy.

She hummed a little tune as she parked in the garage and went inside, making sure to turn on the house alarm after she shut the door.

Halfway to the kitchen to put the steaks away, she felt a sixth sense come over her. Like she wasn't alone. But that was impossible. The alarm was on. And would have been tripped if—she turned toward the living room.

A dark form filled Joe's recliner.

She sucked in a breath.

"Hello, Belladonna."

Claudette. The woman from the cemetery was in her living room. The room should have been dark without the lights on, but the moon and other ambient light from outside and a few electronics made it easy to see. Very easy.

Donna was well and truly freaked out. "What are

you doing in my house? How did you get in with the alarm on?"

Claudette smiled. "You're afraid. Don't be. I told you I would find you and explain things to you more fully. I'm keeping my promise, that's all. It took me longer than expected, and for that I apologize. But I'm here now."

"How did you know how to find me? Never mind. Just get out."

She frowned. "I don't think you mean that. Don't you want me to answer all your questions? Surely you haven't figured out everything already. Have you already made a kill? We don't do that anymore, you know. That's why I had to take care of Raul." She sighed. "That happens sometimes. A turning goes poorly. Not everyone takes to the change as well as you apparently have."

"Stop talking like I have any clue what you mean."

Claudette got out of the recliner in a smooth move that made her seem like she had liquid joints. "I see. You have yet to accept it."

"Accept what?"

She came closer to Donna until only a few feet separated them. "That you are now fully a vampire."

That word. Donna shook her head. "That's not possible."

"You already know it is. Pretending it's not changes nothing." Claudette smiled and showed off gleaming white fangs. "You've seen the signs. Experienced some of the changes. But the transition into the new life can be difficult when you weren't prepared to have to change at all. I understand that."

Donna was about fed up. "So that's why I'm no longer perimenopausal, right?"

"Right. Most come to the new life wanting it, but you weren't given that choice, so of course you must feel some resistance."

"You're talking nonsense. There's no such thing as vampires." But she was down with no more hot flashes.

Claudette vanished. "Isn't there?"

Donna gasped and turned. Claudette was behind her now. "How did you do that?"

"I am a very old vampire. My abilities are vast. Yours will develop over time as well. Your senses have already begun to heighten, as has the increase in your speed and strength, and you may develop a few other gifts as time passes." She shrugged, still looking very much like they were having a conversation about the weather. "Also, you now heal with great speed. Some of these things you have already noticed."

Donna wanted none of this. She just wanted to be left alone to live her life. "None of this is real. You need to leave."

"It's real all right," Claudette said. "But you must still complete the transition. And soon. Your hunger, which I am sure you are feeling, based on the steaks in that bag, will only get worse until you do. Let it go too long, and you will lose your control." Her eyes narrowed. "Bad things happen when vampires lose control."

Donna shoved past Claudette and went into the kitchen, flipping the light on, then dropping the bag of steaks on the counter. She turned, half expecting the woman to be gone. Hoping, actually.

She wasn't.

Donna stared at her. Claudette was even more beautiful in the light. "How is this possible? Vampires aren't real."

Claudette blinked. "Because it is possible. Am I not here in front of you?"

Donna leaned against the counter, her arguments fading fast. Could this really be happening to her? Then a new thought came to her. "Wait a minute. I thought vampires had to be invited in."

"We do."

"Then how are you in my house?"

"You are no longer human. You are in between right now, so that rule no longer applies to you."

Donna frowned. "How convenient." Another thought popped into her head. She crossed her arms. "What about how vampires can't go into churches? I was in a church today. A chapel, actually, but don't tell me that's some kind of exception."

Claudette's forehead furrowed. "It isn't. And that shouldn't be—" Her gaze dropped to the crucifix around Donna's neck. She pointed at it. "Were you wearing that when you were bitten?"

Donna's hand went to the necklace. "Yes. I always have it on."

Claudette's right eyebrow arched. "Interesting. I've only heard of that happening, but I guess it's true. Sacred places shouldn't affect you, then. I'd still tread lightly once you've made the full transition."

"You keep talking about this transition. What does that mean?"

"You need to drink properly to turn fully." Claudette's gaze took on a knowing gleam. "From a human."

"Yeah, I'm not doing that." Donna's lip curled. "Please, can we just leave this for another time?"

Claudette sighed in obvious frustration. "You must."

"Or else what?"

"You will succumb to the thirst. Or you will die."

Donna hated those kinds of threats. "Or maybe I'll go back to being human."

Claudette stared at her. "That won't happen."

"How do you know?"

The vampire growled softly. "Why are you resisting this? Becoming immortal is something most people crave. They would give anything to achieve it. You act like you're being punished."

"Hello! I didn't ask for this." She'd wanted freedom. Not more rules and regulations.

Claudette held up her hands. "I acknowledge that. But there is nothing you can do about it now. Just let me help you get through this, and then you'll see what a gift you've been given."

"Help me? So, like, you're going to take me out to find a victim? I don't think so."

A muscle in Claudette's jaw twitched. "We have the ability to glamour our subjects, making them pliable and taking away their fear. Most humans find it a pleasurable experience, actually."

Donna crossed her arms again. "I find that incredibly hard to believe. Really, just go, I'll be fine."

"You won't be. But…" Claudette was silent for a long moment. "You are not ready for my help. When you are, call me."

"Sure. Using what? The number I don't have?"

"Not that kind of call. You reach out to me with your mind. I'm your sire, we're linked. You call for me, and I'll hear you and come."

Sure, that made perfect sense. Now vampires were psychic. Donna's face probably showed her skepticism, but she didn't care. This was weird. Anyone in her situation would have thought so. "Right. Can you go now? I really want to be alone."

Claudette reached into her jacket pocket and pulled out a business card and put it on the counter. "In the meantime, there is a group you might try."

Donna glanced at the card. "Thanks, but I'm already in therapy."

"It's not therapy. It's a support group for newly turned vampires. It's run by a third-level empath. She's very good." Claudette pushed the card a little closer to Donna. "I will leave you now, but there are a few things you should know, whether or not you choose to believe them."

"Such as?"

"The thirst will win out, but if it gets to that point, you will lose control. Better to drink now while you are the one in charge. Listen for the heartbeat. Don't take too much."

Whatever that meant. "Noted."

"Secondly, you need to surround your house with iron to protect yourself from the fae. They are a vampire's natural enemy."

"Fae? Like, fairies?"

"Yes. And if you think they're like Tinker Bell, you're wrong. They will find you, and they will—"

"I thought werewolves were the natural enemy of vampires."

Claudette let out a low growl. "Do not believe everything you see in movies. There are good and bad werewolves, but they are mostly good and certainly not our enemy. You'll have to figure the rest out for yourself."

"Are you saying werewolves are real too?"

Claudette rolled her eyes. "Surround your house with iron or don't. I'm not sure I care."

She turned to go, then stopped and stared up at the ceiling. "No. I do care. I am your sire, and you are my responsibility. I wish you no ill will, even if you are the most difficult creature I have encountered in the last two hundred years." She glanced back. "Once you transition, stay out of the sun."

"Got it."

Claudette sighed. "You may not believe any of this yet, but you will soon enough. You won't have a choice. When you get there, call me."

Donna nodded, but couldn't keep the sarcasm out of her voice. "You'll be the first."

Then Claudette was gone.

That was a trick Donna wouldn't mind learning.

But that was all it was, right? A trick. Some kind of close-up magic.

Because this couldn't be real life. Vampires were a myth. So were werewolves and fairies. Or fae. Whatever they were called. None of those things were real. They couldn't be. Because that was crazy.

And yet, Donna was struggling to convince herself otherwise.

She picked up the card Claudette had put on the counter.

The First Fangs Club. A Women's Support Group.

A phone number was listed, along with an address and a meeting time. Friday nights at ten.

That was tomorrow night. Maybe she'd check it out. Or not. Donna didn't feel like she was in any kind of headspace to make a decision like that.

All she knew was that she wanted another steak and a glass of wine.

The run could wait until tomorrow, too.

CHAPTER 14

Sleep eluded Donna until almost four in the morning. She finally drifted off, only to be woken up a couple hours later by a throbbing headache and a body racked with pain. The TV was still on and was playing an infomercial for the only frying pan "you'll ever need for the rest of your life."

She groaned as she rolled over toward Joe's side of the bed. What had happened to her? Why did she feel like this? Was this some kind of delayed reaction to the fight at the drop-off? Or was this a brand-new kind of stress reaction?

Lucky, who'd been sleeping in Joe's spot, stretched and looked at her, blinking sleepily.

She scratched his head. "I hope you feel better than I do."

He hissed and jumped off the bed.

"Thanks. Good morning to you too." But she understood why he'd done that. The second she'd started speaking, she'd felt the reason. The fangs were back. She ran her tongue over her teeth. How fun. She stumbled to the bathroom and turned the light on, squinting against the sudden brightness.

The image looking back at her in the mirror was

horrifying. Her face was a wash of dark shadows and deep hollows. She looked malnourished. Worse. She looked like she was dying.

Everything Claudette had said came rushing back.

"No." Donna shook her head. "I refuse to believe anything she said. It can't be real."

Then she curled her lips back to look at the fangs. She pinched one between her fingers and tried to wiggle it. Didn't budge. Okay, so the fangs were real. There was no denying that. But did they mean she was turning into something else?

She didn't want to answer that question.

Her stomach growled, long and low. She *was* hungry. And she had all that steak in the refrigerator. That's what she needed. Some red meat. A good source of iron. That would perk her up. That and some coffee. But then she was going back to bed. Rico wasn't due to arrive until three.

She set the alarm for two, which would give her plenty of time to sleep her way back to normalcy. If not, there was always the hope of a hot shower and a lot of makeup.

She pulled on her robe and took the back steps down to the kitchen. With the light on under the microwave, there was no need to turn any others on, which suited her just fine.

The card Claudette had given her was still on the counter. She picked it up and stared at it for a moment, then tucked it into the pocket of her robe. She got a cup of coffee brewing.

With that started, she turned on the grill section of

the Wolf range so it could heat up. Steak for breakfast might be a little odd when it wasn't accompanied by eggs, but it would be the least-odd thing in her life right now.

The fridge was her next stop. She got out a package of ribeyes. Two of the biggest ones Wegmans had had in the case. A liberal sprinkling of salt and on the grill they went. The instant sizzle and aroma made her stop and inhale.

She turned on the exhaust so the house wouldn't fill with smoke, then leaned in to sniff the steaks again.

Every fiber of her being ached for sustenance. Was this the hunger Claudette had talked about? If so, Donna prayed the steaks would do the trick.

The Keurig sputtered out the last few drops of coffee. She added some cream and real sugar, then took a sip. It was good, but did nothing to assuage the growing urge inside her for something more substantial.

She found the long-handled tongs and flipped the steaks after two minutes. Another two minutes and she pulled them off onto a plate. She wanted them rare and juicy.

She turned off the grill, and while the steaks rested, she fixed Lucky some breakfast. Poor cat. She hadn't meant to spook him with her fangs.

Or had he freaked out because he'd sensed she was…different?

"Lucky boy. Breakfast," she called out. "Here, kitty, kitty."

He appeared at the edge of the kitchen, more likely

drawn by the scent of meat than his canned tuna surprise.

Joe had insisted they give the cat a gangster's name. Lucky Luciano had been Donna's suggestion, and the kids had clung to it, beating out Joe's suggestion of Scarface. As if. What kind of name was that for a sweet kitty?

As a gesture of apology, she cut some steak up for Lucky and put it on a little dish. "There you go, baby." She kept the fangs hidden as best she could while she talked to him. "Mama's sorry I scared you. Friends?"

He gave her a wary glance, then went straight for the food.

Maybe not friends yet, but close enough. She went to her own plate, forgoing the knife and fork and picking up the meat with her hands. She ate over the sink, juice dripping off her chin and fingers.

In minutes, both steaks were gone.

She rinsed her hands and face. She did feel better. And her fangs had retracted. She took that as a sign that, at least for now, things were under control.

How long would it last, though?

She went into the half bath off the powder room and took a look in the mirror to confirm all was well.

It was. The shadows and hollows were gone. So was her headache and the pain in her body. She looked awake and vibrant. And she wasn't tired anymore.

Suddenly, the run she'd put off last night seemed like a great idea. Normally, she'd never attempt such a thing after eating, but then, normally, she wouldn't have downed two ribeyes like they were delicious meaty cupcakes.

Another sip of coffee and she ran upstairs, changed into her cool-weather running gear of leggings and a long-sleeved compression top, pulled her hair through a ball cap, and tied on her sneakers. With her iPhone strapped to her arm and earbuds in, she went downstairs, turned off the alarm, and left through the garage.

The sun wasn't up yet, but the sky wasn't pitch-black either. She had about an hour before the sun breached the horizon. She'd be back home in forty minutes. There was no danger of sun exposure.

Of course, if she believed what Claudette had said, there was no danger until she transitioned anyway. Which she hadn't done yet and apparently wouldn't until she drank from her first human.

She grimaced. The idea was flat-out gross. Drinking blood? From another person? Nope.

Her stomach rumbled, sending a cold chill down her spine. Part of her didn't think it sounded gross at all.

She squeezed her eyes shut and grasped her crucifix. *Please don't let me turn into a vampire.* It wasn't going to happen. She wasn't going to let it. She opened her eyes, turned on her tunes and her running app, and took off on her usual route.

She started slow, like she usually did, settling into a rhythm and getting her breathing right. Then she picked up her pace and decided to test what Claudette had said about getting faster.

The forty-minute round trip through the neighborhood took her seven minutes and twelve seconds, according to her running app, which was now flashing a Personal Best badge.

That wasn't possible. And yet, she'd just done it. She wasn't even sweating.

She ran the loop one more time, really pushing herself on the second go.

Five minutes, thirty-seven seconds, and she was just slightly winded. She stood in her driveway, staring at the time on her app.

She didn't want it to be true. But there was no denying what her phone was showing her.

She swallowed down the sick feeling rising up in her throat. How much longer could she deny what was happening to her?

This wasn't stress. Stress didn't make your skin glow and improve your running time. It didn't make you crave raw meat and give you a surgery-free boob lift.

But she still couldn't wrap her head around the word *vampire*. She didn't want to. It was so foreign a concept, so far off and filled with make-believe, that accepting it felt like admitting she'd lost her grasp on reality.

That wasn't how she wanted to start this new chapter of her life.

More than that, it was unfair. She'd finally gotten the freedom she'd craved for years, and now she had to deal with this new twist? She didn't want it. Didn't want any part of it.

She took a deep breath of morning air, then went back inside feeling completely at sea.

She made a second cup of coffee and took it upstairs, deciding on a quick shower before going back to bed. When she got out, she dried off, pulled on leggings and a big sweatshirt, then climbed under the covers to try to sleep.

Without expecting it to happen, she drifted off.

Pounding woke her up. This time, it wasn't in her head. She bolted upright, thinking she'd overslept and Rico was here. But the time on the cable box showed it was only a little after nine.

Who could be here? She froze. Big Tony? *Please don't let it be Big Tony.* But she could ignore him for only so long.

She really needed one of those doorbell cameras. Joe had refused to let her have one installed, though, claiming it was just one more way for the feds to spy on him. Moron.

With no other option, she grabbed her phone, the gun from the nightstand, and snuck downstairs to look through the peephole. It wasn't Big Tony or Rico, but a man she didn't recognize. His hair was closely cropped, leaving only a dusting of sandy blond on his giant head. The rest of him looked equally as big. And wide. Like a lunk. But not one she recognized. He didn't even look Italian.

He was, however, carrying a big cello and ribbon-wrapped gift basket. The word sympathies was printed on the dark blue ribbon. The basket looked like it was full of sweets and wine.

If he expected a tip, he wasn't getting one. She wasn't putting the gun away just yet, either.

She finger-combed her hair so it wasn't completely wild. Her phone was tucked into her leggings at her back, although she'd almost put the gun there. Instead, she clutched that in her right hand hoping there was no reason to use it.

The alarm was off. She hadn't turned it back on when she'd come in from her run, but there was a panic button on the panel next to the front door. She could tap that if something crazy happened. Well. Crazier.

Or she could just outrun the guy. Or shoot him.

The knocking started again, making her jump. "Coming." She opened the door about two inches and peered out, but kept her foot braced against the door and the gun hidden at her side. "Yes?"

The man smiled. Up close, he was even bigger than he'd looked through the peephole. Like a brick wall wearing a sport coat. "Mrs. Barrone?"

"Yes?"

"I am Yuri Lukin. I was an associate of your late husband's. I am very sorry to hear of his passing." He held out the basket. "I hope you will accept this as a token of my condolences."

"Thank you." But she made no move to take the basket as a little alarm started ringing in her head. Not only was Yuri a Russian name, but this guy had enough of an accent to confirm that heritage. Not straight off the boat, but he'd been born in the motherland, that was for sure.

The alarm, however, wasn't because she'd been unaware that Joe had known any Russians. Of course, after finding Joe's secret room, very little should surprise her.

The alarm was all about the other things she knew. Three in particular. One, the Russian crime syndicate was alive and well in New Jersey. Two, they were exceptionally ruthless. And three, the Russian mob and the Italian mob were sworn enemies.

Yuri continued to hold out the offering. "I was wondering if he ever mentioned me?"

"No, I'm sorry, he didn't." She tipped her head toward the porch. "You can just put that down."

"I see." Yuri frowned, still clutching the basket. "I am afraid he left behind some unfinished business."

Annoyance tensed her whole body. She was not going through this again. "That's too bad. I have to go now—"

Yuri dropped the basket, then his slab of a hand flattened against her door, and he shoved it open, knocking her back as he stepped inside.

She retreated out of surprise, raising the gun. Her hand was shaking. "Get out of my house."

He shut the door and came toward her, hands up. "There is no need for that. This is a simple business matter. Your husband owes my boss money."

She took another step back, sending one longing look at the alarm panel. It was too far away now. And Yuri was in the way. She might actually have to shoot him. "Take it as a loss. Joe can't help you with that. Now go."

"My boss wants the money back."

"I'm sure he does, but it's not my business. Get out of my house." She pulled out her phone with her free hand. "Or I will call the police."

Yuri ignored her threat and came close. "Do you know how much your husband owes my boss?"

"Not a clue, and I don't care." She almost wished it had been Big Tony at her door. She'd much rather shoot him. Hmm. Big Tony. "You know, my husband's boss might like to hear about this. You know who I mean? My *brother-in-law*." For the sake of the moment, Donna was willing to claim him. "Big Tony Villachi."

Yuri nodded slowly, which might have been the only speed at which he was capable of moving his cinder block head. "I know who he is. But this is about your husband and my boss."

"Who is your boss?" She figured she might as well get a name. One more thing to tell Rico.

"Boris Reznikov." In the speaking of that name, everything about Yuri changed. All pretense of friendliness disappeared. The glint in his eyes darkened, and the set of his mouth turned cruel. "And Boris wants his five million dollars."

Five. Million. The familiar figure caused the pit of her stomach to fall to her knees. She sucked in a ragged breath. "That's a lot of money. That I know nothing about."

He popped his knuckles by clenching his fists. "Then you don't mind if I have a look around?"

That assumption ticked her off far more than she could have imagined. "Of course I mind. This is my house. And you are an uninvited guest. Actually, you're not even a guest, because that would imply you might somehow be welcome, and you're not."

She tapped her phone with her thumb to bring the screen to life. "I'm calling the cops." But in the split second she took her eyes off him to look at the screen, he lunged.

He swatted both the phone and gun out of her hands. They went flying in different directions. "No, you are not."

She stared at him, incensed at this intrusion for more reasons than she could count. Her stomach growled, but she had no time for the hunger right now. Especially because anger was the only thing she had to feed it. "Get out. Now. Or I will make sure Big Tony knows that you threatened his sister-in-law. Do you understand me?"

Yuri's beady eyes narrowed. "I understand we are going to do this the hard way."

CHAPTER 15

Yuri grabbed her arm. "Where is your safe?"

"Let go of me." She yanked back, almost getting free. Anger filled her like flame-heated air lifting a hot air balloon. It rose through her with an odd mix of pure calm and hair-trigger crazy. She'd never felt anything quite like it. Except maybe when everything had gone wrong at the drop-off.

"Where is your safe?" he repeated.

Her stomach grumbled again. She stared at Yuri, challenging him with her gaze, but keeping her tone calm. "You need to take your hand off me."

"Or what? You do not control this situation. I do." His grip tightened, and he pulled her close. His breath was sour. Like pickled onions. This close, she could see a vein pulse in his forehead. It was oddly fascinating. "You are a very attractive woman. After you give me the money, I think I will show you just how much I am in control." He grinned lasciviously. "Perhaps you will even enjoy it."

His insinuation made her feel ill. The thought of him touching her more than he already had...she shuddered. "You're not going to lay another finger on me, do you understand?"

He shook her hard, rattling her teeth. "I will do with you what I want."

She shoved at him and kicked him in the shin.

He backhanded her and for a moment, she saw stars. He leaned in. "I am in control. Understand? I am your boss now."

Beside the shock of his assault, his assumption almost made her laugh. It was like her anger had gone all the way around to amusement. He had no idea who he was up against. She tipped her head to the side and back so she could make eye contact with him. His throat was right in front of her. She smiled at him. "Are you, though? Are you *really* in control?"

A moment of confusion drifted through his gaze. No doubt he'd expected her to be scared. Or maybe he'd expected her to break down and take him to the safe. But he wasn't getting anything close to what he'd anticipated.

For the third time, her stomach complained. Her gums joined in with a familiar ache. And the hunger inside clawed at her belly, trying to take over. She held it off. Just.

She spoke carefully, composing her mouth in such a way as not to reveal anything that might show up suddenly and frighten him. She wanted to keep him close just a little while longer. "I'm going to tell you a secret."

His confusion passed. He nodded. "Good. Where is the money?"

"It's in a safe-deposit box." She shook her head. "But that's not the secret."

"What, then?"

She smiled again, tight-lipped this time, and nodded to the urge that was quickly becoming her driving force. Any moment now. "I'm starving."

He frowned. "Why should that—"

She gave way to the hunger. The possession was instant. Her vision sharpened as if a tuning filter had been placed over her eyes. Her fangs punched all the way through her gums, and she opened her mouth, smiling wider.

Yuri yelled something in Russian and jerked back, but she grabbed hold of his sport coat and launched into him, knocking him to the floor.

She rode him down, knees in his gut, taking the air out of him as they landed. He gasped, trying to breathe. His eyes were wide, uncertain, desperate. Hands grasping, reaching for her.

In that moment of helplessness, with his head arched back, she attacked.

Something inside her took control. Something more than the hunger. Something she refused to give a name to. But in this instance, nothing mattered except that she feed.

Her fangs sank into his throat, piercing the vein beneath his skin and giving her exactly what she craved.

He grabbed her arms, trying to wrench her off. His efforts were futile. Her strength was superior, and his fate was sealed.

Time slowed. His heartbeat thumped in her ears, drumming through her with a rhythm that drove her.

She drank to satisfy a thirst that came from deep within her. With the kind of abandon that might have been caused by a hot day and a long run.

Yuri's life force spilled through her. Fleeting images flickered across her mind's eye like old movies shown on a hastily hung bedsheet. They went by too fast to catch much. Then the hunger faded, replaced by a sense of well-being that surpassed anything she'd felt before.

At last, her fangs receded. The hunger was gone. Warmth suffused her. She tingled with it, like champagne ran in her veins.

Or sunlight.

She sat back, wiping her mouth with her fingers. She still sat astride Yuri, who'd gone very still. Something hard and metal dug into her knee as she shifted. His gun.

She took it out of the holster and pointed it at him as she got to her feet. She nudged his leg with her foot. "Get up. It's time for you to go."

He didn't move.

She nudged him again. He was probably in shock. What she'd done to him was enough to stun anyone. "Blockhead. Yuri. Get up."

Still no response.

She sighed and knelt beside him. She shook his shoulder. "Hey. Snap out of it."

His head lolled to the side, eyes open. Unresponsive.

"Uh-oh." Panic set in. She tossed the gun to the side, grabbed his shoulders, and shook him again. Hard. He jiggled with the kind of flaccidity that could be described only as lifeless.

What had Claudette said? Listen for the heartbeat?

Donna pressed her ear to his chest and did just that. Nothing. She sat back on her heels. What else had Claudette said? Don't drink too much.

Holy Mother. Donna feared that was exactly what she'd done. She gasped as the full reality of her actions hit her. "Oh no." She'd drunk from a human. Which meant, according to Claudette, that Donna had completed the transition.

Her internal temperature rose as she ran to the half bath. She turned on the light and stared at herself.

She was radiant. Her eyes were a clear, whiskey brown, unlike the dark coffee color they'd been before. Her skin had a translucent glow that made her seem lit from within. Something was happening. Something inside her.

Energy coursed through her, causing her to tremble.

She went back out to look at Yuri. He'd gone ashen. There was no question about it. He was dead.

The air around her buckled with heat waves. She made it to the couch before her knees gave out. Something was taking place deep within her. A change.

Then everything went dark, and she drifted into immortality.

Lucky's weight on her chest brought her around. He was standing on her, staring down at her with great expectations of something. She squinted at him, barely opening her eyes. "Hi, baby."

She closed her eyes again. She'd dreamed while she was out. Crazy things. Lucinda and Yuri and Joe. Feverish, impossible things.

Lucky pawed at her. She opened her eyes again, wider this time.

Every individual hair on Lucky's black and white body stood out in sharp detail. Flecks of brown and orange decorated his green-gold irises, colors she'd never noticed before. He was purring like a little motor running. The sound filled her ears and carried through her until she could feel it in her chest.

Even his pulse and breath sounds were plain to her.

"Hungry?" She wasn't. She was as satisfied as she'd ever been in her life. More than that. She felt whole in a way she'd never experienced. She sat up, taking Lucky in her arms as she did. His fur was silk and velvet.

She nuzzled her face against his side, luxuriating in the sensation. "Wow, you're soft."

Everything was different. Better. Sharper. Clearer. More real.

She stood, Lucky cradled against her like a baby. Yuri still lay where she'd left him. He'd meant her harm. And yet, she was the one who had caused it. She hadn't meant to. Hadn't understood what she was doing.

Hadn't really been in control.

No excuse, she supposed. But what was done was done. She wasn't going to torture herself over it. He'd been a criminal. Just like the men at the drop-off. Just like her late husband.

She took Lucky into the kitchen and gave him a fresh can of food, then went back out to the living room. She stood there, staring at Yuri's body.

How on earth was she going to move him? He must weigh two fifty. Maybe more. But he couldn't stay where he was.

There was room in the back garden, she supposed. But that meant digging a hole. And then there was his car to think of.

Calling the police would have been the logical thing to do, but logic had left this equation days ago. This problem was hers to solve.

She reached for her crucifix, running her fingers over the metal to comfort herself.

A buzzing sound pulled her out of her thoughts. Her phone. Where had it landed when Yuri had knocked it away? She found it half under the couch. Just an incoming text from Martin's Cleaners.

Her mouth opened slightly. Rico. He was coming at three. And it was ten after two.

Okay, that was a good thing. She'd explain to him about Yuri, and he could help her. He would, wouldn't he?

She looked over her shoulder at the body. How was she going to explain the twin punctures in his neck? "Oh, and by the way, Rico, I'm a vampire."

She swallowed as the last word left her mouth. She'd said it so easily. Maybe because there was no denying it. Not now. Not after all this.

The sense of power it gave her was almost as over-whelming as the crushing weight of acceptance. But why should she feel *powerful*? What did it mean? A vampire? How was that possible?

She didn't know. Just that it was.

Claudette. Claudette could help her. Or the therapy group. That card was upstairs in the pocket of her robe.

Phone in hand, she jogged up the stairs to the bedroom and retrieved the card. She dialed the number. It rang three times before going to voicemail. The message repeated everything on the card. Group name, location, meeting time.

Donna hung up. Maybe it was time to give Claudette a mental ring.

Which was still weird, but whatever.

Donna closed her eyes and sent out a thought. *Claudette, are you there? It's Donna. I need your help. I'm sorry about last night. I know it's all real now. Please get in touch with me. I did something I shouldn't have.*

Donna opened her eyes just to roll them. Did all newly turned vampires sound that pathetic?

Rico was on his way. She'd throw herself on his mercy. He hadn't failed her yet. But a dead body…was that something he could ignore?

A dead Russian gangster, she reminded herself. Who'd intended to hurt her.

She went into the bathroom and turned on the shower, then leaned against the bathroom counter. There was a little smear of blood at the corner of her mouth. She wiped it away. She'd just tell Rico everything. He was an FBI agent. There probably wasn't much he hadn't heard.

If he believed her, great. If he thought she was crazy, then that would just become part of her defense.

She stripped down and got under the hot spray.

Thirty minutes later, she was dressed and back downstairs. She was in a pair of her new jeans, one of her new T-shirts, and an oversize mohair cardigan.

She'd decided against moving Yuri. This was a crime scene, after all, and moving him would be considered tampering with evidence. Although she supposed she'd already done that somewhat by showering and changing clothes.

Rico arrived right on time, pulling up in a step van with a faded plumber's logo on the side. So that was how he was going to hide in plain sight. Smart.

She watched him walk up to her door. He was in a plumber's jumpsuit too. Not a bad look on him, the whole blue-collar thing. There was no sign of the second agent. Kowalski. She was fine with that, considering the circumstances.

She opened the door before Rico could knock.

He tipped his head at the black SUV sitting in her driveway. "You have company?"

She opened her door all the way and stepped to the side so he could see Yuri. "You might say that. Or you might say I did."

CHAPTER 16

"I'm glad Kowalski got called to another case now." Rico stood up from checking Yuri's pulse. "He's dead all right. You want to tell me what happened?"

"Not really. But I'm going to." She chewed on her lip. This wasn't going to be easy. "Could we go in the kitchen? Kind of awkward talking over a dead body."

"Sure."

Rico followed her. She went straight to the fridge. "You want a drink?"

"I'm fine, thanks."

She got a mineral water out and popped the bottle cap off with her thumb, then took a long sip. "I really don't know how to tell you this, except just to tell you. But I first want to say that I don't expect you to believe me. I didn't believe it either. Until today."

He frowned. "Okay."

She set the bottle on the counter. "You might want to sit down for this."

"I'm good."

She nodded. "I'm..." Wow. This was really hard to say. "I killed Yuri. But it was an accident. I...I..." She sighed. This was only hard because she cared what

Rico thought. But that was silly. He thought of her only as an informant. Nothing else.

"Whatever it is, say it. I promise there's not much that can shock me after seventeen years with the bureau. Just come out with it."

Why were these words so stuck on her tongue? "You say there's not much that can shock you, but I don't know…"

"Let me guess." His eyes narrowed. "You're a vampire. Newly turned."

She stared at him like he'd just grown a third eye. "How…how did you know that?"

"I'm right?"

She nodded. She wasn't sure what shocked her more, that Rico had guessed or that he was so nonchalant about it. "You seem so sure. But come on, how did you know?"

He shrugged. "It's my job to be observant and figure things out."

"But a newly turned vampire? That's pretty specific. How did you know the newly turned part?"

He held up his hand and ticked things off on his fingers. "Even though yesterday was overcast, the light seemed to bother you. Sure, you were tolerating daylight, but not like a normal human. The other option was being hungover, and from what I've observed since I've known you, you don't drink that much. Then there was your confession that you were alone at the drop-off. If your strength was recently increased to vampire levels, that would explain how you killed those two men accidentally. The driver's side door you threw the third man against didn't just have a broken window, the metal was staved in. That took an incredible amount of force."

He touched a third finger. "What really got me thinking about it is that you went from being a middle-aged woman in good shape to being a middle-aged woman with the body and face of a twentysomething. In two days. I mean, you look phenomenal."

He thought she looked *phenomenal*. She struggled not to grin wildly. "Thanks."

"You're welcome. But for sure you have the vampire glow. You're all just unnaturally beautiful. Comes with the turning."

Now he thought she was *unnaturally beautiful*. She was going to get giddy about that later. Then she frowned as she thought back to what he'd said. "Wait. Two days? That would mean you saw me on the day of Joe's funeral."

He nodded. "We always keep an eye on those things because everyone shows up. It's a great way to get current pictures and take the temperature of a syndicate. Sometimes we even make a few busts. Anyway, there's no diet program, exercise regime, or plastic-surgery techniques that can create that kind of natural-looking change in such a short amount of time."

She nodded. "If there was, I'd know about it."

"Plus, you smell like a vampire."

"I smell like a vampire?"

He didn't answer, instead tipping his head toward the living room. "Then, of course, there's our friend Yuri out there. He's got two puncture wounds in his neck. Two *evenly* spaced puncture wounds. He's also got a surprising lack of blood coming out of those wounds. In fact, he's at least three shades paler than most of the corpses I've seen."

She crossed her arms. "You've seen a lot of corpses, have you?"

"More than the average person, I'd guess."

"Okay, so you figured me out. But why are you not shocked? I couldn't even accept that vampires are an actual thing until just about an hour ago. And I'm the one who got bitten."

"When did that happen?"

"In the cemetery. The story I told you was true. I just left the more unbelievable parts out. The kid who knocked me down did the biting. And I did pass out. When I came to, there was a woman crouched over me, feeding me blood from her wrist." Donna grimaced. "Thinking about that used to gross me out. I mean, blood. From her veins. That's not normal."

"Neither is being in the Mafia."

She sighed. "No, it isn't."

"So killing Yuri... Is that what solidified the whole vampire thing for you?"

She looked away. "I didn't mean to kill him. I lost control. Claudette said it would happen. That my hunger would get the best of me if I didn't feed soon enough. She was right."

"Were you hungry the night of the drop-off?"

"No. Just mad. And ready to be done with it all. I thought my sudden strength was due to adrenaline."

She glanced at him. "Am I in trouble about that? I have to be, right?"

He exhaled, his gaze distant. Like he was thinking. "No. All good."

"All good?" She realized she sounded a little shrill, but she couldn't help it. None of this was normal, and he acted like he dealt with this sort of thing all the time. "That's not the response I was expecting. At all. Why are you okay with this?"

He scrubbed a hand over his face.

Her mouth fell open. "Wait. Are you a vampire? No, you can't be. You were out in daylight."

"No, I'm not." He cleared his throat softly. "Are you asking me why I'm okay with the deaths of those two guys? Or why I'm okay with you being a vampire?"

"Both."

"The two guys at the drop-off you killed accidentally and in self-defense. I need to investigate what happened here with Yuri a little more. Why was he here?"

"He said he had unfinished business with Joe. Or rather, his boss does. Boris Reznikov. You know the name?"

Rico snorted. "He's the Russian equivalent of Big Tony. Except maybe less cuddly."

She shivered. "Lovely. And Joe was running a deal with him."

"You know that for sure?"

"No. That's just what Yuri said."

"What else did Yuri say?"

"Essentially that he was going to rape me before he left."

A spark of anger flared in Rico's eyes. "Then this was self-defense too."

"How are you going to explain those two puncture wounds and the lack of blood as self-defense?"

"No one's going to care too much how you took out a Russian leg-breaker. Just that you did it and lived to tell the tale."

So far, so good. But there was still something she didn't understand. "I appreciate that. And your help in all this. But there's still one thing I don't get."

"What's that?"

"Why are you not freaked out about the whole vampire part?"

He looked away for a moment, then made eye contact again. "Since I know your secret, I guess it's okay to tell you mine."

A secret from Rico? Every inch of her listened.

"I'm not shocked that you're a vampire. Because I'm a werewolf."

Her mouth fell open as she leaned hard on the counter. "What?"

He nodded. "You know they exist, right?"

"I...Claudette did mention that, yes." Donna was so glad she'd asked about the enemy thing. "I just didn't think the first one I met would be in my kitchen. Or someone I know."

"You're going to have a lot of firsts."

"I guess so. Does the FBI know you're a werewolf?"

"No. But the ability does make me a better agent, so I'm sure they wouldn't mind."

The side of her mouth hitched up in a half grin as she pictured him tracking down a suspect like a human bloodhound.

His eyes narrowed. "I know what you're thinking."

She pursed her lips and said nothing at first. "Can werewolves read minds?"

"No. I just know you had some sort of drug-sniffing dog thing going on."

"More like on the trail of a fugitive, but you were close."

"Ha-ha." Then his expression turned serious again. "This Claudette, she's your sire?"

"Yes. She said that."

"Then why isn't she here helping you? I don't think it's standard to turn someone and just split."

"I sort of asked her to get out of my house. I wasn't ready to accept what was going on. But I did call her today and apologize." *If you could call a mental message a call.* "I'm sure she'll be back."

"Good. You shouldn't get dumped into the deep end like this. There's a lot you need to know."

"Such as? Hey, were you turned into a werewolf? Or born into it?"

"Born. Weres can also be turned, but it doesn't result in as powerful an individual as one who's born into it. In that way, we don't work the way your kind does."

Her kind. How weird. "What things do I need to

166

know? Claudette told me some before she left, but I got the sense there was more. Maybe a lot more."

"You know about the obvious, right? Don't go out in sunlight?"

Donna nodded. "I know that one, yes."

He squinted at the fridge, thinking. "You'll need to find a blood service."

"A blood service?"

"So you can stay fed."

"Yeah, I didn't know about that." Oddly enough, the thought of ingesting blood didn't seem quite as repugnant as it had yesterday. Maybe drinking an entire human had something to do with that.

"There are blood bars in the city too. Maybe even out here. I don't know, it's not my bag."

"I suppose not. Do werewolves eat anything special?"

"No. A lot of meat." He grinned. "You won't run into any vegan werewolves, that's for sure."

She laughed. "Right."

"Did she tell you about the fae? I do know a little about them."

"She told me they're the enemy of vampires and that I need to put iron around my house."

"Have you?"

"Not yet." She glanced toward the window. "I can't exactly run to Home Depot now, can I?"

He looked outside and snorted. "Good thing they're open until nine."

She lifted her hands in surrender. "I don't even know what kind of iron to buy."

"I'd say nails. Then just scatter a perimeter at your property line. Most vampires I know wear a little iron on their person too."

For some reason, that felt like the last straw. She rubbed her forehead, then closed her eyes and pinched the bridge of her nose. "All I wanted was a simple life. Freedom to just live. Now I'm facing a whole new set of rules and regulations. This is *not* what I wanted. Not even remotely."

She felt warmth in front of her and opened her eyes to find Rico standing there.

"Hey," he said. "You can handle this. Sure, there's going to be a learning curve, but once you get the hang of it, you're going to be fine."

She nodded and let out one little sniffle. Which was followed by a deep inhale. Which filled her senses with Rico in a way she'd never experienced before.

A deep, earthy scent washed over her, like a primordial forest after a hard rain. A darker musk danced around her, the essence of every male. Then faintly, a smell that could only be described as *wolf*. Which, thankfully, was nothing like *wet dog*.

She stared at him hard, mouth open to instinctually capture more of his scent.

He stepped back, hands up. "Okay, you're freaking me out a little. I am not dinner."

She closed her mouth, instantly aware that her fangs were out. "Sorry, I don't have any control over that stuff yet."

He nodded. "I know. No harm done. But the weird

eye glow is going to give you away if you don't master it."

"Eye glow? And for the record, I was not going to bite you. I was just...smelling you." Okay, that was embarrassing to admit.

He smiled a little. "I get it. Everything's more intense right now, I'm sure. And yes, your eyes glow when you're, I don't know, really worked up about something."

Great. So he thought she'd been *really worked up* about him. Because telling him she'd been smelling him wasn't embarrassing enough on its own. Wow. This was like going through puberty a second time. "So, uh, when you said earlier that I smell like a vampire? What does that smell like exactly?"

He went back to leaning on the island. "Hard to say. It's kind of a dark, sooty smell with a faint floral note. At least that's what the women smell like. The men have a different undernote that's slightly bitter. Like burnt coffee. Neither one is unpleasant. Just distinct."

She frowned. "So I smell like a florist shop that burned down?"

He laughed, a sharp, sudden bark of a noise. "No, not quite like that." He shook his head. "Tell you what? How about I run to Home Depot for you? I don't like the idea of you being unprotected."

"Thank you. I would really appreciate that. Say, there is one other thing I've been wondering about..."

"Yes?"

"Yuri's not going to turn into a vampire too, is he?"

Rico glanced toward the dead Russian. "Not unless

you tried to revive him with your own blood after you realized he was a goner. Did you?"

"No."

"Then we're good." He headed for the door. "When I get back, I'll deal with the body. And you can give me this new information about the Villachis."

CHAPTER 17

R ico spent an hour getting the nails and then surrounding her property with them, except for the driveway because nails and tires were a bad mix. Despite that he thought there was enough iron in the garage doors and mechanics to do the trick.

Donna couldn't remember the last time a man had done something kind for her solely because he wanted to help her and not gain favor from her husband.

It touched her, but she reminded herself that Rico had a motive. Keeping her safe was important to his case.

Even so, he didn't have to help her with this, so it was still a kind gesture, and she appreciated that.

When he came back in, she was waiting for him in the living room. "Thank you. Would you like a cup of coffee or something?"

"You're welcome. And no, I'm fine. Thanks." He brushed his hands off on his plumber's jumpsuit, then came over to stand at Yuri's feet. "Big guy."

She nodded. "That's for sure."

"Did you check him for ID?"

"I didn't touch him at all. Except for when I did earlier. And ID was the last thing on my mind."

"Right. Okay." Rico bent and checked the man's pockets, finding a wallet in the interior of his jacket. He opened it and looked at the license. "Yuri Lukin. I'll pull his file when I get back to the office, but I'm pretty sure you've done the world a favor."

Curiosity pushed the next sentence out of her mouth. "What are you going to do with him? With his body, I mean?"

Rico glanced over his shoulder at her. "The bureau has some allowances for situations like this. I'll report it, but the body will go into our morgue, and that will be the end of it. For now, anyway."

"The FBI has a morgue?"

"Not as far as anything official goes. But the Organized Crime Unit works a little differently. OCU is its own world. Keeping Yuri on ice is no big deal. And the day may come when his body showing up somewhere will work in our favor. Until then, he's in the deep freeze."

"And you can just do that?"

"I can because it protects you. You're the key to bringing down much bigger fish, so you're a lot higher up the food chain."

"Gee," Donna said with a smirk, "you sure know how to make a girl feel special."

He shrugged, but there was humor in his eyes. "It is what it is."

"You going to put him in the back of your van?"

"Yes."

"You want help carrying him? He looks heavy."

Rico stood, laughing a little. "He looks heavy

because he is heavy, but that doesn't have an impact on people like us."

"Meaning?"

"I'm a werewolf and you're a vampire. Picking up a lunk like this isn't any harder than carrying in your groceries."

She narrowed her eyes at him. "Yeah, I don't know about that."

He stood back. "Have a go."

"It's a dead body, not a barbell."

Rico's expression turned smug. "Chicken?"

She was not about to turn down Rico's challenge, as odd as it might be. She gave him a smug look right back and went to stand beside Yuri. She wasn't even sure how to pick up a guy this size, let alone a dead one. "I don't know where to start."

"Fireman's carry," Rico offered.

She frowned at him. "Like I know how to do that."

"Roll him over, then face him and grab him under his arms and around the back. From there, hoist him to his feet, then bend and drop him over your shoulder."

"You make it sound so easy."

Rico smirked. "Want me to demonstrate?"

"No, I've got this." But did she? It wasn't just Yuri's bulk. He would be dead weight. Literally.

She rolled him over, which wasn't too hard because he wasn't fighting it, then did exactly as Rico suggested. Stuck her arms under his and around his back, then lifted.

Yuri came up to his feet with very little effort. She turned, Yuri slouched over her like the world's worst dancing partner, and shook her head at Rico. "How is this so easy? It's like he hardly weighs anything."

Rico looked proud. There was no other way to describe it. "Told you."

Just because she could, she bent and let Yuri fall over her right shoulder, bending her knees and pressing upright as she lifted him off the ground. "Mary and Joseph. Who would have thought?"

"There's a lot more you're capable of now. You'll see."

She eased Yuri back to the floor. "Amazing. Except for the part where I just had a dead guy draped over me."

"Yeah, well, thankfully it's probably not something you're going to have to do again." He hoisted Yuri, then headed for the front door.

She went ahead of him to open it. "You're just going to carry him out like that? No tarp or anything?"

Rico stopped. "Why? Do you think you're being watched? It's not like the house is visible to any of your neighbors. You sit too far back off the street."

"I don't think I'm being watched. But you came in the plumber's van for a reason."

"Your protection. Pulling up in a bureau vehicle would be dangerous for you." He dropped Yuri back to the floor. "But you're probably right. It would look odd for the plumber to haul a body out of your house. I'll get a tarp. Which, to be honest, is still going to look weird."

"Could you back the van halfway into the garage? There's room."

He nodded. "Let's do that."

"I'll go raise the door."

Rico pulled his keys out. "Be right there."

Ten minutes later, Yuri was loaded up and out of Donna's house. She was glad for that. Having a dead body in your living room was about as undesirable an addition as you could get.

Rico left the van in the garage and came back into the house. "All right. Where's this new info you've discovered?"

A small part of her didn't want to reveal Joe's secret room, but there was no reason not to show it to Rico. He was there to collect evidence against the Villachis. Everything in there was a part of that. He needed to see it.

"Follow me."

She led him to Joe's office and turned the lights on. Then she got the keys out, pulled the book off the shelf, and unlocked the bookcase.

"*The Godfather?*" Rico said. "Really?"

"I know."

When she opened the stash room, Rico nodded appreciatively. He pulled on gloves as he looked into the room. "Nice work finding this."

"Thanks." His compliments always felt like a warm pat on the back. Maybe because Joe had been so stingy with nice words in the last decade or so.

Rico stepped inside the space and let out a long, low whistle. "Quite the arsenal."

She leaned against the opening. The secret room was on the small side for two people. Not that she'd mind being closer to Rico. But she didn't want to crowd him while he was working. "You think some of those guns could have been used in crimes?"

"It's a very real possibility." He put his hands on his hips. "I didn't bring enough evidence bags with me. Some of this is going to have to wait. And some of it's going to have to go in boxes."

"Can you at least get the drugs out of my house? I really don't like having them in here."

Rico turned. "Drugs?"

"Check the cardboard boxes."

He opened the one closest to him. Took a look inside. Nodded. "That will go with me."

"There are two of those. The third one has playing cards in it. Probably marked. But it's the ledgers you're really going to find useful. I think. I looked at the most recent one. Didn't make all that much sense, but it's got names and numbers, dates, all stuff I'm sure you'd find riveting."

He picked one up and flipped through it. He started nodding. "This is definitely going to be a hit. These are case makers, the kind of evidence that puts crews away."

"Excellent."

He looked up at her. "We owe you."

She smiled. "Happy to help."

He kept looking at her, his intense gaze almost hard to bear.

"What?"

He shook his head. "You're a brave woman, Donna."

She laughed.

"I mean it. This isn't easy what you're doing. The burden you're bearing. I feel better knowing about your recently acquired skills, though. Means you're able to protect yourself, that's for sure."

"I appreciate your words. I don't know that I feel like those skills are really skills just yet, but I'm sure I'll get there."

He took a breath and went back to looking around the space, ledger still in hand. "I wish I could get a team out here. Really take this place apart forensically." He paused. "I mean this room. Not your house."

"Thanks for that." She thought for a minute. "Come back as a remodeler. You could easily bring a second person with you. Even a third." She lifted one shoulder. "No one would blink an eye at me wanting to update things in the house. Especially since I'm going to sell it."

"Actually, these ledgers should be enough. Plus, I'm going to take pictures. But I will have to come back tomorrow. Does that work for you?"

"Sure. Just not too early."

"Going out tonight?"

"I'm going to try the support group Claudette told me about." She looked down at her hands, the awkwardness of having confessed such a thing making her break eye contact with him.

"I think that's great."

She looked up. "You do?"

"Sure. If there was ever a moment in your life you could use support, this feels like it."

"Yeah, I suppose so."

He closed the ledger and held it up. "I should get to work on bagging and tagging this stuff so I can load it and get it out of here."

"Right. Well, I'll be…somewhere in the house if you need me. Just yell."

"I won't have to. You should be able to hear me without me raising my voice."

"Vampire thing?"

"Supernatural thing." He tapped his ear. "We all have it."

"Good to know. I'll leave you to it, then." She walked out of Joe's office and meandered through the house, ending up back upstairs. She needed to go through her closet and see if anything still fit well enough to be usable, but something about getting undressed with Rico downstairs didn't feel right.

Her phone vibrated. She checked the screen. A new text from Big Tony.

We need to talk.

That was the last thing she wanted to do. There was only so long she could put him off, she knew that. But dealing with him wasn't high on her list. Not when he was probably the one who'd set her up.

Worse than that, really. He'd hired men to kill her. That was what the evidence pointed to.

She was sure he'd deny it.

Or would he? Maybe he wouldn't. Maybe he'd nod in that steely-eyed way of his, then pull out his gun and finish the job.

Yikes. Was it possible he actually wanted her dead? That was a happy thought. Not. But if it was true, there had to be a reason. What did he think she was up to?

She sat on her bed, pondering that. No way was she meeting him at his house. Or hers. It would have to be a neutral location. When the meeting happened. Which wouldn't be tonight, that much she knew.

But how long could she hold him off? How long until he made another attempt to kill her? Or had he only meant to scare her? She'd never know. Not really. Not with a guy like Big Tony.

And now she had the Russian Mafia to contend with as well.

She scooted back on the bed, pulled her knees to her chest, and hugged her arms around them. Lucky was asleep on Joe's side. The sooner Rico could arrest Tony, the better. That would get one mob boss off her back.

She needed to ask Rico how quickly these arrests could happen, although she already had an idea they wouldn't happen as fast as she wanted them to.

"Donna?"

She looked up suddenly, pulled from her thoughts. The query had reached her ears as if spoken in the same room, but she knew it hadn't been. "Rico?"

"Downstairs. Ready to go."

Wow. He'd been right about the hearing. Extraordinary. "Coming." She ran down, which took seconds, and met him near the garage door. "Hey. Big Tony texted me again."

"Again? How many times has he reached out to you?"

"A few. He wants to talk."

"I'm sure he does." Rico shook his head. "You can't go alone. You need to pick a spot where we can set up a few people, be close enough to intervene if something happens. Which it could."

"I know. I don't want to talk to him at all. Or meet with him. But he won't leave me alone, I know that. Can't you just arrest him already?"

"I wish. It's going to take some time to put this case together. We can't jump the gun. It's got to be hard, actionable evidence. Which these ledgers should provide, but we have to interpret them first."

"What about the way he set me up? That has to count for something."

"It could. But then you'd end up in the thick of it too. Especially because you were a willing participant in that job."

"*For a reason*," she emphasized.

"I know that, and you know that, but how do you think it'd look to a jury?"

She sighed and shook her head. "I can't live like this, waiting for him to knock on my door."

"You won't have to. Not for long. I promise to push this case as hard as I can. In the meantime, maybe I can get a few local uniforms to double up on patrols around here. Just enough to keep him away."

She frowned. "You don't think he's paying off the police? I don't know that he is. But I don't know that he isn't. And I'm not sure I want to roll those dice."

"Listen." Rico bent his head a little. "You have the advantage right now. In a couple ways. For one thing, he doesn't really know what went down at that drop-off, just that you survived and two of his new hires didn't. He's got to be curious. He probably assumes, like we did, that someone else showed up."

"So?"

"So that might be what he's trying to find out. Secondly, he doesn't know what you've become. What you're capable of."

"Neither do I."

"No, but you have an idea. And in a few days, I'm sure the picture will be even clearer. Hold him off as long as you can, and I'll keep working things on my end. If anything breaks loose early, you'll be the first to know."

She huffed out a breath. "I don't like this."

"I know. And I'm sorry. But I'll see you tomorrow and will hopefully have news for you then. Until then… there isn't much else I can do without tipping Big Tony off to your involvement with us. Changing that alarm code would be a good idea. Make sure you have your phone on you too. In case you need to call me. Or the cops."

"I'll do that. I'll be fine." But the words tasted like a lie even as they left her mouth.

There was no way she was going to miss that meeting tonight. But in the meantime, she was calling Claudette again.

Donna needed to know more about her new skills. And how to use them. Especially since staying alive was getting harder every day.

CHAPTER 18

Darkness fell within the hour after Rico left. One of the benefits of winter's approach. It would be even better when daylight saving time took effect.

The first thing Donna did was dig out the manual for the alarm system and change the code. She should have done it sooner, but it had only just occurred to her that Joe might have shared the code with Big Tony. She wasn't sure why he would have done that, but all Big Tony would have had to do was ask.

That was just how things worked in the family.

Once that was done, Donna didn't want to stay home. Not after Big Tony's text. And especially after what had happened with Yuri. But the meeting wasn't until ten. It was in the city, so it would take a half hour to get there, but Donna was itching to leave early. Even if all she did was walk around, she wanted to be someplace else than in this house.

What did one wear to a meeting of newly turned vampires?

Her wardrobe options that fit were still slim, so she went with a pair of her new jeans, her new black T-shirt, and a vintage Chanel jacket that had always been a little snug on her. It fit perfectly now and looked like a million bucks. She added ankle boots and some jewelry, grabbed her purse, then went downstairs to feed Lucky.

"Not sure what time I'll be home, kiddo." She scratched his head while he ate his lamb and rice stew. "Don't let any strangers in, okay?"

He kept eating.

She gave him one last scratch, then stood and went out to the garage, making sure the alarm was on.

As the garage door went up, she stared intently in the rearview mirror, looking for headlights or movement. Any sign that someone was out there. There wasn't anything, but that might only mean she hadn't seen them.

She backed out into the driveway, then sat there until the door was down. She wasn't taking any chances. All the landscape lighting was on, too, which was a lot. The place was lit up like they were having a party.

Good. Creeping around wouldn't be so easy with that much brightness.

She got on the highway and headed for her destination, guided by her phone's GPS app. The drive was nice. Traffic was lighter this time of night, and with her sharper vision, nothing was really that dark.

It was. But it wasn't. She'd never experienced anything like it with human eyes. Was this how Rico saw things as a werewolf? She shook her head. A werewolf. Who would have imagined?

To say her life had changed recently was an understatement.

The idea of this support group made her a little nervous, but mostly intrigued her. Since Claudette had yet to respond to Donna's attempt to contact her, Donna was hoping the group might answer some questions.

Would that make her look like a complete newbie, though? Sure, she *was* a complete newbie, but she didn't want to come off as completely clueless.

Hard to shake the Mafia-born need to be respected, she supposed. Well, whatever happened happened. She needed information, and right now, this group was her best chance at getting some.

The meeting was still almost three hours away, however. She had time to kill and money to spend.

She went straight to 59th Street, parked in one of the nearby garages, then went across to Bloomingdale's. Time to see about filling in the gaps in her wardrobe. She couldn't wear the same two pairs of jeans for the rest of her life.

She walked inside and smiled at the familiar black-and-white-checked floor. The displays hadn't been done for Christmas yet, but even so a feeling of holiday was in the air.

It had been a year since she'd been in this store. She'd gone on a shopping trip with the other wives, all in the name of Christmas, but very few gifts had been purchased. Mostly, it had been about their own wants. Donna was infinitely happier to be here alone.

The scents hit her first. She stood still and inhaled the heady mix of fragrances from the perfume department, the fresh flowers that were displayed as part of the décor, the earthy aroma of leather goods from the shoe and handbag sections, the faint undercurrent of cleaners and floor wax, and the curious note of what she suddenly realized was life.

More specifically, blood. As in what was coursing through the veins of her fellow shoppers.

It made her mouth water in the same way that baked goods used to. She wasn't hungry, but the abundance of it was enticing.

This would be a good way to desensitize herself to such things. Or maybe in a few days, she'd get used to that smell, and it would fade into the background. Either way, she wasn't remotely hungry. Not after Yuri. And she was here to shop.

So that's what she did.

She loved the designer boutiques within the store. Prada, Chanel, Jimmy Choo. They went on and on, each area kitted out with pieces from the line. She swung through Chanel, but she didn't need a purse.

From there she went on to Gucci. She picked up a scarf, breaking the ice with that purchase.

She had about seventy-five minutes until the store closed, so she had to work fast and efficiently. She went straight on to the women's clothing departments, which were on the second, third, and fourth floors.

As she shopped, she realized something had changed. Her taste. Was that a side effect of being a vampire? Things she normally would have gravitated toward, like bolder colors, louder patterns, clothing with lots of embellishments…suddenly those weren't what she was picking off the racks.

Instead, her arms were filled with sleeker designs, a few leather pieces, lots of black, and shapes that were far more body conscious. Maybe it wasn't so much becoming a vampire as it was becoming a size four.

"Can I start a fitting room for you?"

Donna turned to see an older woman waiting on her answer. The saleswoman looked a little tired but was still maintaining a smile. Donna felt for her. The day was almost over, and now here was a customer about to make more work for her.

"Sure." Donna peered at the woman's name tag as she handed her items over. "Do you work on commission, Louise?"

The woman nodded. "Yes, ma'am."

Donna smiled. "I think you're going to have a good end to your night, then."

The woman's smile widened. "Well, I'm not a personal shopper, but if there's anything I can help you with, I'm happy to do it. What's your name, if I might ask?"

"Donna. And I do need help. I need to replace almost my entire wardrobe. If you could add some basics to that pile, that would be great. Keep them simple, but elegant and well cut. Black, dark gray, white, navy, a little red is fine. Maybe even purple. So are subtle patterns. Nothing too crazy, though, okay? And a mix of things. Loungewear, day wear, a nice dress or two. Pajamas. Across the board."

The woman nodded. "I can absolutely do that. I'll get right on it. Size?"

"Thank you. And I seem to be a four at the

moment." As the woman hustled off, Donna went back to picking through the racks. Louise's help would double Donna's shopping time. She'd be outfitted in no time.

Twenty minutes later, Louise ushered Donna into the largest dressing room she'd ever seen. There were so many clothes in it, the space felt more like someone's closet.

"I hope this isn't overwhelming," Louise said. "It's a lot to try on."

"I'll get through what I can," Donna answered. She was about to see just how quickly she could make that happen with her new speed.

Louise pointed to the first rack. "I've arranged everything to make it easier. Pants are here in front, tops behind them, dresses on this rack. I put a few coats on there too. You didn't mention that, but I took a shot."

"No, that's good," Donna said. "I need a coat."

"Great. Behind the coats are some pajamas and nightgowns." Louise looked pleased with her work. "I'll be right outside if you need another size or want to hand a few things out to be put back or taken to the register. Anything. Just give me a shout, Donna."

"Got it." Donna gave her a big smile and rubbed her hands together. "Here we go."

Louise shut the door.

Donna stripped down, hung her things up, then dug in. She worked her way through the pants and tops first. Louise, as it turned out, had a great eye. Donna found things on the rack she never would have picked out because of the way they looked on the hanger. But on her person? Fabulous.

There were even a few pieces with swaths of muted color that Donna knew she would have shied away from if left to her own devices. Now, she was very glad Louise had approached her.

And the coats Louise had picked out were kind of amazing. Especially the steely-blue one with the black leather standup collar and matching knotted leather buttons. Donna put it on and instantly felt six inches taller and like she'd been crowned empress of some exotic winter kingdom.

This was the kind of coat a vampire would wear. She twirled in front of the triple mirrors, watching the skirt flare out as she moved. Too bad they didn't make a summer version.

A small knock on the door stopped her. "Donna? How are you doing?"

Donna opened the door. "This coat."

Louise smiled. "You wear clothes well."

"I'd say you know how to pick things out. So much of this is working. But yeah, this coat is going home with me for sure."

"Excellent. It looks amazing on you. Is there anything else I can take to the register?"

Donna turned to the first rack where she'd been hanging the things she wanted to keep and scooped up about eighteen inches of merchandise. "All of this. Plus the pants and blouse I'm wearing. And I still need to try on the dresses."

Louise's eyes bulged a little, but only for a fraction

of a second. "I'll get to work on these while you try those dresses on, then."

"Thanks." Donna got back to it, shedding the coat and current outfit and stepping into the first dress. It was a slinky column of shimmering black that, while pretty, had looked like a snooze on the hanger.

When Donna turned to the mirrors, there was nothing sleepy about what she saw. "Holy communion." She had no need for a dress like this that clung to every curve. No place to wear a slip of body-hugging fabric that dripped with old Hollywood glamour. Absolutely no reason to buy an outfit that made her look like a femme fatale.

But she already knew she wasn't leaving the store without it. Just for fun, she curled her lips back and tried to make her fangs come out. Nothing. She thought about rare steak and sinking her teeth into Yuri, and bam, there they were.

There was the faintest glow in her eyes, too, and she studied her vampire self, trying to get used to the look. Then she blinked. "Hey, I can see my reflection."

"What was that?" Louise called back.

Donna whipped around toward the door, her fangs disappearing. "Uh, nothing. Just talking to myself."

She put her hand to her chest. Her heart was pounding. So she still had a reflection. And a beating heart. Proof to support what Claudette had said about not believing everything she saw on TV. And another reminder of how much Donna needed tonight's meeting.

She quickly tried on the rest of the clothes, finding

a few more things, although no dresses quite so dramatic as the first, to add to her pile.

At last, she put her own clothes back on and left the dressing room.

Louise was waiting. "How'd you do?"

"Couple more items." Donna handed them over. "I'm very happy. I know the store is closing, and I don't want to keep you, so hopefully I can get out of here without making you late."

Louise hefted the clothing she'd been handed. "Don't worry about a thing. I'm here for as long as you need me."

"Thank you. I have a feeling I'll be back too." She followed Louise to the register.

The saleswoman slipped behind the counter. "I just have to add these last things and wrap them for you, and you'll be all set."

"Great." Donna was already thinking about what she might do with the rest of her time before the meeting. Maybe she'd head toward the location, find a place to park, then look for one of those twenty-four-hour diners and get something to eat. Like chocolate cake. Or a giant black-and-white cookie with a cup of coffee. Now that carbs were no longer the enemy and still appetizing once she was fed, the possibilities were endless.

Or she could just walk around and people-watch. It wasn't like there was ever a shortage of that in the city.

"Ma'am? Donna?"

Donna blinked and looked at Louise. "Sorry. Lost in the clouds."

Louise looked relieved. "I thought maybe it was the total."

"Oh, no. I didn't even hear you. How much is it?"

Louise's smile thinned a little painfully. "$6,627.19."

Donna knew she'd done a lot of shopping, but that was more than she'd anticipated. She tried to keep her cool, however. She took a breath and smiled. "Good thing I brought cash. You do take cash, don't you?"

"Uh…yes, of course."

Donna slipped about half the bills from the bundle still in her purse and counted them out until she had sixty-seven of them. "There you go."

It would be good to get some small bills back in change. Especially if she was going to a diner.

Louise made the change and counted it back to Donna, then gave her a card. "If you ever need anything else, please don't hesitate to ask for me."

"I'd be happy to." Donna eyed the number of big brown Bloomie's bags waiting on her. That wasn't going to be an easy trip to the car. Then she remembered Yuri and realized it wasn't going to be a problem after all.

"Wonderful. Would you like me to call our concierge service and have them assist you with your packages?"

That would be the human thing to do. But Donna wasn't human anymore. "No, thanks," she said. "I've got it."

Louise's brows bent in concern. "Those bags are heavier than you think."

Donna pushed her purse strap onto her shoulder,

then took an even number of bags in each hand, lifting them with ease. "I work out."

She turned, tossed a, "Thanks again," over her shoulder, and headed out. She had no idea what the rest of her evening held, but she was ready for it.

And she realized that she was ready for more than just tonight. Whatever the coming days brought, she would handle it. She hadn't lasted this long or survived this much just to be knocked down by a life change.

Even if that life change was becoming a vampire.

CHAPTER 19

Donna spent another hour wandering the streets with a hot chocolate in hand. The city was beautiful in the evening, all lit up and sparkling. For a few minutes, she let herself fantasize about moving here instead of Florida. Buying a hip apartment downtown. Becoming one of the glamourous folk who shopped in boutiques and bought their groceries at the weekend farmers' markets.

It was fun to think about. But not realistic. The city was still too close to Big Tony. Even if Big Tony and most of his crew got locked up. Except there was no way Rico could get them all. Like Lucinda. She'd still be footloose and fancy-free.

Donna really didn't want to live within a hundred-mile radius of that woman. As far as she was concerned, their familial relationship had ended when Joe died. All they were now was ex-sisters-in-law. And Donna wanted distance. The kind that Florida could give her.

A homeless man was tucked into the doorway of the building she was about to pass. She pulled a hundred off the dwindling bundle in her purse and dropped it in his cup.

"Thanks, lady. God bless you." He looked from the cup to her, his gaze suddenly narrowing.

"You're welcome," she said.

"Vampire," he whispered.

"What? No." She shook her head and moved on quickly. Were her fangs out? Her eyes glowing? How had he known? She glanced over her shoulder.

The man was still staring at her. His gaze held a hard, appraising gleam. Like he was telling her he'd keep her secret, but she'd better not try anything.

She turned away and hurried down the street. In some ways, being a vampire felt a lot like being connected to the mob. Respect came from fear.

That wasn't something she liked. It also wasn't something she could do anything about.

She took the last sip of hot chocolate, then tossed the cup and checked the time. Twenty minutes until the group started. She looked at her map and headed in the direction of the meeting place, taking her time since she was only ten minutes away from the New Manhattan Health and Wellness Center, Floor twelve, Suite C.

As she approached, she studied the building. Double glass doors, simple black granite façade, but that was about all she could see. The rest was covered in scaffolding since part of the building was being remodeled.

A little case of nerves settled over her as she walked through the covered sidewalk to the entrance and went to the elevator bank. She had no idea what to expect, but she knew one thing. She was about to be in a room with a bunch of other vampires.

Right now, all she really knew about vampires was what she'd read in books and seen on TV and in movies. Claudette could tell Donna all day long not to buy into those things, but it wasn't like flipping a switch. Those beliefs were ingrained in Donna. Probably in everyone.

Vampires were part of the culture. No one really believed in them, but at the same time, there was something too real about them as well. And now that Donna knew better—and knew that there were other creatures in the world besides vampires—she realized that almost anything was possible.

She took a breath and pushed the elevator call button, reminding herself that this was a support group she was going to. Everyone was there for the same reason. To get help dealing with this new phase of life.

No one would be there for a free dinner. And even if they were, would one vampire actually attack another?

She had no idea. More proof of how much she needed this group. And Claudette. But Donna was starting to wonder if that was a closed door. She hadn't meant to send the woman packing permanently. It had just all been too much to take at the time.

The elevator doors opened, and she got on, tapping the button for her floor.

"Hold the doors," a voice called out from the lobby.

Donna put her hand out to keep them from closing. "Got them."

It took a moment, but at last, a petite little old

woman made her way onto the elevator. She could have been Betty White's younger sister. Same cloud of white curls, same twinkly eyes, same slightly naughty smile. "Thank you."

Donna's hand hovered over the bank of buttons. "Floor?"

"Twelve, please, honey." The older woman was wearing a black velour tracksuit with a rhinestone zipper and bright white sneakers. Over the jacket, she wore a fluffy white fake fur vest.

Twelve was already pushed, so Donna leaned back.

The woman eyed her sharply.

Donna smiled, studying her elevator companion right back. She realized she might have been wrong about the woman's age. Everything about her indicated she was eighty to eighty-five, but Donna realized her skin was too smooth and firm to be that age.

Or she'd had work done. If so, the doctor ought to win an award. Even so close, it was phenomenal.

"You're coming to the meeting, aren't you?" the woman asked. She had a fanny pack around her waist, and the zipper wasn't quite closed, revealing a crumpled tissue.

"The meeting?" Donna wasn't about to admit where she was headed. Not to this sweet, little old woman. Then she almost laughed at herself. There had to be all kinds of meetings going on in this building. It was a health and wellness center, after all.

The woman stuck her hand out. "I'm Francine Werther."

Donna shook her hand, it was warm and soft and

not the least bit leathery with age. "Donna Barrone. Nice to meet you, Francine."

"You too, kid." The doors opened, and Francine started out. "Come on, Neo gets cranky if we start late."

Neo? Donna walked off the elevator, but shook her head. "I'm not—"

"Yes, you are." Francine didn't even look back.

Donna just kept walking, looking for Suite C. She found it, mostly because Francine was opening the door.

Francine grinned at her. "Told you."

Donna's brain couldn't process the information it had just received. "You're a…a…"

Francine nodded. "Yep." She went in, leaving Donna no choice but to follow.

That sweet little old lady with the fanny pack was a vampire? Sure, that explained the skin, but the idea was so hard to compute that Donna started to wonder if she'd gotten the address right.

A small foyer opened onto a larger setting that looked like a living room. A circle of six armchairs, upholstered in a navy paisley, took up most of the space. On one side was a credenza with a coffee service and bottled water set out. There was a small plate of cookies.

A young black woman with black and purple braids twisted into one central braid atop her head like a mohawk was fixing a cup of coffee. She was in all black. Skinny jeans, T-shirt, sweater over that. All of it ripped or distressed in an artful way. Chunky lug-soled boots and silver jewelry added a street vibe that felt authentic.

"Hi, Neo," Francine called out. "We have a new one."

Neo nodded. "Sensed her when she came in." The young woman turned and leaned against the credenza. She held her coffee with both hands, lifting it to her mouth so the steam rose past her eyes. She gave a little nod. "What's up."

It wasn't really a question, but Donna answered anyway. "Not sure, actually."

Neo snorted. "Then you're in the right place." She glanced at her watch, which looked more like a computer monitor with all the lines of data running across it. "Doc has three minutes."

"She'll be here," Francine said.

Neo shrugged and slunk toward the chairs. She settled into one that put her back to the windows, then she hitched one leg over the arm and slouched down, holding her coffee in front of her like a shield.

Donna took a bottle of water. She didn't need it, but she might want it later, and she didn't want to get up and disrupt the group. She took a chair one away from Neo.

The suite door opened, and Dr. Goldberg walked in.

Donna sat up a little. "La?"

Dr. Goldberg looked at Donna and smiled. "Well, hello there." She laughed softly. "This explains so much. Welcome to the group."

"Thanks. You run this group?" Wait, what had Claudette said about the woman in charge of the First Fangs Club? She was a third-level empath. Donna wasn't entirely certain what that was, but the empath part made sense. Dr. Goldberg was great at her job as a therapist.

"I do," La answered.

Another woman rushed in behind her. "Sorry I'm late."

"You're always late," Neo groused.

The bottle blonde flicked her big dark eyes at Neo with a look that could have killed. "Maybe because I have a life." Her accent sounded Puerto Rican or Dominican, maybe.

"Ladies," Dr. Goldberg cautioned, "this is a safe, civil space. Respect that, or I'll have to ask you to leave."

"Yeah," the blonde added. Her skintight ankle jeans showed off some impressive curves, as did her equally tight, off-the-shoulder black top. Just like Francine, the woman wore a fake fur vest, but hers was long and shaggy and hot pink. She wore pink stiletto ankle booties to match. Even her nails, which were long and pointed, were the same vibrant shade.

"Hoochie," Neo muttered.

"Nerd," the blonde muttered back.

"Ladies, last warning." Dr. Goldberg's voice held a stern tone Donna had never heard before.

The blonde sniffed and went over to the credenza. She opened one of the cabinet doors, which housed a small fridge, and took out a Coke. Then she found a seat next to Francine, who'd put herself beside Donna.

Dr. Goldberg sat between Donna and Neo. She took a notebook and pen out of her bag and set them on her lap. "Does anyone know if LaToya or Meghan are coming?"

Francine leaned in. "Pretty sure Meghan has that charity ball tonight."

The blonde piped up. "And LaToya's out of town this weekend with her boyfriend."

"All right, then, thank you, Francine and Bunni." Dr. Goldberg opened her notebook. "We'll get started, then."

Donna stared at the blonde. Had La actually called her Bunni? She didn't look like a Bunni. Or maybe she did. Also, what kind of vampire name was Bunni?

Dr. Goldberg smiled at all of them. "Welcome to the First Fangs Club. We have a new member this evening, so why don't we go around and introduce ourselves? Neo, why don't you start?"

"Sure." Neo's slouch didn't change. "I was turned three months ago. I have my own cybersecurity business, and I love long walks in dark alleys." She grinned, having apparently amused herself.

Bunni rolled her eyes, but the clockwise direction meant she was up next. She waved at Donna by wiggling just her fingers. "Hi. I'm Bunni Escobar."

That last name sounded familiar to Donna, but she didn't know why, other than the obvious drug lord connection.

"I was turned six months ago. I'm still trying to figure things out. Mostly, like, how not to kill my ex-boyfriend for getting me into this mess." She smiled suddenly. "It's not really a mess, though. It was, when I was first turned, but, like, I'm cool with it now, you know? I mean, we're, like, killing machines. I mean, if we want to be. Which we don't. But it's still cool."

Donna nodded, not sure what else to do.

Francine grinned at her. "I'm Francine Werther, as you know since we met in the elevator. I was turned close to seven months ago. I like crossword puzzles and baking. The best thing about being turned, well, there's a lot of good things about it, but one of the things I really enjoy is how fast I can knit now. Also, not having every joint creak when I move is nice."

Donna grinned.

"Oh!" Francine patted the arm of her chair. "And I was eighty-four when I was turned. Don't I look amazing?"

"You do," Donna said.

She nodded. "Isn't that the craziest thing about all of this? What it does to the way you look? You should see my breasts. Like a twenty-year-old's again." She shook her head. "I have got to get a boyfriend. Well. Another one. I keep wearing them out."

Donna snorted. Francine was a riot.

Dr. Goldberg turned to her. "All right, your turn."

CHAPTER 20

D onna's nerves suddenly returned for the silliest of reasons. She wanted these women to like her. Or at least to think she was cool enough to be friends with. For that reason, she used her full name. "I'm Belladonna Barrone."

The first name she'd struggled with for most of her life suddenly felt right in this context. *Belladonna* was a lot more vampirey than *Bunni* or *Francine*, that was for sure.

Bunni tipped her head, like she was trying to think of something, but Donna kept talking. "I was turned three days ago. It's been…interesting. To be honest, I didn't believe—"

Bunni sucked in a sharp breath. "I know who you are!"

Before Donna could say anything else, Bunni went on. "You're Joseph Barrone's wife. The mobster. Didn't he just get bumped off or something?" She gasped again. "You're Big Tony Villachi's sister-in-law!" Then she laughed. "Sergio would freakin' lose his mind if he knew I met you. Not that I care what that low-life scumbag *pendejo* thinks."

Donna swallowed. The women were all looking at

her. Waiting. She nodded. "He wasn't bumped off. He was killed in a car accident. And yes, I am, or was, Tony Villachi's sister-in-law."

Neo sat up. "For real? The actual mob guy?"

Donna took a breath and raised her chin slightly. She wasn't proud of her former family, but she had nothing to be ashamed of either. Not anymore. "Yes."

Dr. Goldberg held up a hand. "Ladies, I think we should refrain from questions that are overly personal, but I would also like to remind you that what is discussed in group stays in group."

"It's okay," Donna said. She appreciated La's efforts, but Joe's reputation was what it was. Especially in this area. She made herself smile, lips tight. "I know from our sessions that the best results come from honest, open work. And I need this group to work for me. Becoming a vampire wasn't something I planned. Frankly, it wasn't something I even thought possible."

Neo nodded. "Yeah, I feel that." She reached across Dr. Goldberg to offer Donna her closed fist. "We got you."

Donna hesitated, then realized what Neo wanted and tapped her fist against the other woman's. "Thank you."

Dr. Goldberg smiled. "Excellent work, ladies. Donna, would you like to tell us how you were turned? Only if you feel comfortable, of course."

"Sure. I went to the cemetery to see Joe." She snorted. "To give him a piece of my mind, actually. I was mad. About a lot of things."

"I hear that," Bunni said.

Donna continued. "While I was there, I was attacked by a young man. A vampire. Not that I understood at the time that that's what he was. I thought he was some Goth freak hopped up on whatever drug the kids are doing these days. He bit me. I mean, who does that?"

Francine leaned in, smiling. "We do. But not without consent."

"I'll remember that," Donna said. "Anyway, I passed out. When I came to, there was a woman crouched over me." She swallowed, thinking back. "She was feeding me blood from her wrist, which should have been disgusting, but it wasn't. Then she said she had to go catch the vampire who'd bitten me, that he'd gone rogue and shouldn't have done that, and that she'd find me later and explain. After that, I passed out again. The second time I came to, I convinced myself I'd been the victim of a couple of weirdos cosplaying in the cemetery, and I'd just gotten caught in the middle of their crazy game."

Bunni looked unconvinced. "But you had to know something had happened, right? You had to know you were different."

"I didn't. Not really. I had a lot of other stuff going on. More than just my husband's death. Stuff I can't really talk about."

"Mob stuff?" Neo asked.

Donna hesitated. "Nothing I can talk about. But it was heavy enough that what happened in the cemetery got put on the back burner. In fact, even when

Claudette showed up—that's the woman who saved me—I wasn't ready to hear what she had to say, because I couldn't make myself believe that she was telling the truth."

"Claudette?" Francine asked. "I think she's Meghan's sire." She clapped her hands. "You're blood sisters, then! How fun. And how nice to have such a high-ranking sire."

"High ranking?" Donna asked.

Francine nodded. "Claudette is the vampire governor of New Jersey."

Donna just looked at her. Everything still had a very surreal quality to it. She wasn't sure what surprised her more. That Claudette had turned another woman in this group or that Claudette was *someone* in the vampire world. But then, she was the one who'd given Donna the card for the First Fangs Club, after all, so maybe that was her way of being responsible?

Dr. Goldberg made a note. "Donna, are you feeling overwhelmed?"

She nodded. "I am a little. I have so many questions. I feel…like a newborn. In a way. It's very unsettling."

Francine patted the air in front of her like she was trying to reach Donna. "We have a group text. We'll add you. Then you can reach out to us anytime you like."

"That would be great. Thanks," Donna said.

Dr. Goldberg uncrossed and recrossed her legs in the opposite direction. "Francine, why don't you tell Donna your turning story? I think it would be good for her to hear some other experiences."

"Sure," Francine said. Her eyes lit up, and Donna got the sense that telling this story was something the woman really enjoyed. "My third husband, Artie, may he rest in peace, was a movie producer. He left me buckets of money and a beautiful townhouse on the Upper East Side. After he died, I got a little lonely, so I turned the basement into an apartment and rented it to a nice young man. A musician. Artie would have loved him. I didn't charge him a whole lot, because musicians are always broke, and he was a sweet boy. Anyway, I never saw Lionel all that much, except for Monday nights when he would come up and we'd have movie night. So much fun. Mostly, though, it was just nice to know someone else was around, you know?"

Donna nodded.

"Plus," Francine said, "Lionel's very handsome. So that didn't hurt. Anyway, a couple years after he moved in, I got very sick." Her smile disappeared. "To make a long story short, the doctors told me I had maybe six months to live."

It was Donna's turn to gasp. "How awful."

Francine folded her hands in her lap. "It was. Just because I'm an old woman doesn't mean I'm ready to die. Lionel was devastated when I told him. He wept. Actually cried. I was so touched. And then, a couple days after I told him, he came up to see me again. He had an answer, he said. A sort of cure.

"Of course, I was interested, so I listened." Francine's smile returned. "He explained to me that he was a vampire and if he turned me into one, I could live forever, and my cancer would be cured. I thought he'd been smoking too much reefer, but it was such a kind offer that I said it sounded lovely. All the while, I was thinking if only it was possible!"

Bunni laughed, and Neo let out a little snort.

"Well," Francine said, "he took that as my agreement and bit me. Next thing I know, I was a vampire."

"Wow." Donna shook her head. "I guess you believed it then."

Francine nodded. "Oh boy, did I. Kicked that cancer right to the curb. I only went back to see the doctors one more time, just to make sure it really was gone, then I figured I didn't need them anymore."

"I have to ask," Donna said. "Does Lionel still live in your basement?"

Francine's grin went a little lopsided. "Not exactly. He's moved upstairs now."

"Oh. *Oh*," Donna said. "Good for you."

Francine gave a little snicker. "Very good for me. We have an open relationship, though."

"Very modern." Donna admired Francine. She was definitely living her best life and making the most out of becoming a vampire, but then, she'd had a choice. Donna hadn't.

"Bunni, would you like to share?" Dr. Goldberg asked. "Your story is very different than Francine's."

"Sure," Bunni said. She leaned back, her hands resting lightly on the arms of the chair like she was holding court. "I was with my ex-boyfriend, Sergio, and his crew while they were scoping out a new warehouse location."

"For their drug-packaging business," Neo said with an eye roll.

Bunni glared at her. "Yeah, so? I'm done with them now, so get over it." She huffed out a breath before going on with her story. "The warehouse was abandoned, or so they thought. But there were some big containers in there. Crates. Couple of Sergio's boys opened one up to see what was in it."

All cockiness left her expression as she remembered back. "I know now it was a den. A vampire sleeping spot. Opening the crate woke them. Two of them attacked."

Her hands came together in her lap. "Sergio and his crew ran. I got left behind. Hard to run in heels, you know?"

Donna nodded, sympathetic.

Bunni's gaze filled with the resolute look of someone who'd accepted her fate. "I thought I was going to die. I *was* dying. But one of the vampires figured out that what had happened wasn't intentional and took pity on me. He saved me. Made me one of them."

"That's amazing," Donna said. "You got lucky. If you consider being turned lucky."

"I do," Bunni said. "Better than being dead." Her eyes narrowed. "Now I'm going to do good things with my life."

Dr. Goldberg's pen was poised to write. "What are those good things, Bunni?"

Bunni hesitated. It was clear what she wanted to say

was not what she thought she should say. "I don't know why taking out Sergio and his crew would be such a bad thing. He left me for dead."

"And they're drug dealers," Neo added.

"Ladies, we've discussed this," Dr. Goldberg said. "The way forward needs to also be the way up. Revenge only takes us backward and down."

Bunni's lids fluttered in what looked like a barely suppressed eye roll. "Yeah, well, he's selling dope to little kids, and the cops can't pin him on it, so I'm supposed to just let that go?"

Donna leaned forward. "Can you give the cops the evidence they need to arrest him and his gang?"

Bunni shrugged. "I tried, but he's got a cousin on the force that got wind of the raid, and Sergio cleared out the house before the cops got there. He's wired up good. They have all kinds of protections in place."

Donna nodded. "I understand that."

Bunni grinned. "I bet you do."

"Maybe you need to go bigger. Talk to the FBI."

Bunni seemed to think about that. "Yeah, maybe. You think they'd listen to me?"

Donna lifted one shoulder nonchalantly. "I know a guy. I could ask him. Would you be willing to wear a wire? Get Sergio to incriminate himself and his gang?"

"Sure," Bunni said. "What have I got to lose? He can't hurt me anymore." Then her expression turned coy. "How come you know a fed?"

Donna paused. Telling the truth might not be the best thing to do, but she was tired of dancing around it and giving vague answers. Dr. Goldberg had already pointed out that what was said in group stayed in group, and Donna chose to believe that. "Because I wanted out of my life and away from my husband and his horrible family. To do that, I needed protection. I could only figure out one way that I could make that happen. Turn state's evidence against the Villachis."

Neo, Bunni, and Francine looked at her with sharpened gazes that seemed, at least to Donna, to be filled with respect.

Francine was the first to speak. "You're a brave woman, Belladonna. You're going to do just fine as a vampire."

"Yeah," Neo said. "Respect. That's hard-core."

Bunni nodded. "It is hard-core. And if you can do it, I can do it. Will you talk to your friend for me? Or would you maybe go with me to see him?"

"I would be happy to," Donna said. She hoped she hadn't spoken out of turn and that Rico could actually help Bunni. And did she need to tell Bunni that Rico was a werewolf? What was the protocol on that?

The group was helpful, but what she really needed was for Claudette to get in touch with her. Or find some kind of a manual. Did such a thing even exist?

Maybe she should write one. *Everything You Ever Wanted to Know About Becoming a Vampire But Were Afraid to Ask.*

At some point, she did need to start thinking about earning her own money. The insurance was only going to last so long. Were there any rules about writing a book on being a vampire?

She sighed. There was so freakin' much she didn't know.

Becoming a vampire was like going through puberty all over again. And not in a good way. If there was a good way to go through puberty.

CHAPTER 21

"More great work, ladies," Dr. Goldberg said. "Why don't we talk about your highs and lows this week?"

Donna kept her internal struggle to herself awhile longer.

Neo, still slouching, raised her hand. "I got a high. Just got the blood supplier on East 58th as a new client, and as a bonus, they're hooking me up with a half-price membership."

"Well done, Neo," Francine said.

"Thanks." Neo looked at Donna. "You been to one of those yet? You've been turned for a couple days now. You're going to need to eat."

"No," Donna said. "I didn't even know such things existed until recently. Claudette's not even the one who told me. I think she's mad at me. She hasn't answered my call yet. Although I suppose being governor keeps her busy."

"Why do you think she's mad?" Neo asked.

"When she showed up at my house, I wasn't in the right frame of mind to accept everything she was telling me. I basically asked her to leave, and she did. I got over all of that the next day, though, and I called her back like she said to do, but she hasn't shown up yet."

"Probably just busy. Or maybe teaching you a lesson," Neo said. "Some sires can be divas. Not saying Claudette is, just that it happens. Don't worry. We'll help."

"Great. How often do I need to…feed?"

"At least every couple of days," Francine said. "But more when you're young. So maybe even tonight. You can come over to my place if you'd like. I have plenty on hand."

"That's kind of you, but I really need to get my own source," Donna said. Then it all started to feel heavy. And despite her newfound strength, she wasn't sure she could handle it.

Frustration settled over her. "I feel like I'm never going to get the hang of this. Like I'm going to screw up and accidentally kill myself—or worse, someone else—by doing something wrong. I didn't ask for any of this, you know. I just wanted my freedom back. To live a life where I wasn't constantly looking over my shoulder."

She pressed a hand to her chest. "I'm not a bad person, but people think I am because of who I am. And who I'm married to. *Was* married to. And now I'm a vampire. A freakin' vampire!" She tossed her hands up before shaking her head and slumping back into her seat. "I didn't ask to be turned into a monster. How is this fair? It isn't. Not even the tiniest bit."

No one said a word, and she realized her rant had shut the group down. Had the word monster offended them? Or was it something else she'd said? Didn't matter now. What was done was done. She grabbed her purse. "I'm sorry. I should go."

"No," Neo said. "Don't go."

"No, don't," Francine echoed.

"Yeah," Bunni said. "Stay. We get it."

"We do." Neo looked at Donna, all bravado gone from her demeanor. "We've all been there. Well, maybe not Francine as much, because she had a clue about what was happening. But yeah, I think we all had a point where we felt like we'd been given more than we could handle."

"That's how I feel," Donna said.

Bunni leaned forward a little. "I had a couple days where I wished they'd just let me be dead."

Neo, despite the opening, didn't snap back. Instead, she nodded solemnly.

"Did you feel that way, Neo?" Donna asked. "Like you wished you'd just died instead?"

Neo stopped nodding and stared at the table in the center of the space. Her gaze was distant and bitter, and for the first time that night, she looked vulnerable.

Donna decided to ask a different question. "How were you turned, Neo?"

For a moment, she said nothing. Then she cleared her throat. "I was in Belgium for a big cybercon. Out on the town, having fun...a little too much that last night. Made a wrong turn on my walk back to the hotel and ran into a group of rogue vamps."

The faraway gaze went deeper. She shook her head. "They were cruel. They wanted me to be afraid. I was too. Terrified. After a couple minutes of torment, they attacked. Drank me nearly dry and left me for dead."

No one in the group said a word. Donna got the sense that Neo didn't tell this story often. Or ever.

She started again. "I lay there, staring up at the stars, my life fading away, and I was powerless to do anything about it."

She rubbed a hand across her face like she was trying to wipe away the memory. "Thankfully, like most of you, another vampire found me and took pity on me. In my case, it was three vampires. Brothers who spent their nights in the Belgian streets looking for victims of the *gedrocht*, the monsters who attacked me. It took blood from all three of them to revive me, that's how little I had left."

Suddenly, she smiled and sat back, the worst of her tale apparently over. "It's pretty rare to have three sires. I'm hoping it means I end up with three special abilities."

"You're very fortunate to be alive," Donna said. She made a mental note to come back to the *special abilities*. "I guess that's the takeaway here. We could all be dead. But we're not. That second chance just comes with the burden of learning to live in a different way."

Dr. Goldberg nodded. "That's a very smart way to look at it, Donna. Very smart. This is a second chance."

Bunni pursed her lips. "To right wrongs."

Dr. Goldberg frowned.

Bunni shrugged. "What? Donna's gonna help me do things the forward way. Right, Donna?"

"Right," Donna said. "Can I ask a question? About

those special abilities that Neo mentioned? Claudette said something about that too. That sometimes vampires develop other abilities. What kinds of things are we talking about?"

Francine chimed in. "Lionel can levitate. It's very useful if you need something off a high shelf."

Donna laughed. "I could see that it would be."

Neo crossed her arms. "My sires can all read minds. Not deep, probing stuff, but enough that they can get the measure of a person. They said it's how they knew I was worth saving."

Bunni rolled her eyes but said nothing.

"It's what they told me," Neo added sharply.

Donna found it all fascinating. "I'd love to be able to read minds. Can you do that, Neo?"

"Not yet. Just because my sires can doesn't mean I'll get that ability. Or any ability. It's not a guarantee. And there's no rhyme or reason to when you get one either. Mostly, they seem to come in the first year. But I also know a guy who got the ability to become invisible on his tenth anniversary of being turned."

"That would be a cool thing to do." Donna thought about how easy it would be to eavesdrop on Big Tony if she was invisible. "Has anyone ever gotten more than one?"

"It happens," Bunni said. "Meghan said Claudette can perfectly imitate a baby's cry, and she can shrink herself down to the size of a gnat."

Donna frowned. "Neither of those seem like especially useful powers. Maybe the shrinking one." Was that how Claudette had gotten into the house without setting off the alarm?

Francine shrugged. "They're not levitation, that's for sure."

Neo laughed. "Yeah, there are definitely some great powers and some not-so-great ones. Although I guess shrinking yourself could be useful, and being able to cry like a baby was probably a good way to lure unsuspecting humans to their death, back when there were no rules about consent."

Donna looked at her. "There are rules? Who made them? I need to know this stuff. Are there consequences for breaking them?"

Neo held up her hand and ticked her answers off on her fingers. "Yes, the Immortus Concilio, and yes."

"Whoa. Back up. The Immortus Concilio?" Donna didn't like that. It sounded way too mobby.

Dr. Goldberg held up a hand. "Our time is almost up, but this is an important conversation. Is anyone willing to continue this with Donna?"

"It's really Claudette's job," Bunni said. "If she's not going to do it, Donna should file a grievance. But yeah, I can hang out for another minute."

"I appreciate that," Donna said. "But I think if someone could just tell me what the Immortus Concilio is, I'll be good for tonight. And maybe give me the name of a blood bank. Then I'll be set. I'm sure Claudette will call soon."

Francine nodded. "I'm sure she will. The Immortus Concilio is a group of seven vampires who oversee vampire activity across the globe. Nearly two hundred years ago, they declared it unlawful for a vampire to take a human life, even for sustenance."

Donna's mind went to Yuri. She might already be in trouble. "Are there any extenuating circumstances allowed?"

Francine looked around the group. "There could be, I suppose."

"Self-defense?" Bunni offered.

Neo nodded. "I think that would be okay. Or if the human was especially terrible. Like, I think there's a special exception for high-ranking criminals." She laughed. "Why? You thinking about having a drink of Big Tony?"

Donna's lip curled back. "Ew. No. Way too much garlic in him anyway. Or isn't that an issue?"

"Depends," Neo said. "Some can tolerate it, some can't."

Francine raised her hand. "Repeats on me something awful."

"And there are other rules? I need to know these. Or at least get a copy of them."

"Claudette—" Bunni started.

"I know," Donna interrupted her. "But I don't really want to wait on Claudette when there could be something I need to know now."

"Basically," Neo said, "don't kill humans, don't kill other vampires, don't start trouble with the other supernatural races—unless they're fae, and then you can have at it. Also, don't tell humans about vampires or any of the other supernaturals unless they're sworn to secrecy." She looked at Francine. "Did I miss anything?"

"No," Francine said. "You got all the big ones."

Dr. Goldberg closed her notebook. "That's our session, then. We went a few minutes over, but that's understandable. I'll see you all next Friday." She stood. "Have a great week."

"You too, Dr. Goldberg," Francine said. Then she turned to Donna as Bunni and Neo said goodbye. "Would you like to come up to the house? I'll give you some blood to take home."

Neo got up and stretched. "I can take her to Lifeline." She hooked her thumb back behind her. "It's just a couple blocks up. Then she can stock up and see about setting up her own account."

Donna nodded. "I think that would be good. Not that I don't appreciate your offer, Francine. I really do. It's very generous. But I feel like I should get enough to last me awhile, you know?"

"Oh, sure, honey." Francine got up, unzipped her fanny pack, and pulled out her phone. "We still need to get you onto the group text."

"Right. That would be great." Donna stood as well, waiting until Francine had the appropriate screen up, then rattled off her cell number.

Francine tapped a few more buttons, and Donna's phone vibrated. "There you go. I just sent an intro text to the group."

Bunni had walked Dr. Goldberg to the door, but she returned now and joined them. "You really think your

FBI friend can help me? I want to nail Sergio, but he's slippery as an eel."

"I'll reach out to him tomorrow, I promise." Donna held her phone up. "And I have your number now, so I'll let you know what he says."

"Great." Bunni gave her a big smile. "See you guys later. I gotta party to go to. Nice to meet you, Donna."

"You too, Bunni."

She wiggled her fingers at them and sashayed out of the room.

Neo frowned as she watched Bunni go. "She's a freaking piece of work, that one."

Donna had to ask. "What's with the bad blood between you two? No pun intended."

Neo shrugged. "She's low-rent. I don't like her. She's dumb. And phony. Running with those gang-bangers, then acting like becoming a vampire turned her life around." She sucked air through her teeth. "I just think she's full of it."

Donna's brows lifted. "You must not think much of me either, then. Seeing as how I was running with gangbangers of a sort."

Neo's expression shifted, and she shook her head. "I...no, that's not what I meant. You're different. You're a lot more sophisticated." She sighed and frowned toward the door. "Bunni just gets on my last nerve."

Donna nodded. "Hey, I get it. Some people are like that." Lucinda, for example. "But she strikes me as a woman who could use a friend. I know I could." She smiled at Neo and Francine, thinking what unlikely women they were to be those friends, and yet, here she was thinking they were exactly who she wanted to spend time with.

Were vampires really that different than mobsters? These women seemed different than that. They weren't caught up in ill-gotten gains and getting one over on somebody, but then, she'd just met them. She prayed they truly were different. Because she hated feeling like she'd traded one prison for another.

CHAPTER 22

F rancine put a hand on Donna's arm. "Anything you need, you just reach out."

"Thanks. I really appreciate that."

"C'mon," Neo said. "We can walk over to Lifeline and get you hooked up." She laughed. "Pun intended."

They all headed out to the elevator.

As they rode down, Donna's thoughts got the best of her, and she laughed softly.

"What?" Neo asked.

"Every once in a while, it just hits me how crazy this is. I guess it still hasn't sunk in that I'm a…a vampire. See? I almost can't bring myself to say it."

"You'll get there," Francine said. "Everyone adjusts in their own time."

Donna nodded. "I'm really glad I met you ladies. It's already helped."

Francine beamed. "That's what First Fangs Club is all about. Helping our sisters adjust."

The elevator touched down on the first floor, and the doors opened. They all got off and went through the foyer to the sidewalk. Francine waved as she headed in the opposite direction. "See you next week."

"Bye," Neo answered.

Donna waved. "Next week." She and Neo stood on the sidewalk. She looked at the other woman. "Which way?"

Neo grinned. "Listen, I will absolutely take you to Lifeline, but if you're in the mood for something a little *fresher*, I know a place we can go first."

Donna wasn't exactly sure what that meant, but she had an idea. "You mean…"

Neo nodded. "Right out of the vein."

Donna couldn't stop her face from showing her horror. "I don't know."

"They're willing. It's not like anything's happening that's not supposed to." Neo leaned in. "Trust me, there are a lot of humans that get off on it. Big-time. In fact, some of the older, wealthier vampires have live-in feeders."

"Feeders? As in people who live with them for the sole purpose of feeding the vampire?"

Neo nodded. "Feeders, blood babies, donors, assistants, whatever you want to call them. Although assistants usually do more than just supply blood. It's a symbiotic relationship. The vamp pays their bills, gives them a place to live, all that. And the feeder supplies them with an unlimited supply of blood." She shrugged one shoulder. "It's a sweet deal if you can afford it. Not sure I'd want a human living with me, though."

"Yeah, me either." Donna's lack of knowledge about her new lifestyle became more and more evident with every minute she spent with Neo.

"So you wanna hit up Redline or no?"

Tentatively, Donna nodded. "Okay." How else was she going to learn?

Neo grinned. "Cool. Word of warning, cover is steep. Not as much for us as it is for the humans. But that's partially how they weed out the riffraff."

That was interesting. "What do you consider steep?"

"Seventy-five bucks. I don't go to blood bars very often, but I thought it would be fun to take you to one since you're new and all. Kind of a special occasion."

"That's nice of you." Donna already knew she'd pay Neo's cover. That was just the polite thing to do, especially when Neo was doing this for her.

"This way." Neo got them walking again.

"Are there a lot of these places? These blood bars?" Donna slipped her hand into her purse, pulled two hundreds off the bundle, and tucked them into her jacket pocket, ready to go.

"There's a good handful in the city, by which I mean five or six. Deep Six is pretty good. Kiss Club is a pit. I don't think they test their donors at all. Crimson is *the* show. I mean, it's super bougie. You have to be a member or know a member to get in there. And membership is, like, fifteen grand a year."

"Ouch."

"Yeah. I went about a month ago when my sires were in town. They took me." Neo shoved her hands in her pockets. "Where do you live? If you don't mind me asking. Some vampires aren't big on giving out that kind of info."

"I don't mind. I'm about an hour away in Jersey. East Verona. Near Westbrook."

Neo whistled. "That's a nice place, right? Lots of expensive homes and private schools. I did a job out there once for a guy who needed some heavy-duty encryption for his business."

Donna nodded. "It is. But very controlled. The Villachis have a lot to do with that. Big Tony likes it that way."

Neo was quiet for a moment. "I've never met anyone in the mob before."

Donna slanted her eyes at the woman. "You might be surprised. The family's reach is far."

Neo's brows rose, but she didn't say anything more about it. Half a block more and she pointed ahead. "There's Redline."

There was no line, just a small square in front of the door, roped off with standard burgundy velvet. Within that square sat a large man Donna assumed was the door guy. Another, smaller man stood outside the ropes, showing his ID.

Neo slowed. "Hang on. Let him go in first."

"Okay."

When the human entered, Neo approached the bouncer. "Hey, Marcus. This is my friend Donna."

"Neo, Donna." Marcus nodded. His muscular build made it appear that his head sloped directly into his shoulders, but his pale eyes against his dark skin really caught Donna's attention. He looked otherworldly. "I still need proof, ladies."

The Southern accent surprised Donna.

Neo turned to her. "Show him your fangs, or make your eyes glow."

"I don't know if I can." She gave Marcus a nervous smile. "I'm new to this."

He smiled back, showing slightly larger-than-normal canines with wicked points. "You can do it, sugar. Think about blood."

She nodded, but that was easier said than done. While she'd popped her fangs out with no trouble in the Bloomie's dressing room, being put on the spot made it feel impossible. "I'm trying."

"Hang on," Neo said. She faced Donna. "Look at me." Then she bared her fangs, her eyes lighting up like embers.

Without meaning to, Donna reacted, lips curling, fangs jutting out.

Neo looked at Marcus again. "There you go."

He unhooked one side of the rope separating them. "Welcome to Redline. Cover is seventy-five each."

Before Neo could pay, Donna handed Marcus the two bills she'd put in her pocket. "Keep the change."

"Thank you." He tipped his head in gratitude as he opened the door for them. "Y'all have a good night."

"Hey," Neo said. "You didn't have to do that."

"I wanted to," Donna said. "My way of saying thanks for the extra help."

"That's really nice of you. I appreciate that. And with that tip, Marcus will remember you."

Donna just nodded as she looked around. Being married to Joe had definitely taught her the power of overtipping.

The bar was decent inside. Very clean. Dimly lit but in a way that was more atmospheric than shady.

Textured gold walls were broken up with black leather booths along one side and a marble-topped bar along the other. Battery-operated candles flickered in mercury glass globes on each table and spaced along the bar.

Some kind of European trance music played loud enough to make eavesdropping impossible. Or maybe it was the faint but purposeful hum that lay under the tracks. Like a supernatural white noise.

The staff wore all black with red ties. That made it easy to see who was an employee and who was a patron, but there were also a number of humans in street clothes. Humans. Interesting that, without really trying, she could pick out who was a vampire and who wasn't.

An older woman approached them. Human. "Welcome to Redline. I'm Caroline. Would you like a booth?"

"Yes," Neo said.

She smiled at them. "Follow me."

She took them to one, waiting as they sat. "What can we get you this evening?"

Donna looked at Neo, hoping she'd take the lead. She did. "Male. Wait. Is Hector here?"

Caroline nodded. "He is. I'll see if he's available." She looked at Donna. "And for you?"

"I have no idea. This is my first time."

Caroline smiled. "I understand. Do you prefer a male or female donor?"

"Male, I guess."

"Very good. Do you have an age preference?"

Was that a thing? Apparently. "No. Any age is fine. Within reason. No kids. But then, you probably don't let kids in here. Do you? No one too young." She took a breath. "I'm sorry, this is all really new to me."

Caroline's smile turned sympathetic, and Donna wondered if she was the most pathetic vampire the woman had ever seen. "Not to worry. I have someone in mind. What recovery package would you like to order?"

Donna had no idea what that meant. She looked at Neo, clueless. Caroline seemed to understand. She presented them with a menu board.

Recovery packages were apparently for the humans. There were four of them: Bronze, Silver, Gold, Platinum. Bronze was cookies and orange juice. Platinum was fresh fruit, imported chocolates, champagne, and pineapple juice. She pointed to the Platinum, but looked at Neo. "What do you think?"

"Yeah, let's do Platinum. Hector loves chocolate."

Donna nodded to Caroline. "Two of those. Or one, if that's enough for two."

"Very good." Caroline took the menu and left.

"Thanks," Neo said. "But we're splitting that check."

"No, we're not. I ordered it. I'm paying." Donna leaned across the table. "But isn't this bizarre? We're ordering people. Is that not weird? Because it seems weird to me."

"It only seems weird because you still don't think of yourself as a vampire. That will change."

Donna wasn't so sure about that.

Neo went on. "Also, we're expected to tip when we're done."

"How much?"

"Up to you, but I think twenty percent is about the minimum."

"Thanks for telling me." Donna's nerves were up. She wasn't sure she'd ever get used to this. "Is Marcus, the guy at the door, a vampire?"

"No, werewolf. He's a good guy."

Caroline returned with two men. The younger man, a Latino, greeted Neo with a grin. The older man was handsome and graying at the temples, but incredibly fit. Everything about him, from his gorgeous dress shirt to his expensive watch and alligator belt, said *money*. Interesting. "Here are your gentlemen for the evening. Let me know if I can do anything else for you."

"Thanks, Caroline." Neo patted the seat next to her. "How've you been, Hector?"

He took the seat. "Great. You?"

While they chatted, the older man gestured to the spot beside Donna. "May I join you?"

"Yes, please." He was very good-looking and certainly seemed willing, but it still felt odd to her.

He smiled. "I'm Pierce, by the way. Caroline said this is your first visit to Redline."

"Hi, Pierce. I'm Donna. *Oh!* I just got it. Pierce. That's funny."

"What?" He frowned. "No, my name really is Pierce. Like Pierce Brosnan."

"Oh." She stopped smiling. "Sorry, I just thought—"

He laughed. "I'm teasing you. In here, I get that all the time."

She pressed her fingers to her forehead, smiling again. "I walked right into that one."

"You looked tense. I just thought it might break the ice a little."

"Yeah, I am tense. I was only turned a few days ago."

His brows rose. "So you really are new to this. I'm honored to be a part of that journey."

His sincerity was touching. "Thanks for being understanding. To be honest, I don't really know what comes next."

Pierce's gentle smile made that seem okay. "It's really up to you. Some patrons like to talk a little, some like to get right to feeding. I serve at your pleasure, so whatever you'd like is fine with me."

She'd never had a man speak to her like that. It was heady. She shot a quick look at Neo and Hector. They were chatting away. "I wouldn't mind talking to you a little."

He nodded. "Wonderful. I certainly wouldn't mind talking to you. As I'm sure you can imagine, I find your kind endlessly fascinating."

"Is that why you do this?"

"In part. But this is also a pleasurable experience for many of us. Myself included." He went silent then, seemingly lost in thought.

She probed gently. "Why else?"

He glanced at her, then away just as quickly. "I'm attracted to the power. Serving a woman such as yourself creates a thrill in me unlike anything I've ever experienced before."

She sensed there might be more to it than that, but didn't want to pry. "Can I ask what you do for a living?"

He made eye contact again. "I'm a lawyer."

That surprised her. But then things started to make sense. Like his nice clothes and expensive watch. And how a powerful man might really enjoy a more powerful woman.

"You're shocked by that," he said. "I can see it in your face."

"I am," she admitted. "But intelligence is a wonderful quality. So let's call it more of a pleasant surprise."

He smiled again. "Thank you. I like that." He stretched his arm out and rolled up his sleeve, then put his hand on the table before her, wrist up. "I am yours, whenever you are ready."

In a sudden attack of the senses, she could instantly hear his heart beating and the thrum of the blood in his veins as the rich scent of that blood just beneath his skin reached her nose.

Her fangs extended and her mouth opened. She couldn't tear her gaze away from his wrist. "I'll do my best to be gentle."

He leaned in to whisper in her ear, "I don't care about that."

CHAPTER 23

She took his wrist in her hands as if cupping water and brought it to her mouth. She was vaguely aware of him closing his eyes and leaning back against the booth. Then vaguely aware of Neo preparing to do the same thing with Hector.

Donna opened her mouth wider, pressing her fangs into his wrist. The flesh was warm and soft and smelled faintly of whatever soap he'd used. She took the moment in, because it was another first. But her hunger rose up like a beast, so she didn't linger long.

Still, she was aware of what she was about to do. She decided a decisive bite would be better than a hesitant one, so she drove her fangs in. The instant they broke his skin, he let out a soft moan. The sound was a mix of pain and pleasure.

More pleasure, if she had to bet.

Which was good, because she couldn't have stopped if she wanted to, a feeling that scared her a bit, but she was lost to the sacrifice. He was willing, and somehow, that made the blood sweeter.

Yuri had been bitter in comparison. The taste of fear, she now understood. Pierce was a fine wine. Yuri had been scummy pond water.

But this was not Yuri. Although something similar was happening. Images were once again flashing through her mind. Maybe that was just what happened when a vampire drank from a human. She had no idea.

Afraid to repeat her first mistake, she made herself disengage. She could have had more. A lot more. Even so, she was sated and warm with the life she'd taken in.

A sweet calm filled her, like lounging in the sun on a day when there was nothing else to do. It was the purest sense of relaxation she'd experienced, elevated beyond what she'd felt with Yuri.

She turned her head to the side. Beside her, Pierce looked at her, eyes a little sleepy. His gaze shifted to his wrist, still in her hands. "The wounds. You have to run your tongue over them to heal them."

"Oh." She did as he said, cleaning away the last of the blood. The punctures sealed up and disappeared. "Wow."

Pierce smiled. "You are amazing creatures."

She licked her lips. "And you taste so much better than the first guy I had." She laughed, a little light-headed from the feeding, but too deliciously warm to care. It was blissful. "Pretty sure I've never said that to anyone before."

"It was my privilege to be your first here at Redline."

Neo finished up with Hector, and a moment later, a server showed up with a silver tray loaded with an array of chocolates, fresh fruit, and small pastries. Behind her was a second server bearing a champagne bucket filled with ice, a bottle of whatever champagne had been part of the package, and a third server with a carafe of pineapple juice.

As the servers set things up and opened the champagne, Donna looked at Pierce. "I hope this is okay. Would have been better if I'd been able to ask you what you like."

"This is perfect," he assured her. He accepted a glass of half champagne, half pineapple juice from one of the servers, but offered it to Donna.

"No, thanks," she said. "I have to drive home."

"You know," he said quietly, "with your new metabolism, you can drink that entire bottle of champagne and barely feel it."

"Really?" Kind of sad that a human knew more about being a vampire than she did. "Okay, I'll have a glass."

He handed her his, then took a second from the server, who then prepared glasses for Neo and Hector. When she was done, the young woman looked at them. "Anything else I can get you?"

Donna shook her head. "I think we're good."

Neo nodded. "Same, all good here."

Donna held her glass out to Pierce. "Thank you. And cheers."

He clinked his against hers. "Same to you. I would love to see you again. In fact…" He dug into his shirt pocket and took out a business card. "Here's my contact information. I hope that's not too bold of me, but I like you. I'd be happy to serve you again."

She set her glass down and took the card.

Pierce Harrison, Attorney at Law. Criminal Defense.

The firm listed was one of the biggest ones in the city. And he was a partner. She raised her eyebrows at him. "This is impressive."

He smiled and saluted her with his glass. "Thank you." He took a plate and put some fruit and chocolate on it. "I try to only defend the innocent. Thankfully, I've reached that point in my career where I can be a little picky."

"That must be nice." She tucked the card into her purse. What would he think of her if he knew who she was connected to? Probably not much. That made her sad.

Then an image flashed through her mind again. One she'd seen before when she'd been drinking from him. She decided to test a theory. "Did you have a husky when you were a kid? A big one with blue eyes? Named Mocha?"

His lips parted in surprise. "Yes. I haven't thought about Mocha in ages. How did you know that? I could see if you'd read my mind, I know some vampires have that power, but I wasn't thinking about him."

She shook her head. "I don't know. It just came to me." She didn't want to tell him she'd seen it while taking his blood. That felt like revealing too much.

"You're just turned," he said, "so it's early to get your special power, but it does happen."

She sat back to ponder that. The same thing had happened when she'd drunk from Yuri. But the pictures she'd seen had been of Yuri, Joe, and Lucinda. Those images had come back to her as she slept afterward. She'd thought they were dreams.

Now she wasn't so sure. What if they were memories? Was that possible? And if it was, what did it mean that she'd seen Yuri with Joe and Lucinda?

Nothing good, that much was for sure. Like that Yuri had met with the brother and sister before Joe's death. The implications of *that* were deeply disturbing.

"Is everything okay?" Pierce asked.

She nodded. "Just remembering some things I need to take care of. I should probably go."

He looked disappointed. When was the last time a man had genuinely wanted her to stay? She didn't even care that it was most likely because she was a vampire. He nodded. "I understand."

She put her hand on his arm. "I would very much like to see you again. Can I call you sometime?"

That perked him up. "Absolutely. My personal number is on the card."

"Wonderful." She reached across the table toward Neo as Pierce slid out of the booth to let her exit. "Hey, I have to run. Thanks so much for bringing me here. See you next week?"

Neo nodded, her smile lazy and sated. "You know it. Stay safe, Donna." Then she sat up a little. "What about the blood service?"

"I'm good for now. I need to find one near me anyway."

"All right," Neo said. "Talk to you soon."

"You too." She took her purse and left the booth, Pierce offering her a hand as she did. "Thank you."

"I would ask if you'd like me to walk you to your car, but I know you don't need the protection."

"No, I don't," she said. Neo's words about tipping came back to her. But this man was an attorney. A well-paid one, judging by his clothing and the firm where he was a partner. She reached into her purse for a hundred, all the same. "But it's still a kind offer." She kissed his cheek and pressed the bill into his hand. "Thank you again."

He looked down at the money. "This is kind of you, but I'd rather see you again."

She smiled. He was utterly charming. "You will. Good night."

He took her hand and kissed the back of it. "Good night, my queen."

His words swirled through her head like a drug, intoxicating her. She left the club floating, giving Marcus a big smile on the way out.

"Have a good time?" he asked as he opened the ropes for her.

"Yes," she nodded. "Do you know Pierce Harrison?"

"I do. Good guy. You need a lawyer? He's kind to our community."

"I don't need a lawyer." Not yet, anyway. "I was just thinking about using him for…feeding." Such a weird thing to say.

Marcus tipped his head. "Was he your donor tonight?"

"He was. Very nice man."

Marcus smiled. "You're just his type too. He likes sexy, sophisticated women. Emphasis on *women*. Pierce isn't into millennials, if you catch my drift, sugar."

"He likes older women. More his age?"

"Yep. You want him now and then? I bet he'd jump."

"So he'd be safe to be alone with?"

"As a Brinks armored truck." Marcus leaned in. "Between us, I think what he really wants is a vampire sugar mama. You know, some vampire queen to keep him in her home and treat him like her personal buffet. Crazy, right? 'Cause he's this powerful attorney, but hey, the heart wants what the heart wants."

Donna felt like her storehouse of interesting information was now overflowing. "I'm not there yet, but good to know."

"You got it, sugar. You come back now, all right?"

"I will. Maybe next Friday."

"Cool." He winked at her.

She smiled back and headed to her car. The walk was uneventful, despite the late hour. She thought about Pierce. About his willingness, his desire, really, to serve a vampire.

In all honesty, there was something very exciting about that. A man at her beck and call. A man whose sole focus would be her needs, her desires, her well-being.

She could see how helpful it would be to have a companion who could go out in the sun too.

She reached her car. In a few minutes, she was headed home, navigating city traffic, which was ever present no matter the hour, and her mind returned to the idea of getting some help.

That's what she was calling Pierce in her mind. Help. That was a safe term. But what kinds of things would he expect from her? Besides being taken care of financially. Or would he not expect that as much, since he probably had his own money?

She shook her head. Why was she thinking about these things? She was in no position to keep a man in her house. Not with everything else going on. The Villachis. The Russians.

Rico.

She sighed. If there was ever a man she'd like to keep in her house, it was him. But he wasn't about to get involved with her. She was much too tainted. She knew that.

Still, maybe once the Villachis were behind bars, he'd reconsider. What was the agency's policy on dating former informants? She had no idea.

She groaned. There was too much going on in her head to think such thoughts. Which reminded her about the thoughts she'd had involving Joe, Lucinda, and Yuri. That might be worth mentioning to Rico. Maybe he could see if any connection existed among them.

Worth a shot, she thought.

What she needed to do most of all, however, was get ahold of Claudette and get the rest of her questions answered. That was looking less and less likely to happen, though.

Claudette, where are you? I'm sending up the mental bat signal for the third time. Respond already!

If she didn't, Donna was going to have to reach out to the First Fang girls. And as helpful as she knew they would be, she still hated coming off as such a clueless newbie. At least now she knew they wouldn't hold it against her.

Forty minutes later, she turned onto her street, not quite ready for bed, but not knowing what else to do with herself. Now that she was a night owl, she supposed she'd have to start rearranging her schedule accordingly.

Maybe she'd go for a run.

She pulled into her driveway and approached the house.

A strange car was parked in front of her garage.

She slowed.

And Big Tony got out.

CHAPTER 24

She froze. She wasn't ready for this. Her heart was pounding, her chest felt tight, and her hands had gone clammy. She clutched the crucifix around her neck and prayed for deliverance. But regardless of how that request was answered, she had to prepare to get herself out of this.

All the powerful vampire feelings she'd been having were gone. All she wanted to do was throw the car in reverse and stomp on the gas.

But doing that wasn't going to solve anything. Not unless she ran Big Tony over, because he wasn't going to go away so easily.

Instead of running, she gave the crucifix a quick kiss and parked alongside his vehicle. Normally, she would have opened the garage and parked inside, but she didn't want to give him the opportunity to go into the house.

So the driveaway it was. She got out, feeling a little nauseated from nerves. Even so, she tried to keep it light. "Tony, hi. What are you doing here? Is everything all right?"

He squinted at her, reminding her that in this darkness she had the advantage. "I was about to ask you the same thing. You're out late."

She nodded. "Support group in the city. Highly recommended. Couple of us went out for…drinks after." He didn't need to know who'd recommended it. Or what it was in support of. Or the details of those drinks. He'd never believe her anyway.

His eyes narrowed a little more, like he wasn't sure he believed her. As if *he* was someone to judge her for lying. "You haven't returned any of my calls or texts."

"I realize that. I'm sorry. Things have been hard lately. Very unsettled. That's a big part of why I went to the group tonight."

He took a step forward, but only so he could lean against the back of his car. His gaze raked her in a shameless appraisal. "You look good. Real good. Like you tightened up all over. You lose some weight?"

Yeah, that wasn't weird or creepy. She barely kept the disgust off her face. "A little. Grief does that to you."

"Right." He nodded again, then went silent like he was waiting on her to fill in the gap.

She wasn't about to volunteer anything, so she played dumb. "Well, thanks for coming to check on me. I'm going in. It's late, and I need to go to bed." She looked him right in the eyes with intent. "See you at mass tomorrow."

Her words had no effect on him. He took another step forward before she could go anywhere. "Listen, about the drop-off. I know things didn't go as planned."

She crossed her arms. Finally, they were getting to

the reason he'd showed up. "Do you? Do you know that the men I met there tried to kill me?"

His mouth opened, his brows bent in consternation. "What?"

Her turn to scowl in disbelief. "You didn't know that?"

He scrubbed one meaty hand over his face. "That ain't what I hired them for."

"So you did hire them?"

"I ain't gonna—"

The sound of rapid footsteps filled the night air, then they faded, and Claudette walked out of the shadows. She glanced at Big Tony before looking at Donna. "Who is this?"

"Tony Villachi. Head of the Villachi crime family. My former brother-in-law."

She nodded. "We need to talk, but I'm guessing this needs to be taken care of first."

"It does," Donna answered. "But it's my business. I'll handle it."

"Well, do it later. We need to talk now."

Donna's explanation of who Big Tony was clearly hadn't made an impression on Claudette. Or she didn't care. Either way, there was no putting him off so easily.

He flicked his gaze at Claudette. "Look, sweetheart, I don't know who you are, and I don't care. I got business with Donna. That comes first. You girls can have your chitchat later."

"Girls?" Claudette glared at Big Tony like he was an insect that had dared her not to step on him. After her withering glance, she turned to Donna. "I don't know or care what's going on, but I'm your sire. I'm supposed to help with these kinds of things. You want me to kill him?"

"Whoa." Tony immediately reached for his side, no doubt for the gun tucked in his belt, but Claudette was faster.

She reached him before his hand crossed his navel, taking him by the throat with one hand. Then she held him slightly off the ground. "You don't amuse me, human."

The toes of his polished black loafers just touched the ground. He barely managed to squeak out, "What the—"

"No killing," Donna said. That would be harder to explain to Rico. He'd probably frown on Big Tony's premature death, seeing as how the mob boss could end up singing like a canary once the FBI started making arrests. "I didn't think that was allowed anyway. But it would be nice if someone could make him tell the truth. Any chance you can do that?"

A look came over Claudette that was a mix of self-satisfaction and *watch this*. Instantly, she lowered Big Tony to the ground and faced him so she could look into his eyes. "You're going to answer some questions for us."

There was something lyrical about her voice suddenly. A quality that made it impossible to ignore.

Big Tony seemed to feel the same way. Maybe more so. His eyes rounded, his pupils growing larger as his jaw slackened. He nodded.

"What do you want to know?" Claudette asked.

SUCKS TO BE ME

Donna spoke up instantly. "The truth about the drop-off. Did he set me up to be killed?"

"Did you set Donna up at the drop-off to be killed?"

"Not killed," he muttered. "Kidnapped."

The word sent a shockwave through Donna, even though she'd thought at first that that's what the men had planned. The first guy had seemed like he was trying to shove her into the trunk. She joined Claudette, standing at her side. "Why did you want me kidnapped?"

"Why did you want Donna kidnapped?" Claudette repeated.

"Because I suspect she's talking to the feds. I wanted to find out for sure."

Donna's hand went to her crucifix again. "Why did he think that? Who told him? Never mind, don't ask him that yet. Ask him what was in the duffel bag for the drop-off."

"What was in the duffel bag for the drop-off?"

"Fifty Gs. Payment for the job."

"Payment for who?" Claudette asked on her own.

"The guys."

"Names," Claudette said.

"Good," Donna said.

"Al, Turo, and Sam."

Those were the right names, and two of those guys she'd accidentally killed. Donna shook her head, trying not to think about that right now. If there had been money in the bag, then who replaced it with newspaper? Vinnie? He'd delivered it. Didn't mean he'd been the only one with access to it, though.

Claudette looked at her. "Are we done here?"

"No. Ask him why he thinks I'm talking to the feds."

Claudette sighed and made eye contact with Big Tony again. "Why do you think Donna is talking to the feds?"

"Joe thought she was. Thought she was going to flip, send us all up."

Donna grimaced. She'd had no idea Joe'd suspected her. Not even an inkling. "One more question. Ask him who else had contact with the duffel bag besides him and Vinnie."

Claudette barely contained her boredom. "Who had contact with the duffel bag besides you and Vinnie?"

"No one," Tony said. "It was in my office until I handed it off to Vinnie."

Which meant Lucinda could have gotten to it. Or possibly one of Tony's other lunks, if they were around. But Lucinda was looking pretty good.

Un-freakin'-believable.

"We done now?" Claudette asked.

"Yes." Donna was fuming. Could Lucinda be behind this? It was certainly a possibility. She'd like to get Claudette and Lucinda together. See what the old battle-ax had to say for herself then. "You can let him go now."

"Good." Claudette kept staring into Big Tony's eyes. "You're going to forget me, our entire conversation, and why you came here in the first place. What you will remember is that you desperately need to get home and that Donna is not talking to the feds and that she should be left alone. Do you understand?"

He nodded. "Go home. Leave Donna alone. She's not talking to the feds."

"Good boy." She released him. And disappeared. Or she'd gone gnat sized.

Big Tony blinked at Donna. Then he looked around like he had no idea where he was.

"Thanks for stopping by to check on me," Donna said. "But I really need to go in and get to bed. It's very late, and I'm sure Lucinda will be wondering where you are. Probably worrying herself silly already."

"Uh, right." He looked relieved to find out what he'd been doing. Then he seemed to remember who he was, and his chest puffed up. "Lucinda only worries about what I tell her to worry about. You take care now."

"You too."

He got in his car and drove off.

Donna watched him, shaking her head. If only Claudette hadn't—

"Now," Claudette said as she walked out of the shadows again. "Why haven't you reached out to me? If you think you can do this alone, that little incident should prove otherwise."

"What are you talking about? I've been calling for you mentally, like you said to do, since the day after you first showed up. Three times already. You're the one who hasn't responded. You also didn't tell me you're the vampire governor of this state."

"I don't usually reveal that right away for personal reasons." Claudette's gaze narrowed. "But let's be clear, I come when my children call for me. I haven't heard anything from you."

"That's not my fault." Donna crossed her arms again. She was not taking the blame for this. "Maybe your hearing is going."

Claudette frowned. "Try it now, while I'm standing here."

"Fine." Donna spoke her sire's name in her head. *Calling Claudette. Come in, Claudette. Can you hear me, Claudette?* "Well?"

"Nothing. Maybe you're not doing it right. Are you using my name?"

"Yes. I just said it three times in my head. How else would I call for you? How could I possibly be doing it wrong?"

"I don't know, but it's not working. That's very odd. Maybe that crucifix is messing up the signal."

"Sure, that's what it is. Jesus doesn't want me talking to you." Donna rolled her eyes, although maybe that was true. "Hang on." She took her necklace off and set it on the trunk of the car. *Claudette, Claudette, Claudette.* "Anything?"

"Nothing. At least we know it's not the crucifix."

"And at least you're finally here." She put the necklace back on. "I do appreciate the help with Big Tony. Perfect timing. I really need to learn that glamouring thing." She decided to leave out the part about praying for intervention. "Why don't you come in so we can talk?"

"Fine. And the glamouring takes time and practice."

"Good to know." Donna opened her car door, pressed the visor button to open the garage door, and headed inside. She could move the car in after Claudette was gone.

Claudette followed.

Donna turned the alarm off as soon as they were inside, then flipped on some lights and went into the kitchen. "Can I get you anything? A glass of wine, maybe? We can sit in the living room then."

Claudette hung by the kitchen's entrance. "No, but speaking of, what are you doing for sustenance? I can tell you've made the transition, so I know you've had blood."

"About that..." Donna decided wine sounded good. She poured herself a large glass of Pinot Noir and walked past Claudette to reach the living room. She settled on the couch, kicking her shoes off before tucking her feet underneath her and taking a long sip of her wine.

It wasn't Pierce's blood, but it was good.

Claudette wandered in. "Well, what about it?" She sat in one of the chairs facing the sofa, crossing one long leg over the other.

Donna sighed. "I'm pretty sure I did something I wasn't supposed to."

"Which is?"

"The day after you were here, I had a visitor." Donna stared into her wine. "Not a nice guy. Basically broke into my house. Threatened to do some pretty awful things to me. I got mad. And I was hungry. So—"

"Tell me you *just* bit him."

Lucky came running in and jumped up on the

couch. Donna scratched his head with her free hand. "Not exactly."

"You *didn't*." Claudette's rounded eyes and gaping mouth spoke volumes.

"If you mean that I didn't drain him to death, then sorry, but yeah, that's exactly what I did. I absolutely didn't mean to. I couldn't control myself. The hunger just took over."

Claudette closed her eyes and appeared to be calming herself. Or trying to. When she opened them again, her jaw was tight and the tendons in her neck stood out. "That is a violation of the highest—I warned you about that."

"Unfortunately, I don't think you did *exactly*. You never came right out and said the hunger would make me accidentally kill someone."

Claudette got up from her seat to pace the room. "*That's* why I can't hear you. This isn't good. You broke the psychic tether between us."

"By draining him dry?"

Claudette whipped around, eyes gleaming the way Donna had seen hers react during high emotion. Claudette was obviously mad. "Yes. There are consequences for such actions."

"Like what?" Donna knew all about consequences.

"I shouldn't even tell you this, because you'll probably think it's some kind of supernatural windfall, but chances are good you'll end up with a bonus power because of this."

"And that's a bad thing?"

"Yes. It can be." She stomped toward the piano.

"That's why the council outlawed such killings centuries ago."

"The Immortus Concilio?"

Claudette stopped pacing. "Yes. How do you know about them?"

"I went to the First Fangs Club tonight. That group provided a wealth of information. That's how I found out about you being governor."

Claudette looked slightly green. "You didn't tell them what you did, did you? That you killed a man accidentally?"

"No, it didn't come up."

She exhaled, hand on the baby grand. "Good."

"Listen, I didn't know. And I certainly didn't intend to kill this guy, but he threatened me with physical violence. He wasn't a good person. A Russian gangster, actually."

"That could play in your favor. Still, the council may not think that's enough of a reason."

"Why would they think anything about it unless you tell them?"

"These things have a way of getting found out." Claudette looked around with the slightest bit of panic about her, nostrils flaring. "I don't smell anything. What did you do with the body?"

CHAPTER 25

"Do you think I have it tucked behind the sofa?" Donna's brow furrowed at Claudette's insinuation. How dumb did she think Donna was? Maybe that was better left unanswered. "A friend took care of it."

Claudette arrowed in on Donna again. "What kind of friends do you have that take care of dead bodies for you? Oh wait, you're married to the mob. I forgot. Do they know you're a vampire? Can they keep their mouths shut?"

She really hadn't been paying attention when Donna introduced her to Big Tony. "I am *no longer* married to the mob, thank you very much. And yes, my friend knows. And yes, he can keep his mouth shut. He's a werewolf, so—"

"How are you already friends with a werewolf?"

"Can you sit down?" Donna took a much-needed gulp of wine. "You're making me nervous, which is ruining the nice buzz I got from Pierce."

Claudette blinked at her. "You drank from another human this evening? Did you kill him too?"

"Yes. And no. He was a donor at Redline. All perfectly aboveboard. It's a vampire bar in the city where you can—"

"I know what Redline is." She plopped into a chair like the fight had been taken out of her. She rubbed at her brow. "So you've just completed your transition, but you've already made your first kill, become friends with a werewolf, and had your first donor at a blood bar." She threw her hands up. "I'm not sure what you need me for."

"I still have a lot of questions." Claudette had also been very handy with Big Tony. "Speaking of, how do I learn to do that thing you did outside? The whole Wonder Woman Lasso of Truth thing? Because that would really come in handy."

"Practice. It's a power that builds with time. You have to keep eye contact and hold them in thrall." Claudette shook her head slowly, like things weren't processing all that quickly. "I have some questions too. The werewolf who took care of the body, is he trustworthy? Are you sleeping with him?"

"Very trustworthy. He's FBI. And whoa, *no*. Why would you ask that?"

Claudette's lazy smile spoke volumes. "The werewolf-vampire relationship has long been a rather charged one. For whatever reason, we seem to be very attracted to one another. Maybe because we're pretty high up on the supernatural food chain, and that makes us compatible, but I think it's also because werewolves mate for life with their own kind, so they tend to avoid serious same-species relationships until they're ready to settle down. Until that time, they often seek out vampire partners. I know it's probably counter to most of what you've learned from Hollywood and books, but trust me. Every vampire should have a werewolf partner once in her life."

Donna sat there, speechless.

Claudette seemed amused by that. "How did you meet your wolf?"

Rico certainly wasn't Donna's wolf, but she answered anyway. "I've been working with him to put my husband and his criminal family away. He's the fed that Big Tony thought I might be talking to. I am. I have been. My husband was right. But I had no clue Joe was wise to that."

Claudette leaned forward, her gaze clouded with confusion. "So your husband's family really is Mafia?"

"Late husband. That's whose grave I was at the night you saved me. And yes, they're Mafia. Did you think I was kidding? Big-time crime family. The man in my driveway was the head of it, Big Tony Villachi. My former brother-in-law." Donna swallowed another sip of wine. It wasn't having any effect, proving Pierce right about her new tolerance for alcohol. "I've wanted to get away from them for years. Rico, the FBI werewolf, was my out. He was building a case, and I was going to turn state's evidence in exchange for going into WITSEC."

"So what happened? Who killed your husband?"

"Fate. Karma. God. I don't know, but he was in a car accident. It was perfect, really. I got my way out and didn't have to leave everything behind to do it. I have two kids. Grown, but that doesn't mean I wanted out of their lives. I have a sister I love very much too. Going into witness protection was an incredibly hard decision, but I thought it was the best way to protect them."

Claudette nodded. "But now you don't have to?"

"I hope I don't have to go into hiding now, but I'm still working with Rico to put the Villachis away." Lucky curled up at her side. "That's why he's so willing to help me. He needs me. And I need him. I won't really feel safe until Big Tony and his crew are locked up. Especially now that I know Big Tony tried to kidnap me. Which probably would have led to me getting whacked."

Claudette sat back. "You had a very complicated human life."

"Had? Just because I became a vampire doesn't mean it suddenly got simple. In fact, becoming a vampire only made things more difficult." She untucked her feet and stretched them out to rest on the coffee table.

"You need an assistant."

Donna's mind went to Pierce as she looked at Claudette. "You mean, like, live-in human help?"

"Yes. If you can afford it. Most vampires with some age can, but..." She glanced around. "I'm assuming you can, too, based on this house and the Mercedes you drive."

"I have some money, yes, but that seems like such a strange thing to do."

"Do you have a gardener? A maid service? Someone who treats your house for pests? It's not that much different."

"Yeah, but I'm not having sex with any of those people."

Claudette's brow furrowed. "Who said anything about sex?"

Donna shrugged. "I don't know. It just seemed like... The donor at the bar tonight? He seemed pretty interested in that kind of setup, but I got the impression he'd expect more. Like, that kind of more."

"Some do. Some don't. It's all about ground rules." She smiled slowly, like she was about to reveal a great truth. "Remember, we are vampires. Superior to humans. Naturally, there are those who will fear us, and they should. We are killing machines."

Donna had already killed more than she'd ever intended.

"But," Claudette went on, "there are also those who revere us and want to worship us."

That was definitely Pierce.

"Find one of them to assist you, and your life will be infinitely easier. Of course, you'll have to pay them. And they don't all want money. That's why you need to set rules up front."

"So sex, then."

"*No.*" Claudette rolled her eyes. "Do all middle-aged women have their minds stuck in the bedroom? We are vampires. Human assistants usually want to be paid in blood. Money, too, but mostly—"

"My mind isn't—what?"

"Vampire blood is like the Fountain of Youth for humans. It's why you need to keep your new status to yourself, or you could find yourself being hunted.

Anyway, giving your assistant allotments of your blood is how you keep them strong and healthy. It gives them an edge against whatever they have to deal with. It's a big reason why most of them take the jobs."

"Do you have an assistant?"

"I'm the governor. I have several."

"Oh. Right." And just like that, Donna was considering giving her new lawyer friend a call.

But not yet. There was no way she was calling Pierce for anything more than a meeting at Redline until the Villachis were dealt with. So she just nodded at Claudette. "I'll keep all that in mind. In the meantime, can you answer some more questions for me?"

"That's what I'm here for, but the sun will be up in a few hours, so I can't stay long."

"Why don't you just spend the night? I have plenty of guest rooms."

Claudette seemed to consider it. "Is the house sunproof?"

"The windows have room-darkening shades, and there's one room that's on the north side that gets no sun. We always jokingly call it the dungeon."

"All right. I'll have to let my people know where I am. Wait. Did you put iron around your house like I told you to?"

"Yes. Actually, my werewolf FBI friend did it for me since it was daylight."

Claudette nodded appreciatively. "I had a werewolf lover once. He was a lot of fun. He eventually decided it was time to find a mate of his own kind, though."

"Yeah, again, Rico's not my lover." Not that Donna

was against the future possibility. Especially now that she'd learned about their supposed compatibility. "We have a professional working relationship."

Claudette shrugged. "Whatever. I'll stay the night."

"I didn't see a car out front, so I don't know where you parked, but if you want to put it in the driveway, you're welcome to. Or you can have my space in the garage since I haven't pulled my car in yet."

"I didn't drive. I ran."

"You…ran? From where?"

"My house."

"Do you live close?"

Claudette hesitated. "In the area. What other questions do you have?"

Donna understood her sire wasn't ready to share specifics. Seemed odd, considering Donna had drunk the woman's blood, which was about as intimate as you could get, but she wasn't going to pry. Claudette had to have her reasons. Maybe it was a security thing, being governor. "I have so many… How old are you?"

"Closing in on three hundred."

"Wow." Donna let that settle over her. "You've seen a lot in your time."

"I have."

"Is your sire still around?"

Claudette's gaze narrowed ever so slightly. "Why do you want to know that?"

"Just curious."

"She is, and that's all you need to know. If all goes well, you'll never meet her."

That was a curious thing to say, but before Donna

could ask another question about Claudette's sire, she held up a finger. "I'll take a glass of that wine after all. So long as it's decent."

"Do I look like a woman who'd drink bad wine? Life's too short for that. Or it was." Donna got up. "Be right back." She took her glass with her to the kitchen, refilled it, then poured a generous one for Claudette. What kind of a sire did Claudette have that she'd act so oddly about her? That question was going to stick in Donna's head for a while.

When Donna returned to the living room, Claudette was looking at photos on the baby grand in the corner. Without turning, she asked, "These are your children?"

"Yes. Do you have any? Human ones, I mean."

"No. I managed to avoid that."

Donna ignored the comment. Her children were the best thing that had ever happened to her. If Claudette didn't understand that, her loss. "They're both grown now." Donna held out the glass. "Christina's in college, and Joe Jr. is in the Air Force."

Claudette turned to accept the wine. "You can't tell them, you know."

Donna found that hard to believe. "So they're just supposed to accept without reason that their mother no longer goes out during the day?"

"If they don't live with you, it shouldn't even be an issue." Claudette sniffed the wine. Her brows rose in apparent appreciation.

Donna wasn't convinced. "Except when they come to visit. Or wonder why I can't visit them."

"You can visit them. You just need to travel at night." She took a small sip of the Pinot Noir, then nodded. "This is good. Next question."

Her responses hadn't solved anything concerning her children, but if Donna wanted to tell them, she was going to tell them. Nothing came between her and her kids. Claudette wouldn't even need to know. And if she did find out, well, she'd just have to get over it. Donna asked her next question. "Am I dead?"

Claudette looked at her and laughed. "No, not technically."

"But I thought vampires were the undead. Dead, but not."

"Yes and no. We are immortal, but we can be killed by various means."

"Yes and no? What does that mean? I still don't get the dead-undead thing. My heart is beating. I'm breathing. I feel very much alive."

"You are. Because you haven't truly died yet."

"Didn't I die in the cemetery?"

"No. You came close, I think, but you still had a pulse when I found you. Although, any longer and you would have expired, I'm sure."

"Would you still have been able to save me?"

"Yes. But there's a time limit on that."

Donna only gave that a moment of thought. There was still so much to learn. "Then I can still die? Or not?"

"Yes, you can. The first real death you suffer, and that might not be for many, many years, you will physically die. But that's it." She shook her head. "All that will happen is that those physical things you just described—the beating heart, the breathing—will cease. It's nothing to be alarmed about, though. Vampires don't need a pulse and functioning lungs to exist."

"So, let's say I get shot. I die. But I don't."

"Right."

"Let's say I've already died that physical death. Then I get shot. What happens then?"

"Nothing. A bullet can't kill a vampire. It'll still hurt, but unless it's made of wood and a direct shot through the heart, you'll be fine."

"A wooden bullet through the heart can kill me?"

She nodded. "A certain type of wood, yes. But it would have to be a pretty direct shot. Most hunters prefer crossbows and wooden stakes."

"There needs to be a handbook for all this." Then Donna stared at her. "Hunters?"

"Vampire hunters."

Donna took a big slug of her wine, then went straight to the couch and sat down. "I did not sign up for this."

Claudette laughed softly. "It's not as if they're out roaming the streets looking to pick us off. A hunter only goes after a vampire who's gone rogue. Unless it's a fae hunter, but that's a different story entirely."

Donna gave her a sharp look. "Define rogue."

"Essentially a vampire that's drained a human to death or—oh. I see your point." She took her seat again. "Look, it's not as if the human you drained is going to be missed exactly, is it? And you said your friend was going to deal with the body. I'm sure it's all fine. Other than the fact you severed our tether. That could be problematic."

"About that. Don't you have a cell phone number you can give me?"

"I do." She frowned. "But I don't really like giving it out."

"Maybe you can make an exception." Donna knew there was a tone in her voice, but she didn't really care. She needed a lifeline. Although, now that she had the First Fangs Club women, maybe she didn't. Still, it would be nice to get in touch with Claudette if she needed to.

"I'll make sure you have it before I leave. But you need to know that if you step out of line, it's my job to correct that. It's expected of me, actually."

"Thank you. And I understand. Speaking of rogues, what did you do to that vampire in the cemetery?"

Claudette looked away. "What I had to."

"Which means?"

She was silent for a long moment. "I put him down."

"Because he bit me?"

"Because he bit you and basically drained you to death. Trust me, had I not intervened, you would have died. He was on a rampage and about to make a second kill when I caught up to him. Fortunately, I didn't need to turn that one."

"I'm sorry. That had to be hard."

Claudette nodded. "I had such high hopes for him. But I had no choice. If the council had found out..." She shook her head.

"What would have happened? If the council had found out."

"They would have stepped in. Taken care of things themselves. And I would have been in trouble for it."

"How would they know?"

"They know."

"Do they know about me?"

"Yes. We're required by vampire law to register any new vampires we create."

Donna stared at her. "You registered me? How did you know who I was?"

"I went through your purse. Found your ID."

Nothing about that made Donna happy. She wanted to be less connected to the vampire world, not more. Mary and Joseph, being a vampire was as complicated as being human.

"Settle down," Claudette said. "I can see you're upset. All vampires get registered. It's a good thing, I assure you."

"If you say so." Donna still felt a little pouty about the whole thing, but what was done was done. "What made him go rogue? Why did he attack me?"

"Full moon didn't help, but it was because he'd had some bad blood." She looked at Donna again. "*Never* drink from a dead body."

Donna nodded. "I won't. I promise." Yikes. She made a big mental note never to cross that line. "Is it safe to get blood from one of those blood services, then?"

"Yes. They get their blood from living donors, and they are well vetted. Trust me, if they weren't, word would get out, and that would be the end of them. Literally and figuratively. We don't tend to accept things, like humans trying to take advantage of us, with much grace."

"Got it. Can we go back to the ways to die? I don't need to know how you killed the rogue, but it would be useful to know what can kill me."

"You mean besides me and the council?" Claudette laughed, then swallowed the last of her wine and held out her empty glass. "Sure, I'll tell you a few. But first, do you have more of this?"

"I do." Donna got up to get a refill. She was totally second-guessing the invite to have Claudette stay over. Why had she offered? Were the answers really worth it? The woman had basically just told Donna that it was her job as sire to "put down" Donna if she screwed up.

And if she didn't, the council would.

Donna shook her head in disbelief. And here she'd thought being a Mafia wife was dangerous.

CHAPTER 26

Two more hours of conversation and two more bottles of wine, almost exclusively consumed by Claudette, and the woman was finally showing signs of sleepiness. Or maybe that was the wine kicking in?

Donna didn't know how much it would take to give a three-hundred-year-old vampire a good buzz, but two and a half bottles seemed like a substantial amount.

Whatever the reason, Claudette was ready to turn in, and Donna was good with that. Neither of them spoke while Donna led her to the guest room. Something else Donna was okay with. There was so much new information in her head, so much to process, that she was done talking. Plus, she still wasn't used to being up until the early hours of the morning, and she was feeling a little tired.

Besides, Rico would be back in the afternoon, so she needed to be awake when he— crap. Rico would be here while Claudette was here too. Was that going to be an issue?

Donna opened the guest room door. "Here you go. Listen, my FBI friend is going to be here in about ten hours or so to work on the case. I see no reason for that to affect you, though."

Claudette gave her a strange look. "Neither do I. At my age, I sleep very hard. Like I'm dead. If something happens that wakes me up during daylight hours, it's not going to be pretty for anyone. So unless the house is on fire, don't disturb me. Understand?"

"You're not to be woken up. Got it." Apparently, being three hundred not only made you cranky, but also gave you a big case of I'm A Diva.

Claudette looked around the room, then faced Donna, her hand on the doorknob. "I like to feed when I arise. You do have blood on hand, don't you?"

"No." Donna gave her an incredulous look.

Claudette rolled her eyes like the weight of the world lay upon her shoulders and it was all Donna's fault. "Lakewood Consumer Products. They're a local blood bank that does home delivery for vampires. Look them up and get it worked out. You need a service anyway."

Donna frowned. She did need a service, but she hated being bossed around. Suddenly, she wasn't all that sad about the severed psychic tether. Not being mentally connected to Claudette was sounding like more of a gift, frankly. "I'll get on it when I wake up."

Claudette shook her head. "Do it now. They're open twenty-four seven. Then you can have a delivery sent in time for me to feed."

Donna opened her mouth to respond, but Claudette abruptly shut the door, leaving Donna in the hall.

What an entitled piece of work. Even for being the governor. Donna glared at the woman on the other side of the door, a thousand different snappy responses building up inside. But instead of saying anything, she ground her teeth together and stomped back downstairs to wash the glasses and feed Lucky.

She got his food dished out, then ran the faucet for hot water. Claudette's demands were still frosting Donna's nerves, but she had to let it go. Claudette would be gone tomorrow. And Donna *did* need to work out her own blood supply. But wow, the woman was a real pill.

The kind made of arsenic and rat poison.

She rinsed the wineglasses and set them on a mat to dry before getting her phone out and calling the company Claudette had told her about.

It took five minutes and a credit card to set up delivery. Donna wasn't sure what Claudette's blood-type preference was, so she ordered a variety pack. Somehow, that would probably still be wrong. But it would give Donna a chance to see what she liked for herself.

At least it was done. Donna turned the lights off and went upstairs to bed. She set her alarm just in case. It wouldn't do to have Rico's arrival wake her up.

But as she lay there, on the verge of sleep, Claudette's words about the werewolf-vampire relationship came back to her. Did Rico feel like that? Was he interested in her? Would it take the case being closed for him to act on those feelings?

It certainly made her wonder.

Of course, she had no idea what Rico's personal life was like. For all she knew, he already had a vampire girlfriend. Or maybe he was married. Mated. Whatever his kind called it. Just because he'd never mentioned a wife didn't mean there wasn't one. He didn't wear a ring either, but that meant nothing. Joe had never worn one.

She frowned. Joe had had a series of girlfriends, too, the cheating, two-timing scum bucket.

She sighed. Maybe getting Pierce to move in would be a good idea. He was a handsome man. Different than Rico. More James Bond than Dirty Harry. Both had their appeal. But she didn't need protecting, did she? She needed someone to help her navigate this new life.

Pierce could do that. He was clearly capable and smart and literally worshipped her. Plus, he could keep her alive.

She thought about that for a moment, then realized Claudette had never said anything about drinking a werewolf's blood. Was that okay?

She groaned. Why did everything end up in a new question? There really ought to be a book. Or a supernatural Wikipedia, where all her questions were searchable. Why wasn't someone working on that? Neo would be perfect. Donna was going to talk to her about it next week at group. The woman obviously already knew about computers and…

Donna woke to the soft beeping of her alarm. Was it

really time to get up? She felt like someone had piled sandbags on top of her. It must be because her body clock was adapting to her new physiology, and that didn't include being awake during daylight hours.

Then she woke up a little more, opened her eyes, and realized that those sandbags were warm. And purring. Lucky was sleeping on top of her, stretched out along her body from chest to hips. "Morning, you silly beast."

He lifted his head and chirped at her.

Someone wanted breakfast. Or lunch, as the case might be. She'd set her alarm for two, and Rico was due at three again. Didn't leave her much time to get ready, but since she could move with remarkable speed, that shouldn't be an issue.

Hopefully, Claudette would stay asleep.

Donna slid Lucky off and got up. Funny how the first thing she used to do when she got out of bed every day was some gentle stretches, then she'd baby her hips and feet until they warmed up and the stiffness disappeared. Those aches were gone now. "Better living through vampirism," she muttered on her way downstairs.

Lucky got fresh water and a new can of food while her coffee brewed. She took the coffee upstairs and drank it while she went into her closet to pick out something to wear.

"Ugh." She shook her head as she remembered that all her new purchases from Bloomie's were still in the car, which was in the driveway. If she'd moved it into the garage like she'd intended, getting her things out wouldn't be an issue.

Now, however... She went to the window and peeked through the side of the shade. Fairly overcast, but patches of blue were visible. Dare she risk it?

For that new marine-blue cashmere sweater with matching skinny jeans? Yes, she dared. But she'd be smart about it. So, dressed in leggings, hoodie with the hood up and well over her face, and sunglasses, she went downstairs again and opened the garage.

She stood there for a moment, staring into the daylight.

It wasn't far to go. She'd jump into the car, drive it into the garage, and be done. What would that take? Thirty seconds, tops? Less with her speed? And most of the time, she'd be in the car, which would provide protection. Keys in hand, she dabbed the button to unlock the Benz, then crossed herself and dashed out into the open.

She cringed as she broke into the light, expecting searing heat or pain or *something* to shoot through her nervous system and let her know she wasn't supposed to be out at this time.

But nothing happened. She wasn't about to stand there and test her good luck, however. She yanked the car door open, pushed the start button, shoved it into drive, and got the car into the garage before something changed and she burst into flames.

Once in the safe zone again, she leaned back and exhaled. Her heart was pounding, but it was quickly slowing to normal. Why hadn't there been any pain? At the very least, she'd thought there might be a few visible wisps of smoke coming off her.

But there hadn't been a sign of anything amiss.

She got out of the car and walked back to the line of demarcation between the shadows of the garage and the brightness of outside. Could it just be because the sun was hidden behind some clouds? Was that enough protection?

It would be nice if overcast days were safe. New Jersey had a lot of those during the winter.

She'd have to ask Claudette about what constituted dangerous levels of UV exposure. Because Donna realized she'd done something pretty stupid before she'd known about this vampire thing.

The rest of Joe's cash, more than four million of it, was locked up in a safe-deposit box in a bank that did not have evening hours.

Major vampire fail.

She stood there for a moment longer, looking outside. The urge to tempt fate was strong.

In a burst of impulsiveness, she pushed her sleeve back and stuck the tips of her fingers into the light.

Nothing happened.

She reached farther, putting her whole hand out.

Still nothing.

It made no sense. Was the UV risk cumulative? Like could she handle a few minutes, but after ten she'd combust? She didn't have time for more tests, Rico was on his way. But she would find time soon. Because she had to get to the bank, somehow, eventually. How amazing would it be if she could go out during the day?

She grabbed her shopping bags, chastising herself for not keeping more money handy as she closed the garage door and went upstairs. But there was a spring in her step. Her life would be a lot easier if she could get outside while the sun was up. She wouldn't be greedy. There'd be no sunbathing. No showing off. Just running errands. Basic necessities. Things like that.

She smiled all the way through her quick shower. Afterward, she added a touch of makeup and changed into a new outfit. Then she was ready for Rico. So. Ready.

Even if he wasn't interested in her, he was nice to look at.

She took her empty coffee cup and went downstairs. She was tempted to test the outside again but didn't. No sense in getting crazy and accidentally setting herself on fire. She stayed by the door to watch for him, though. Her plan was to open it before he rang the bell. A little insurance to keep from waking Claudette.

He was punctual, as always, showing up again in the plumber's van.

She let him in with a smile. "Good morning. Well, afternoon for you."

"Afternoon. How are things?"

She closed the door. "Interesting. I have some—"

His nostrils flared, and he looked toward the upper floor. "There's another vampire in the house?"

She nodded. "Yes. My sire. And I'd really like her to remain asleep."

"Got it. Sorry, what were you going to say?"

What had she been about to say? Things to tell him. Right. She'd start with the one he'd probably find the most interesting. "Big Tony was here last night."

Rico's brows shot up. "What happened? You look all right. Did he survive? You didn't kill him, did you?"

She wasn't sure if he was kidding or not, but she went with kidding and gave him a *yeah, right* look. "No. But Claudette showed up and used her vampire powers on him to get him to answer some questions truthfully."

Rico nodded. "Good use of that skill. What did you find out?"

"Basically, Big Tony was behind the ambush, but it wasn't his plan for me to be killed, just kidnapped so he could find out if I was talking to the feds, something he suspected because Joe also apparently suspected that."

"How?" Rico frowned. "We've been very careful."

"No clue."

"You're sure he was telling the truth?"

"Under Claudette's spell, I have to assume so. He claimed there was fifty thousand dollars in that duffel bag, so whoever took that money is the person who wanted me dead." She gave him a meaningful look. "I think that's Lucinda. I guess it could also be Vinnie, but it's a known quantity that Lucinda hates me."

"I have accounting looking into her finances. So far they haven't come up with anything that isn't also tied to Tony."

"Well, I have something else for you to look into." She brushed her hair back from her face and gave him her second bit of new info. "I think I've come into one of my extra vampire powers."

"Oh?" Rico's interest seemed piqued.

"I get snippets of people's memories when I drink from them."

His eyes narrowed. "Is this about Yuri?"

She nodded. "Yes. I didn't understand what I was seeing at the time, but now I do. And I saw Yuri with Joe and Lucinda. The two of them must have made a deal with the Russians."

"That's pretty heavy stuff. If they were going behind Big Tony's back…" He thought a moment. "What could they have been up to? Just a deal? I don't think Lucinda would have risked so much for a simple deal. It had to be more."

"I think so too. But how much more?"

"That's my job to figure out. Maybe those ledgers will help. Speaking of, I should get the rest of the stuff out of the stash room."

"Right. Come on." She led him back to Joe's office, then opened the bookcase to give him access. She sat on Joe's desk while Rico started bagging things. Instead of coming right out with her third thing, she decided to test the waters. "Have you ever heard of a vampire who can walk in the sun?"

He was crouched down. At her question, he leaned back on his heels to look at her. "Do you know one?"

"Don't answer a question with a question. Has it ever happened? That you're aware of."

"I'm not exactly a vampire expert, but yes, I've heard of it. It's rare. Takes all kinds of things aligning at the time of turning to make it happen. Pretty sure the Immortus Concilio would want to know if there's a vampire who can do that." His gaze was pinned on her, like he was watching her for some telling sign. "So would every pack leader I know."

CHAPTER 27

"**P**ack leader? As in werewolf pack?"

He nodded. "Your kind have the council, witches have covens, fae have courts, we have the pack. *Packs*, really. Each state has one, but there are smaller, local ones inside each bigger state pack. And then US werewolves as a whole are considered one pack, as are those in Europe, the United Kingdom, and so on."

"Good to know there are also witches." She held up a finger. "Just as an aside, my sire is the vampire governor of New Jersey."

His brows lifted. "Good for you. Politics was never my thing. What I deal with in the bureau is more than enough."

"I hear that." She tipped her head. "Can I ask why the pack would want to know if there's a vampire who's immune to the sun?"

He stood, his gaze growing more serious. "Think about it, Donna. A vampire who can daywalk isn't constrained by the normal perimeters of vampire natural law. What else might that vampire be able to do? The trouble a vampire like that could cause... It wouldn't be good."

What else might that vampire be able to do? Walk

on sacred ground, for one. And Claudette had already told her that was a rare thing. Could the crucifix be what was making her sunproof too?

When she didn't immediately respond, he turned toward her fully. "Is it your sire? You can tell me."

For what reason? So he could report the info to his pack? She had enough to worry about with Claudette and the council. Suddenly, Rico didn't seem like quite the ally she'd thought he was. Not in vampire matters at least. She shook her head. "No."

She didn't say anything more, just pondered his words. What could she say? *Hey, I don't think the sun has any effect on me?* Not now. Not after what he'd just told her. She finally shrugged. "I'm still learning all this. I was just curious."

"I get that. It's got to be hard not being able to go out during the day. I have to say, that part might make me stir crazy." He went back to work. "But then, maybe it wouldn't. We run at night. So I'm not exactly all about the daytime either."

"Mm-hmm." She couldn't shake the feeling his response had given her, though. The feeling of being alone again. And wishing she'd never gone to that cemetery. The thought that she was immune to the sun's harmful effects had seemed like such a good thing. Now the weight of knowing that such a vampire would be considered a threat—information she wasn't even a hundred percent sure of—felt like a suffocating blanket.

Every new day of being a vampire just made things worse. What was next? The council would want to see her? She was registered, after all. Why wouldn't they come knocking? Was that even a thing? Home visits? She really hoped not.

With a sigh, she pulled her legs up to her chest and wrapped her arms around them, pressing her forehead against her knees. She closed her eyes and prayed for the strength to get through this. Maybe she should go see Cammie. Tell her everything and let her impart some words of wisdom.

At least Cammie would have her back.

A warm hand touched her shoulder. "Hey, are you all right?"

She looked up into Rico's deep-brown eyes. "I don't really know. Being a vampire is even harder than being married to a mobster." She sniffed. "I didn't ask for this."

"I know." Genuine concern filled his eyes. "I'm so sorry this happened to you. But look on the bright side. Tony and his crew are pretty powerless against you now."

She nodded. "I suppose that's true. But having you put them away would accomplish the same thing. And protect my family."

"I will. It's just going to take longer. And with you being a vampire, I don't have to worry about you so much." He smiled. "Just them."

A partial smile was all she could manage. "Thanks." It was nice that he worried about her, but he had an end game, and without her, that game would be lost.

"It'll get better."

She held on to her little smile for him, but she

wasn't sure she believed that platitude at all. "Do you like being a werewolf?"

"I do. But then, it's all I've ever known."

"Oh, that's right. You were born into it."

He nodded, then tipped his head. "Do you want me to ask around and see if there are some other vampires you can talk to?"

She shook her head. "No, but that's kind of you. I have my support group. What I'm dealing with now is just stuff I'm going to have to work through on my own."

"Okay. If you change your mind, let me know."

"I will, thanks." The doorbell rang, making her jump. If that woke Claudette up, she was going to kill whoever it was. Figuratively. She hopped off the desk.

"Expecting someone?"

"No." Then she remembered she was. "Actually, I am. A blood delivery. I should let you work anyway."

She went to answer the door. The delivery man was dressed in jeans and a black polo shirt with the Lakewood logo on it. Could have been for an HVAC company or insurance, but she supposed that was the point. A logo that clearly said "vampire blood-delivery service" would get a lot of odd looks. She opened the door.

A black cooler, also bearing the Lakewood logo, sat at his feet. "Delivery for Belladonna Barrone."

"I'm Belladonna."

He held out a small tablet. "If you could just sign."

She scrawled her name on the line with the stylus, then he picked up the cooler and handed it to her. "On your next delivery, we'll exchange this empty cooler for a new full one. And you don't have to take your delivery during the day. We can come anytime."

"Thanks, but this worked out."

"Well, we don't need you to sign now that we have your signature on file. You can just leave the cooler in a designated spot, and we'll pick it up and leave the new one in the same location."

She nodded. "Good to know. I might do that."

"Just let the office know what you'd like."

"I will. Thanks."

He gave a little wave and left. His car was a nondescript blue compact SUV. She could just make out stacked coolers in the back through the tinted glass.

How many other deliveries was he making? And how many other vampires lived around here? She probably couldn't guess, because if they didn't go out during the day, she doubted she'd seen them much.

She shut the door gently, then took the cooler into the kitchen and set it on the counter while she made room in the fridge.

There was a lot in there to clean out. Especially now that food wasn't her main source of nutrients anymore.

She pulled the trash can over and got to work. Didn't take long, because most of it was funeral food, and she was done pretending she was going to eat any of it. Besides, it all just reminded her of Joe and her human life.

Somehow, that seemed so far away now. Even though it had only been a few days.

The trash can was filled in about five minutes. So

was the sink—with dishes to be washed and returned. What a pain. But she'd get them done. Returning them would be harder. She unloaded the cooler, which also contained a slip of paper with directions for heating if a warm product was desired. She put that in the junk drawer for later, because cold blood didn't sound all that appetizing. Then she stacked the thick plastic bags on an empty fridge shelf.

She glanced at the cooler and thought about what the man had said about deliveries. Maybe she'd return all the dishes at night. She could leave them on people's front porches with a note of thanks.

That would be simple enough. And it would come with the added bonus of not having to talk to anyone.

She smiled as she hauled the trash bag out to the receptacle in the garage. She brushed her hands off and stared into the three other bays that held Joe's Cadillac Escalade, his vintage Ferrari, and his black Mercedes that matched hers.

All three were getting sold. It was just one more thing she had to take care of. But the cars definitely had to go.

She glanced at her Benz. In fact, she was going to sell hers too. Then she'd buy the car she really wanted. A Tesla. With windows tinted as dark as the law would allow.

Staring at the car reminded her of the duffel bag with the cut-up newspaper. She went straight back to Joe's office. "Did you find any of Lucinda's prints on the bag from the drop-off?"

Rico came out of the stash room with two paper

bags tagged as evidence. "Not that I've heard. I'll check when I get back to the office, though."

"Thanks."

"You know she probably wore gloves, if she was involved at all."

"I know."

He lifted the bags he was holding. "I have to put these in the truck, then I'll be back for the rest. I'll have the room cleared out today."

"Excellent. Do you want me to help you carry anything out?"

He made a face. "Into the daylight?"

She realized her mistake and laughed it off, shaking her head. "I haven't adjusted to the whole no-sun thing yet."

He smiled and headed for the door. "Don't worry, I won't let you turn yourself into ash accidentally."

"Thanks," she called after him. But she rolled her eyes at her slipup. She had to be more careful. She couldn't have Rico thinking she needed to be reported. But would he? Sure, she could see him reporting Claudette. A sunproof vampire governor would be something. But Rico needed Donna. At least until all of this with the Villachis was over.

She sighed. She didn't know what he'd do. Rico was a rule follower. That was sort of a big part of being an FBI agent. It would be better for her to keep her mouth shut and her secrets to herself.

Then there'd be no decision for him to make.

She left the office and went back to the kitchen to start on washing the funeral dishes. If she wasn't around Rico, she couldn't say anything to incriminate herself. Besides, the sun was inching toward the horizon, which meant Claudette would be up soon.

Hopefully, her waking up wouldn't overlap with Rico's visit. Call it a hunch, but the two of them meeting didn't sound like the best idea.

She ran hot water into the sink, squirted soap in, and got busy. Out of habit, she put gloves on, but she had to wonder if the hot water would be unbearable now that she was a vampire. Did that increase her tolerance to heat and cold?

She pulled one glove off and stuck her hand in. Very hot. But not so much that she couldn't take it.

Even so, she dried her hand and slipped the glove back on. No sense ruining her manicure.

Rico came in when she was finishing up the last platter. It was pressed green glass and had held a walnut coffee cake drier than the Sahara during a drought.

He leaned on the counter a couple feet away. "Don't you have someone to do that?"

"Yes, we have a cleaning service, but I'm not going to let these sit here until they come." She gave him a little side-eye. "What? You think I don't do dishes?"

He laughed. "I don't generally think of any vampire doing dishes, I guess. Anyway, I'm done. The truck's packed. I'll get everything filed and in process when I get back. Hopefully, we'll get all kinds of new evidence from this stuff."

"I hope so too. Don't forget to check about the duffel bag."

He nodded. "You worried about Lucinda?"

"She feels like a loose end right now. And if she's the one who tried to have me killed, then yes. I'm worried about her. Wouldn't you be?"

He hesitated. "If you think she's going to come after you again—"

"I do. Why wouldn't she? Especially if she and Joe were really together on this deal with the Russians. Whatever that might be."

He seemed to give that some thought. "And if she's got the Russians' money… Yeah, we'll prioritize that. In the meantime, if she does come after you—"

"If who comes after her?" Claudette walked into the kitchen from the back steps. Her hair was scraped back into a high ponytail that accentuated her already blade-like cheekbones. She smiled at Rico, showing off her fangs. "Well, now. Hello there, Mr. Wolf."

His smile in return was much more reserved. "You must be Claudette."

"I must be." She stopped a few inches away from him and looked up, still smiling. "I understand you've been very helpful to my new protégé. I appreciate that."

"I'm sure you do, seeing as how you left her hanging. Surprising behavior for a governor." Rico's eyes flashed with a moonlit glow that, for a moment, transformed his gaze into that of a wolf's.

Claudette's smile disappeared.

Crap. This was exactly what Donna didn't want. "It wasn't her fault," Donna said. "I wasn't calling her right." She waved her hands next to her head like it was all so confusing. "That mental-link thing takes some practice."

Neither Claudette nor Rico looked like they believed a word of that, but she didn't care. She just wanted to diffuse the situation.

She made herself smile. "Thanks again for everything, Agent Medina." Couldn't hurt to remind Claudette that Rico wasn't just a werewolf.

He finally stopped staring Claudette down and turned toward Donna again. "You're welcome. I'll be in touch." He turned on his heel and left.

Claudette watched him go, suddenly smug. When the front door opened and closed, she looked at Donna, brows raised. "He's hot. Typical wolf, though. Ready to fight at the drop of a hat over something that's not even his business."

"I am kind of his business."

"If you say so." Claudette shook her head. "They're like that, though."

"Like what?" Donna asked.

"Protectors. That's just the wolf DNA."

"And vampires aren't?"

Claudette shrugged. "We're not a species that tends to group up. The wolves are pack animals by design. They protect each other. It's how they survive. Vampires tend to be solitary. Not that there aren't exceptions, but nests are rare."

"So a nest is a group of vampires? What's a den?"

She nodded. "Yes, a nest is a group that lives together like family. It happens. But like I said, it's rare. A den is just a group sleeping place." She looked at the empty cooler, now on the island. "What kind did you get?"

"The variety pack since I don't know what you like."

Claudette smiled as she turned toward the refrigerator. "Good job. I guess you can teach a middle-aged woman new tricks."

CHAPTER 28

That comment triggered every single nerve in Donna's body. She was pretty sure if she had been a wolf, she would have snarled. She clamped her jaws together, though. This was her sire and the governor.

Then she had a second thought and unclamped. Why should it matter who Claudette was? The comment was disrespectful, and Donna was fed up. "What's that supposed to mean?"

Claudette was riffling through the bags of blood in the fridge, reading the labels, maybe to see what kind they were. She didn't look at Donna as she answered. "What's what supposed to mean?"

"That crack," Donna snapped back. "You think I'm dumb because of my age? That all middle-aged women are dumb? Is that what you're trying to say?"

Claudette closed the refrigerator and turned, a bag in her hand. There was a little surprise in her gaze, but a flippant tone in her voice. "I was just making a joke. Relax."

"No," Donna said. "You weren't just making a joke, and I won't relax. You were making a comment. About me. About women my age. Like we're somehow insignificant because of where we are in life. If that's a joke to you, maybe you should explain how it's funny."

Claudette opened her mouth, but didn't say anything.

Good, Donna thought. Better the woman be quiet than dig herself deeper. Because Donna was not done talking. "Let me tell you something, you have no idea what I've been through in my life. None. You think you're special because you turned me into a vampire? That's nothing. I've created life. Twice. Then given birth to it. Twenty-six and thirty-seven hours of labor, respectively."

Claudette looked like she would have backed up, but there was no place to go since the fridge was behind her. "You're right. That is an admirable—"

"Admirable?" Heat built in Donna's body. The kind of heat that had to be let out. "I'm not talking about saving the whales or remembering to use my cloth bags when I get groceries." She leaned in, the reflection of her glowing eyes visible in Claudette's own wide gaze. "It makes me a warrior, do you understand?"

Claudette nodded rapidly.

"There is no fiercer, tougher, stronger creature on this earth than a mother. And for you to act as if I'm less-than because of some preconceived notion you have about middle-aged women is insulting. Especially while you're under my roof. Even more so because if you're the governor who represents me, you'd better learn to treat me with respect." Donna stabbed her finger at Claudette. "Don't. Do. It. Again."

Claudette swallowed. "I'm sorry. I won't."

SUCKS TO BE ME

"Good." Donna went back to her dishes, her internal steam dissipating. "Now have your breakfast and get out of my house. I need some alone time."

"I'm still your sire, you know. No need to be—"

Donna whipped around, glaring at her. "Stop talking while you're ahead. And don't forget to leave me your number. In fact, go write it on the memo board over there."

Claudette frowned, but did as Donna asked. Then she came back over, bag of blood in hand. "Do you mind if I heat this up?"

Donna almost smiled at the suddenly respectful tone. "Not at all. What do you need?"

"A bowl of hot water that I can submerge this in."

"Second cabinet on the right under the Keurig. And there's an Instahot at the sink, so you can get all the hot water you need."

"Thank you." Claudette went about her task. "Do you want me to warm one up for you?"

Donna turned to hide the smile she could no longer restrain. "No, thanks. I'm good for now."

Claudette set the blood to warm. "I'll be back in a few minutes."

"Okay." Donna nodded and kept drying the dishes she needed to return. She listened as Claudette went up to the guest room. A few moments later, she heard the door shut, followed by very muted talking. She couldn't make out the words—her vampire hearing stretched only so far—but it sounded like Claudette was on the phone.

Whatever. She was allowed. Probably telling her

assistants she'd be back soon. Or maybe she was calling a friend to complain about Donna. Let her. She might be three hundred years old, but for a woman in such a high position, she was acting like a teenager.

When Donna was finished drying all the funeral dishes, she made a list of which one belonged to whom so she wouldn't forget where they all went. Then she sat at the island and dashed off quick thank-you notes to each of the women who'd brought the food. The notes got taped to their respective dishes. Once she was done with that, she packed the dishes in two totes and loaded them into the car.

By the time she got back to the kitchen, Claudette had returned.

Donna took a seat at the island. She nodded at the warming bowl. "Do you pour that into a glass or just bite the bag or what?"

"You can do either. Whatever you want."

"Good to know. So do you want a glass?" Donna was feeling generous toward this new, sedate version of her sire. Who knew that all it'd take to straighten her out was to stand up to her? Dr. Goldberg was right. Donna was a much stronger woman than she realized.

Well. She wasn't going to take herself for granted anymore. At least, she was going to do her best not to.

"No, I'm good." Claudette took the bag from the water, dried it with the kitchen towel, then sank her fangs into it. A few minutes later, the bag was empty.

Claudette put the deflated bag into the trash and used a paper towel to wipe her mouth. "Thank you for your hospitality."

Donna couldn't take it anymore. She stood up abruptly, making Claudette step back. "Okay, enough with this scolded-puppy routine. You were out of line, and I corrected you. Let's move on, all right? No hard feelings on either side."

Claudette's gaze turned wary. "Just like that? You're not still mad?"

"Yes, just like that. And no, I'm not still mad. I said what I needed to say. Things happen. You recalibrate and move on. How have you lived this long without understanding that? How do you operate as governor? It's how humans survive."

Claudette shrugged. "I've been a vampire so much longer than I was ever human, I think I just forgot."

Donna nodded. "I can understand how that might happen." She stuck her hand out. "Friends?"

"Friends." Claudette worried her bottom lip between her teeth as she shook Donna's hand.

Donna wasn't sure what that meant. Maybe Claudette's newfound hesitancy was just something she was going to have to deal with in her own time. Had none of the vampires she'd ever turned stood up to her? If so, the woman had a lot of learning ahead of her. Donna was done being a pushover.

She was also curious how Claudette had been elected. Or maybe becoming a governor worked differently in the vampire world.

Claudette cleared her throat. "I'm leaving. It's dark enough now. Lots to do. Call if you need me."

"Right," Donna said. "One second before you go." She didn't exactly mistrust Claudette, but she wasn't convinced the woman wanted Donna to contact her. Donna went to the memo board, plugged in the number Claudette had written there, then sent a text to it.

Claudette's phone chirped.

"Excellent. Now you have my number too," Donna said. She started to add the number to her contacts, then realized something. "I don't even know your last name. What is it?"

With a guttural sigh, Claudette said, "Martine."

"Great." Donna finished tapping it in. "Now we have each other's info. Let me walk you to the door." She couldn't shake the feeling there was something else going on, but she wasn't about to psychoanalyze Claudette's issues. The woman could pay for therapy like everyone else.

She saw Claudette out, then shut the door, but peered through the sidelights. In trademark style, Claudette was there one minute, then seemingly gone the next.

Donna made a mental note to work on her speed, because that was impressive. Maybe it was something that got better with time. Lots of vampire skills seemed to work that way.

Lucky had plenty of food and water, so without further delay, Donna grabbed her purse and headed for the garage. The sooner those dishes were returned, the sooner she could close that chapter of her life and rid herself of the last remaining connections to those who knew her as Joe's wife.

It felt oddly liberating to leave the house, maybe

because she'd been stuck inside during the day. Even if the sun wasn't her enemy, she couldn't let Rico or Claudette know she was potentially immune, and that made her feel trapped in a way she hadn't anticipated.

She'd test the theory for real tomorrow. She'd get up while it was still full-on daylight, and she'd go out on the back deck. Hopefully, there would be sun, because she wanted to know once and for all what the truth was.

Her plan was to test with and without her crucifix on. There was nothing else she could think of that might be protecting her. Certainly her turning hadn't been unusual in any other way, or Claudette would have remarked on it.

A little purple remained in the sky, so she stopped at the local coffee shop and got something rare—a salted caramel latte with extra whip. Why not? Burning calories didn't seem to be a problem anymore. If anything, she was burning too many. Might as well indulge.

She sat at a table near the window, watching the sky go full black. Amazing how much she could still see despite the dark. As night truly descended, she took her drink to the car and got back on the road.

She made her first few deliveries without incident, parking a house away, then leaving the dishes and notes on the front porches of those who'd brought them. Most of the houses had lights on inside. Keeping to the shadows, she peered into a few windows, reminding herself what family life was like. As much as what she *was* witnessing was family life.

Regardless, she never wanted to become like Claudette, so removed from humanity that she forgot how to be human. That would be terrible.

Car headlights streaked past as a car drove by behind her. She ducked before she could be seen. Time to get back to it.

A few houses more and only one remained. The one she least wanted to go to.

Tony and Lucinda's.

Maybe she'd just stick the dish into their mailbox and be done. Lucinda had brought banana bread, so the loaf pan would easily fit. Donna hadn't tried the bread. With her luck, Lucinda would have laced it with some kind of poison. Or laxatives.

Donna parked several blocks away, which ended up being behind the Villachis' house. She knew Big Tony's house and knew there was an extensive security system. They also had a dog, if it could be called that. Nero was a Chihuahua mix. What the rest of him was, Donna wasn't sure, but he hadn't gotten the pretty parts, that was for sure.

She'd rarely seen him when his teeth hadn't been bared or he wasn't yipping at something. To add insult to injury, Lucinda constantly had him dressed in ridiculous outfits. She posted pictures of the mutt on her social media and got cranky if he didn't get enough likes.

The last outfit Donna had seen was a studded biker jacket with a matching leather cap, which only succeeded in making the poor beast look like a lost member of the Village People.

Loaf pan tucked under her arm, she locked her car and started the trek toward the Villachis'. She wished she could see Lucinda's face the next morning when she found the pan and realized Donna had been there. She smiled just thinking about how irritated that would make Lucinda, if for no other reason than it would remind her that her plan to bump Donna off had failed.

The houses in this development were well spaced on large acre-and-a-half lots. Lucinda's was an estate lot, meaning it was double that. A dense thicket of trees separated the Villachi house from its neighbors, exactly like Big Tony wanted.

Probably to prevent the very thing she was doing. Sneaking up on them.

She moved past the house that backed up to the Villachis' property, then disappeared into the woods between. She picked her way through, impressed with her ability to move silently. That had to be a vampire skill, because she'd never been this quiet in her human life.

At the tree line, she stopped. The Villachi house was a monstrosity of Tuscan design. It oozed Mediterranean motifs wherever possible.

During the building, Donna had heard ad nauseum from Lucinda about every single thing inside the house that had been imported from Italy. Tiles and chandeliers and fireplaces. On and on.

Sad, really, because on their own, the things were beautiful. But together they were like a woman in head-to-toe leopard print. Too much was too much.

Donna had to go around and leave the pan on the front porch. Leaving it in the back of the house would create panic. The fact that someone, even if it was Donna, had breached their security, would cause an uproar.

She wasn't looking for more drama. Just to return the pan.

Satisfied she could stay clear of the motion sensors that would flip on the security lights, she started around to the front as quickly as she could.

The speed she achieved in seconds made it almost impossible for her to stop in time to avoid Lucinda, who was in the front yard with Nero.

The little dog snapped and snarled as Donna came to a halt inches away from him. He was wearing a black hoodie with rhinestone letters that spelled out Thug Life.

Yeah, so thuggy. The poor thing.

Lucinda, thankfully, was occupied with something on her phone, so she missed Donna's inglorious arrival. She looked up at Nero's commotion, however. "Donna. What are you doin' here?"

"Hi, Lucinda." Donna held out the pan. "Just returning your loaf pan. Thank you for the banana bread. It was very kind of you."

Lucinda glanced past her, looking both annoyed and baffled. "Where did you come from?"

"My house." Donna knew that didn't explain the lack of a vehicle. "Just out returning all the dishes people brought over." She forced a congenial smile. All she wanted to do was leave. This wasn't about not being a pushover. It was about not making a bad situation worse. "You have a good night. Give my best to Tony."

As soon as the last sentence left her mouth, Donna realized it might have been better off not said. She turned, hoping to walk away.

Lucinda grunted. "Hold up, Barrone. You ain't going nowhere."

CHAPTER 29

Donna reminded herself how, just about two hours ago, she'd faced down Claudette with great results.

This was really no different. Sure, Lucinda was crankier (maybe) with slightly worse people skills and was more likely to attempt physical harm, but Donna could handle that. Especially with all her new skills.

She fixed an innocent look on her face and turned around. "Was there something else, Lucinda?"

Her unkempt brows furrowed in obvious annoyance. "Where's your car?"

Too mentally fatigued to come up with anything else, Donna decided to go with brutal honesty. "Parked around the block. I was hoping just to leave the dish and go so that I could avoid running into you, seeing as how we aren't exactly BFFs."

Lucinda hesitated, clearly not expecting such a truthful reply.

Donna took advantage of the woman's rare speechlessness. "Have a good night. See you around." She turned for the second time and actually got two steps away before Lucinda found her words again.

"You're right. I don't like you. You think you're all that. And now you come over here, showing up unannounced. You sure you weren't looking for Tony?"

Donna sighed. The woman was exhausting, and Donna had already surpassed her tolerance level for crap today. She spun around, full of the same ire that she'd unleashed on Claudette earlier. "Did you willfully choose to ignore what I just told you? I was trying to avoid seeing *you*. That includes your disgusting pig of a husband, who treats everyone around him like they owe him something. I want nothing to do with him. Or you. As for thinking I'm all that...you know what? Sometimes, I do think that. Other times, I feel like nothing I do goes right. But that's just being human." She stalked closer, her anger growing with the kind of force that would soon breach her control. "You should try it."

Nero sniffed Donna's leg, but Lucinda was the one who snarled. "How dare you talk to me like—"

Donna poked a finger into Lucinda's fleshy upper chest, cutting her off. "While I'm doling out advice, let me give you a little more. Watch yourself. I know what you did. What you're involved in. You think you can come for me? Try it. See which one of us survives."

Lucinda reared her head back in shock, giving herself three extra chins.

"I'll give you a hint." Donna leaned in and tried to will a little of her new vampire power into her eyes, hoping for the slightest glow to spook Lucinda. "It's not going to be you, Lucy."

Lucinda gasped in plain indignation. She opened her mouth wider and screamed, "Tony. Tony, get out here."

Donna gave her a big smile. Then pulled a Claudette and disappeared with as much speed as she could muster.

She was in the middle of the tree line when she heard Lucinda's front door open and Big Tony's response. "What?"

He sounded cranky. Donna leaned against a pine to listen.

"Belladonna was just here."

"For what?"

"To return my loaf pan."

"Why is this a problem? She's gone now, ain't she?"

"She threatened me," Lucinda whined.

"With a loaf pan?" An exasperated sigh. "Leave her alone, will ya? She ain't over Joe's death, and you're harassing her. Of course she's going to threaten you. You probably started it."

Donna smiled. Was that the result of the power Claudette had used on him? If so, that was pretty cool. Donna stuck her hands in her pockets and left, no longer interested in what else the Villachis had to say. They were all going down, Rico would see to that. She'd give him whatever help he needed.

She got in her car and went home, filled with a sense that everything was going to be all right. She was a new creature now. She had to accept that for all the good and bad it might bring her. Just like everything else life had thrown at her, she'd get through it. She'd find her way. Or make her way, if the path ahead didn't suit her.

That was what she'd always done. Becoming a vampire wasn't going to change that. And if she worked at it, this could be a good thing. It was already giving her more confidence.

Telling Joe Jr. and Christina was going to be hard, though. Cammie too. But Donna would. Wasn't like she'd chosen this new life. And while they might not like it, they would get used to it. They all would eventually. She still wasn't there herself.

In a year, she'd probably look back and think how silly she'd been to worry. She hoped, anyway. A year from now felt so far away. Like such a long time to have to survive.

She would. She knew that. She just had to focus on the positives. On accepting who she was. And owning this new power. That was key.

She turned onto her street. She knew exactly what she was going to do to kick off the next phase of accepting her vampire self.

She pulled into the garage and went inside the house, setting the alarm as soon as the door was shut. Lucky ran to greet her. She scooped him up and kissed his furry face. "How about we have a glass of wine and catch up on some movies, huh? What do you think?"

He butted his head into her chin, which she took for a yes. Maybe it was a boring way to spend the night, but nothing said becoming a vampire meant you had to suddenly turn into a party animal.

That had never been her style, and it wasn't about

to be. Although, she might go out a little more than she used to if the company was right.

"I just have to do one thing first." She put Lucky down and got her phone out, pulling up Pierce's number. She stared at it for a moment, then tapped Call while she was still riding the high of telling Lucinda off.

It rang a couple times before he answered. "Harrison speaking."

She smiled. He sounded powerful and in command. She liked that, especially knowing what she did about him. "Hello, Pierce. It's Belladonna."

A small intake of breath. "Hello, beautiful. What can I do for you? Name it."

"You can take me to dinner. Tomorrow night. I thought we might get to know each other a little better that way."

"It would be my pleasure. I'll make the arrangements and text them to you now that I have your number. Would that suit you?"

"Perfectly. Have a good night."

"I will now."

Still smiling, she hung up. That new little black dress was going to come in handy after all. She poured a glass of wine, then on a whim grabbed the bottle and took them both upstairs. Lucky followed. She put the wine on her nightstand, took her makeup off, and started to do her evening skin care routine.

She stopped as she was about to slather herself in serums and moisturizers made specifically for eyes, neck, and cleavage.

Did she need to do all this now that she was immortal? That was another question for Claudette, but Donna doubted her sire spent time on her skin. Francine would know. Donna screwed the lid back onto her eye cream and set the jar aside. Maybe Cammie would want all of this stuff. Or maybe not. Nuns weren't known for their extensive beauty rituals.

Maybe Christina, then. She was young, but it was never too soon to take care of yourself. Donna shrugged. So many new things to consider.

She brushed her teeth, then stood in front of the mirror, practicing with her fangs. Out, then away, out, then away. She did it a few times more, until it got easier. Not quite smooth yet, but getting there. She repeated what she'd done at Lucinda's, too, just to see if she'd really managed to get her eyes to glow.

They did. Just a hint. In fact, Lucinda probably wasn't sure what she'd seen. It almost looked like light was reflecting off Donna's eyes. Like a cat caught in headlights. It was a cool effect. Lucinda had to be wondering what had gotten into Donna.

Thinking about that made her eyes glow a little harder. Interesting. Was that tied to emotion? She tried thinking about Lucinda's attempt to have her killed.

Donna's eyes lit up like sparklers.

Good to know. She calmed down, smiling as she changed into her new navy silk pajamas from her Bloomie's spree, then settled into bed and turned on the television. She was searching through the on-demand movies when her phone buzzed with a text from Pierce.

She read what he'd sent and smiled. Meridian was a great restaurant, and he'd offered to send a car service for her, providing her with the company's phone number so she could give them her address. She could get used to that kind of treatment.

She sent him a quick text back. *Well done. See you at eight.*

She found a rom-com she hadn't seen and started it.

Lucky jumped up on the bed and settled in to clean himself.

She scratched his cheek. "Lucky Luciano, you're the only gangster I could ever really love."

The wine was gone and the movie almost over when her doorbell rang. She paused the movie and checked her phone. No one had texted about coming over.

So who was downstairs?

There weren't many people who'd show up at this hour. And it was highly unlikely any of them would be bringing good news.

Reluctantly, she put her slippers and robe on and went to see who it was. She took her phone, but left her gun, feeling more confident in her ability to defend herself with her new vampire skill set. Even so, she really needed one of those camera doorbells. Especially now that Joe wasn't here to tell her no because he was sure it would be used to spy on him.

The lights were on outside, but all she could see through the sidelights was a dark shape. Even vampire eyesight couldn't see clearly through frosted glass. She checked through the peephole anyway. One person. And not a particularly menacing one, either.

A sleek black town car sat at the end of the drive, and at her door was a gorgeous young man in a black suit. Another one, dressed alike, stood by the door of the sedan. None looked particularly Russian. They were all slim too. More like members of a college swim team than European lunks.

Had the Jehovah's Witnesses upped their door-to-door game?

She turned off the alarm and opened the door. "Yes?" She realized instantly they were vampires.

The young man on the right spoke. "Our mistress, Artemis, wishes to speak with you."

Then he turned so he was perpendicular to the front of the house and facing the garage. Like an old-fashioned footman who'd done his job.

The young man at the car opened the door.

Out from the dark interior stepped a woman who glowed with the immortality of a vampire. Her skin was golden brown, her hair a mass of reddish-bronze ringlets, and her eyes gleamed like polished obsidian. Her dress was black chiffon that looked casually destroyed but had probably cost more than Donna could imagine. A gold snake, sparkling with gems, wrapped her right bicep. Donna had never seen anyone like the woman in her life.

"Who is Artemis?" she asked the young man. Though, on a certain level, she knew. Artemis was a very old vampire. Greek, Egyptian, Assyrian, or something else, Donna didn't know. But the ancient-vampire part was plain.

The young man didn't respond, merely held his position as if commanded to do so. Which he probably had been.

Artemis made her way to Donna's door, her walk so smooth she might as well have been gliding.

Donna's heart was in her throat. She had no idea what this was about, but the woman approaching emanated power. Donna took a breath and stood her ground, waiting.

Artemis stopped just outside the house. "You are Belladonna?"

Donna nodded.

Artemis smiled. She had a smaller set of fangs next to the standard large ones. "I am Artemis, daughter of Zenos. Sire of many." Her eyes shone like burning coals. Donna was helpless to look away. She knew the woman was exerting power over her, but could do nothing to break the hold. "I wish to speak to you, new one."

"Yes, of course. But why?" Donna managed to get out. "Why me?"

"Because my child, Claudette, told me about you. And now I am here to see what must be done."

"You mean you're Claudette's sire?"

"Yes."

Claudette's words—*if all goes well, you'll never meet her*—came back to Donna. A new feeling rose up in her. Panic. She shook her head. "There is nothing to be done."

Artemis's gaze intensified. "You think you are in danger."

"Aren't I?"

"That's for me to decide." Artemis moved closer, stopping at the door's threshold.

So her fate was in this woman's hands? That didn't seem fair. "How do I know you're telling the truth? That you're going to be fair?"

Artemis's smile widened. "Claudette was right about you. About your boldness. But what she finds troublesome, I find interesting." She brought her hand to her mouth, punctured the tip of her index finger with a fang, then held out the bead of blood to Donna. "Take it. You'll see."

Donna hesitated, but only for a moment. She licked the drop of blood off Artemis's finger and instantly knew the woman was on the up and up. Donna couldn't see a memory, like she had with Yuri and Pierce, but she got a sense that the woman before her was not her enemy. How had Artemis known that would work? Obviously, because she wasn't the newbie Donna was. "You can come in."

"You understand I waited for your invitation out of courtesy, not need."

Donna nodded. "Yes. It was kind of you."

"Courtesy is not something Claudette excels at." Artemis gestured toward the car, and the young man by Donna's front door retreated to it. Artemis stepped inside. "You must forgive her. She still has much to learn."

Donna just stood there. If Artemis thought

Claudette had a lot to learn after three hundred years, she must think Donna was brainless. Awesome. But Donna tried to reserve judgment until she heard more. In the meantime, should she offer the woman a glass of wine? Blood? This was uncharted territory. "I don't hold any ill will toward her. I know I'm not the easiest person at times."

Artemis smiled as she looked around at the house. "You know a lot about yourself. That is one of the benefits of your human age, I suppose. I like that."

"Thank you. Yes, it is my age. It's taught me a lot."

"You will be a very powerful vampire." Artemis stopped her appraisal and returned her attention to Donna. "That is why I'm here. We must talk about your future. About what you've done. The council is troubled."

So the council knew? "But you're not?"

"I am nearly fifteen hundred years old. There is very little that troubles me. Or excites me." Her smile reached her eyes, and she laughed suddenly. "That's also why I've come. You are interesting. There is so little these days I can say that about."

"Fifteen hundred years old?" That was unfathomable. The woman hadn't just seen history being made, she *was* history. And she was Donna's grandsire, as it were. Also, she had come to see Donna. In person.

In any other circumstance, Donna imagined a visit like this would be considered an honor. At this moment, honored was the last thing she was feeling. Worried was more like it. Because of Claudette's words, but also because life connected to the Mafia had taught her that when the boss wanted to talk to you, something was about to change.

Maybe for the good.

Most likely for the bad.

CHAPTER 30

Regardless of what was about to happen, Donna needed to step up her hospitality. If for no other reason than to stay on the woman's good side as much as possible. "Would you like some wine? Or blood? Or something else?"

"Blood. I have traveled a long way." Artemis's eyes narrowed, and she glanced toward the outside. "This house is protected against the fae, yes?"

Donna nodded. "Yes. It's surrounded by iron. Claudette made sure I did that."

"Good. Because if I am here long enough, they will come. I apologize, but it cannot be helped. They are attracted to my power like insects to a flame. My assistants will take care of them, though, should they arrive."

Donna gestured behind her. "The kitchen is this way. Or I can just go get the blood and bring it to you..."

Artemis laughed softly. "You are unsure how to act around me. You needn't be. I am not some capricious creature who strikes down on a whim those who displease her. My children are precious to me." Her smile turned wry. "Also a great responsibility at times, but what is life without responsibility?"

"Very true." Donna headed toward the kitchen. Artemis followed. Donna turned the lights on and went for the fridge. "Do you have children, then? Or did you mean children in the vampire sense?"

"Both, but for now, in the vampire sense. You are one of my children. Claudette told me how your turning came about." She took a seat at the island, shaking her head slightly. "I imagine that was a difficult thing for you to accept. Being turned is hard enough when it is anticipated, but when it is not…"

Donna nodded. "It was hard. Still is, if I'm being honest." Artemis was an incredibly scary being, but Donna already liked her more than Claudette. She felt like the woman was on her side. But maybe that was Artemis's plan. Donna opened the fridge. "Do you have a preference for type?"

"No, but thank you for asking. Anything will do."

Donna chose the bag of B positive. If only for the not-so-subtle message that accompanied it. She filled a bowl with water from the Instahot, then submerged the bag to warm it. "It'll just be a few minutes."

Artemis nodded. "Your home is lovely. You live here alone?"

Donna nodded. "Just me and the cat. My husband passed away recently, but my children have been out for a while. College and the military."

"Both admirable pursuits. You must be proud."

"I am." Donna wondered if Artemis hadn't offered

311

her condolences because Claudette had already told her about Joe.

Artemis shook her head. "I turned Claudette too young, but I had no choice. She would not have survived otherwise. Still, her youth when she was turned is often her downfall." She seemed to study Donna intensely then. "You are better suited for what lies ahead."

"Thank you." Donna wasn't sure what that meant, but she was happy Artemis thought so well of her. And as much as she wanted to know the real reason for this visit, Donna was glad for the small talk. "Can I ask how old you were when you were turned?"

"Thirty-four. But I had five children by then, and in my time, thirty-four was, as they say now, the new fifty. Although in my day, fifty was the new ninety."

Donna laughed. "I can already tell you have the kind of wisdom that comes from experience."

"I do my best."

"How many vampire children do you have?"

"Many. But it's a number in flux." The happiness left her face. "Between the fae, the hunters, stupid mistakes, and infighting, our numbers rise and fall. My hope in coming here was that I would find in you someone more levelheaded. I know you are new to this life, but I often find myself in need of someone I can count on. Claudette is..." Artemis frowned. "Not always so reliable."

Donna had seen that firsthand. "What are you asking me to do? It sounds like you want me to take on some kind of responsibility. I'm not afraid of that, but I don't think I'm ready for it either. I know so little about being a vampire. I don't even know if I should keep using moisturizer or not!"

"I am not asking you to assume any role yet, just looking forward to the future. I am definitely thinking about how you might serve. If things go as I imagine they will."

Whatever that meant. "What is your position, exactly? If that's okay for me to ask."

"I am the Queen of North America." Artemis waved her hand. "But I am getting ahead of myself. Nothing will happen until this incident has been dealt with."

"Incident?" Donna played dumb while she took the bag out of the hot water and poured it into one of the big red wine goblets always on hand.

"Claudette told me you severed your tether by killing the first human you drank from. Is this true?"

So there it was. The real reason Artemis was here. Donna delivered the glass. "Yes. It's no excuse, I suppose, but I didn't know that my actions would erase the tether. I didn't know a lot of things. Like the importance of my first feeding. Or how out of control my hunger would be. Or the extent of my new power and strength. You know, there should be a handbook for new vampires. Especially when their sires don't pony up the kind of important info they need. Yes, I went too far, but it was unintentional. I don't think I should be punished for that. Plus, the guy I *accidentally* killed was a criminal. He would have done me serious harm if he'd lived. Maybe even killed me."

Artemis took a long drink before answering. "Can this be proven?"

"Yes. He was a known Russian gangster, and he claimed my husband owed his boss money. I have no doubt he would have hurt me if he thought that would help him find the money."

"Is there anyone who might testify to this on your behalf?"

"Sure, I think. The man who helped me with the body. He's a werewolf. And an FBI agent."

Artemis nodded and drank some more.

Then Donna realized what she'd asked. "Testify? You mean like in court?"

"Yes. There is going to be a trial."

Suddenly weak-kneed, Donna put her hand out, found the island countertop, and leaned against it hard. "Is this before the Immortus Concilio?"

"Yes."

Donna couldn't believe this was happening. "What happens if I'm not cleared of wrongdoing?"

"You will be put down."

Ice filled Donna's body. "Put down? You mean killed."

"Yes. But I will do it so quickly you will not suffer."

"That's really why you're here, then. To bring me to trial?"

"More or less. You are ultimately my responsibility. But you do not seem like the kind of woman who would run."

"I'd like to think I'm not. I've never been on trial for

my life before." She took a few deep, shuddering breaths. "I guess Claudette was too chicken to face me over this, hmm?"

Artemis smirked. "She does seem a bit scared of you, which is also interesting to me, but this wasn't something she could have handled. She's already had one child go rogue on her. To have a second do that in such a short period, well, the council does not look upon that favorably. She had no choice but to turn this over to me."

"You're who she called. From my guest room." Donna shook her head, feeling betrayed that she'd offered Claudette hospitality only to now realize the woman had stayed over probably just to keep an eye on her. "That little—what happens to her if, I mean, *when* I'm exonerated, and they realize what a crap job she did as my sire?"

"She will be punished. Her title stripped. She may be banished for a set period. Or another decision will be made. You will be promoted to her position. It is all according to the council's rules."

"What do you mean another decision—wait a minute. I'd be governor?" That was insane. Was that how vampires ran things? That seemed ludicrous. "I have no experience."

"Being the governor of the state isn't like being a human governor. Not exactly. It's more about keeping things peaceful. If a vampire goes rogue, you may have to send hunters after them. If there is a dispute that cannot be settled, it will come to you for a decision. If there is something you cannot handle, you turn it over to me."

"That still seems like a lot of power for a woman who hasn't even been a vampire for a week. Speaking of, when will this trial take place?"

"Three nights from now."

"That's kind of soon, isn't it?" Like really soon.

"Vampire justice moves swiftly. Will you not be ready by then?"

"I guess I have no choice." A sudden idea came to her. "Am I allowed to have an attorney?"

Artemis hesitated. "There is no rule against it."

"Then I'm bringing one. Where will this trial take place?"

"Right here, in your home. It will be done via video-conference."

"Who knew vampires were so modern? Will you be staying here until then? To keep an eye on me?"

"Do I need to?" Artemis asked.

"No. I give you my word on that."

"I believe you. So no, I will not be staying. But you must understand two things. If you do not appear for trial, it is an automatic admission of guilt on your behalf. Hunters will be sent after you. Also, if I return for the trial, and you are not here, I will make it my personal mission to find you, and then it would be best for you to pray the hunters get you first. Is that understood?"

Donna nodded, hoping she didn't look as terrified as she felt. "Very much so. Three days from now. So Tuesday night. I will absolutely be here."

Artemis smiled. "Very good. I will see you then."

She got up and made her way to the front door. Donna followed, because it felt like the thing to do. One of Artemis's assistants was there, waiting.

Artemis greeted him with a question. "Any sign of the fae?"

"Not yet, mistress."

Donna called out to her as she left. "What if I need to reach you? What if I have a question before the trial?"

Artemis turned to look at Donna one last time. "Those are valid concerns." She glanced at her assistant. "Florian."

"Yes, mistress." He dug into his suit pocket and pulled out a business card, then handed it to Donna.

The card was matte black with shiny black printing, and the only information on the card was Artemis's name and a cell number. Donna had to tip the card toward the light to read it. "Thank you."

"You're welcome. Three days."

Donna nodded. "Three days."

Artemis walked to her car, where the second assistant opened the door. Artemis got in, then he got in after her. The first assistant got into the front passenger's seat, making Donna realize there was also a driver.

As the car pulled away, Donna memorized the license plate, then she typed it into the Notes app on her phone.

She was going to be as prepared for this trial as

possible. She'd only just decided to embrace this new way of life.

There was no way she was going down without a fight.

CHAPTER 31

As soon as Artemis left, Donna drank what was left of the blood in the goblet so that it didn't go to waste, then went straight back to her bedroom and her wine.

She sat in bed, sipping wine and just thinking for a good ten minutes, forming her game plan.

She'd text Rico as soon as she woke up tomorrow. She didn't want to do it now. She wanted to catch him actually on his phone. Except she wondered if what she had to talk to him about was really the kind of thing that should be recorded in texts. He had an FBI phone. Those texts undoubtedly would go into a database somewhere.

Better that she ask him to come over. Or she'd go see him. She sighed into her glass. Except she couldn't, because she wasn't supposed to be able to go out in the sun. Which was something else she had to figure out for sure.

So she'd text him, tell him she had an urgent matter to discuss with him, and ask him to come by. That was Rico sorted out.

Then there was Pierce. She was pretty confident he'd be willing to represent her at the trial, but then again, maybe that would be getting too involved in vampire life for him. She wasn't sure. The thought of arguing before the Immortus Concilio was either going to thrill him or send him running.

Either way, she was going to make that request in person, too, so it would have to wait until dinner. For which she was going to look as irresistible as possible.

When her glass was empty, she set it aside. She ought to sleep, but sunrise was still hours away, and it felt like the afternoon to her. And with everything on her mind, sleep felt impossible. There was too much to think about, too many scenarios to run through, too many possibilities to explore.

The only one she wasn't going to think about was being put down by Artemis if she wasn't cleared at trial. Because that would not be an acceptable outcome.

So she did the only thing she could think of. She put on her running gear and went downstairs. She hadn't turned the alarm on after Artemis had left, but she would when she got back.

She stood in the garage, doing a few stretches and getting her playlist right. With that done, she opened the door and headed out into the night. It was cold enough that she could see her breath. She blew out a plume of vapor as she left the shelter of the garage.

Something whizzed past her.

She ducked instinctively, turning toward the direction the thing had gone. It was too big to be a bat.

Her eyes found it, even in the darkness.

The creature was thin and angular, with cheekbones like razors and wings of iridescent membrane that gleamed in the ambient light. Its dusky skin was stretched drum-tight over its bones, making the being look gaunt. She knew without question this was the fae she'd been warned about.

Maybe a run wasn't such a good idea. "What do you want?"

"The old one," the fae answered.

"Long gone," Donna said. "Now leave me be. I've done nothing to you or your kind. You have no cause to bother me."

It hovered a couple feet off the ground, wings beating furiously. "Not yet, you haven't."

"What do you have against my kind?" That was another question she needed answered. Why did the fae hate vampires so much?

It smiled, revealing a mouthful of pointed teeth. The thing was a nightmare. She was adding more iron to the perimeter as soon as possible. And getting herself some iron jewelry. "You are young. And worthless."

Then it was gone with the same kind of speed Claudette liked to show off.

Donna stood there for a moment, listening for it to come back. For the flutter of wings, any sign it might return. But all she heard were the sounds of the night.

She went back inside, set the alarm, then ran up to the exercise room and did five miles on the treadmill. She finished with a few therapeutic rounds with the heavy bag. She would have preferred the outside run, but the image of the fae lingered.

Her newfound courage didn't extend to becoming

the victim of a fae attack. Plus, getting to punch something had been a bonus.

When she was finally good and sweaty, she quit and went back to her bedroom. Lucky had never left the bed. Actually, she wasn't sure if he'd even woken up.

She filled the tub with steaming hot water and tossed in a muscle soak bath bomb, then got another glass of wine before stripping down and climbing in.

She stayed in the tub until the water lost all useful warmth, then she got back in her pajamas and went to bed.

Her alarm woke her up at two. She texted Rico immediately. *Can you come by today? Urgent news to discuss.*

If that didn't get her the desired response, she'd call.

Next, she got dressed and went downstairs to feed Lucky and make coffee. While that was brewing, she went to the sliding doors that opened onto the enormous back deck and took a hard look around.

She didn't know the rules of the fae. Were they nighttime-only creatures, like vampires? Or could they handle sun? She needed to know that. She needed to know everything about them. It was the only way to defend herself.

Behind her, the Keurig sputtered out the last drops of dark roast. The smell was divine. But she had something else on her mind.

She turned off the house alarm and unlocked one of the sliders. She opened it just enough to slip through. The sun wasn't high enough in the sky to reach over the house yet, so half of the deck was still in shade.

She inched forward, toward the line of sun. Her pulse picked up with each step. When she was a foot away, she stretched out her arm.

Her fingertips felt the warmth, and she jerked back. A second later, she realized all she'd felt was the sun's rays, not her skin bursting into flame.

She repeated the action, this time leaving her fingers in the sun.

Nothing happened.

She went farther and farther out, testing her ability to withstand the UV rays, until at last she was fully bathed in sunshine.

How was this possible? She tipped her head up and let the warmth cover her. It felt glorious, especially since she'd assumed it was never going to happen again.

She returned to the shade, took off her crucifix, then inched toward the sun again, fingers out.

When the sun hit them, blisters formed almost immediately. With a yelp, she pulled her hand back, the pain making her eyes water.

That answered that. But would any crucifix do or just this one? That was a question for another day. She put the necklace back on, kissed the crucifix, then went inside for some burn salve and her coffee.

Rico had returned her text. *Four okay?*

Yes, she texted back. *Perfect. Thank you.*

With Rico squared away and nearly two hours before his arrival, she did what needed to be done. A run to the bank to retrieve more cash. With her crucifix firmly in place.

Twenty minutes later, she was home again, this time with two hundred thousand that she tucked away in the safe in the walk-in closet. She wasn't sure what Pierce would charge her, but she figured that should more than cover his retainer.

If not, she'd get more. Now that she knew she could, it wasn't such a big deal. She just hoped he didn't care that it was Mafia money.

She had a second cup of coffee and called Cammie. The blisters were already gone. The call went to voice-mail. "You've reached Sister Mary Lazarus Immaculata. Please leave a message at the beep and have a blessed day."

"Cammie, it's Donna. I'd love to see you soon and talk. Let me know what your schedule is like, okay? Love you." She wasn't ready to have the vampire conversation with her kids yet, but soon. After the trial. After she'd survived and there was a reason to tell them.

Next, she reached out to Neo. She thought about using the group text, but considering there were two women on the group whom she'd never met, she wasn't sure how smart that would be.

Neo picked up on the second ring, but there was sleep in her voice. "Yo, what's up?"

"Neo, hi, it's Donna. I'm sorry I woke you. I can call back later."

"No, it's cool, I'm up. What's going on?"

"I screwed up, and I'm being put on trial before the Immortus Concilio. I just need someone to talk to."

Neo let out a soft curse. "I'm awake now. What happened?"

Donna explained about Yuri and Claudette and then Artemis's visit. Neo's first response was a low whistle. "Girl, that is messed up. You were protecting yourself."

"I think so too. I just hope the council sees it that way."

"Hey, do you want me to be a character witness?"

"You would do that for me? You've only known me a couple days."

"Yeah, but first impressions don't lie. You're no killer." She laughed softly. "Plus, I have *always* wanted to see the council. Just tell me where and when."

"Let me talk to my attorney about having character witnesses, and I'll let you know. To be honest, it hadn't occurred to me, but I think it's a great idea. I just don't know what he'll think. But thank you so much. I'm honored that you'd do that for me even when you haven't known me long."

"That's what friends do, right? And we're friends."

Donna swallowed down a little knot of emotion in her throat. How long had it been since she'd had a true friend? "That's what friends do. I'll talk to you soon."

"Hey, you know Francine would do it, too, I'm sure. You want me to reach out to her?"

"I…okay, sure. Thanks again."

"Hang in there, Donna."

"I will." She hung up and took a breath. She'd never expected Neo to make such an offer, and it touched her. It also got her thinking. Who else could she ask to speak for her? La? Dr. Goldberg had known her a long time, so that could be good. Donna had another idea, but it might cause more problems than it solved.

Best she talk to Pierce first and see if he was even willing to represent her.

When Rico arrived, she wasn't feeling quite so desperate. Neo's offer had boosted her mood significantly. She'd reached out to Dr. Goldberg, too, who'd very apologetically told Donna she would be out of the state at a one-day wellness conference, but said she'd write a letter and email it to whomever Donna wanted.

She welcomed Rico in with a smile, noting the plumber's truck was out front again. People were going to think there was something critically wrong with her pipes.

"You look surprisingly cheerful for someone with an emergency."

She closed the door behind him. "I had some unexpected kindness come my way, and it's picked me up a bit, but things are actually pretty serious. Let's sit." She went into the living room, her expression much more sedate now, and he followed.

When he took a seat, she began. "I'll keep this brief and to the point. I'm being put on trial in front of the Immortus Concilio for killing Yuri and severing the tether with my sire. I need whatever proof you can give me that he was a known Russian gangster and would have done me harm."

Rico stared at her for a long second. "Donna, that's serious."

"I know. That's why I asked you to come over. And

why I'm asking for your help."

He raked his hand through his hair. "Should I ask what happens if you lose?"

She gave him a quick, bitter grin. "You're out a witness."

"As in—"

She nodded. "As in I will be put down, to paraphrase my sire's sire. Who, by the way, happens to be Artemis. Name ring a bell?"

"The Queen of North America?"

"That's the one. But get this, if I win, I take Claudette's position as governor." She shook her head. "Vampire politics are as crazy as human ones."

Rico wasn't amused. In fact, he looked downright miserable. "Do you get to have an attorney?"

"Yes. I have a meeting with one in a couple hours." Rico didn't need to know it was a date.

"Tell him I'll be your first witness."

"You're sure about that?"

"A hundred percent. I need you, Donna. You're a key witness in my case against the Villachis. I can't have the Immortus Concilio deciding to end you. This is bigger than them and whatever nonsense rule you supposedly, and accidentally, broke. Plus, I don't want to see anything bad happen to you. You're good people."

Once again, she was touched by the unexpected offer and kind words. "Thank you. I'll let you know what my attorney says."

Provided Pierce agreed to represent her. Which she really, really needed him to do.

CHAPTER 32

Donna had never dined at Meridian before, but the moment she entered, she felt like she'd been wrapped in a warm, intimate embrace. It had the aura of a private club. Dark wood, dark leather, white linens, low lighting, touches of brass and crystal, soft jazz, and a staff that was somehow attentive and unobtrusive and knew what you wanted before you did.

It was the perfect place to discuss personal business, and considering that Pierce was an attorney, it seemed logical this was the sort of place he'd bring her to.

Not that he'd brought her here, exactly. The arrangement had been for her to meet him at the restaurant, something she approved of. Really, he'd done everything right, setting the evening up so that she didn't have to reveal any personal details about herself to him.

And while she appreciated how private he'd allowed her to remain, that was about to end. He was moments from knowing exactly what was going on with her.

Which was why she'd taken so much time getting ready. Every detail about herself was as perfect as she could make it. From the amazing little black dress to her hair to her Louboutin stilettos, she'd done her best to present the image of a confident, sophisticated vampire woman.

As much as she imagined that looked like.

Donna walked in and found him waiting for her at the bar just off the small foyer.

His eyes lit up when he saw her, and he smiled like he'd just found out he'd won the lottery. It wasn't a bad way to be greeted. Certainly better than any greeting she'd gotten from Joe in the last decade.

Pierce held out his hands to her. "You look like a goddess. But then, you are one."

She smiled and took his hands, her small clutch tucked under one arm. "That's very kind of you. You look very handsome yourself." He did too. She knew suits, and the one he was wearing was no doubt custom-made and expensive.

He leaned in and kissed her cheek. "Thank you, my queen."

In that moment, she panicked a little, thinking there was no way he'd represent her once he found out she wasn't the perfect vampire he imagined her to be. After all, she'd broken one of the most sacred rules of her kind. Would that shatter Pierce's image of her? It seemed highly possible.

When he pulled back, he frowned as he looked at her. "I've made you unhappy. I shouldn't have kissed you without permission."

"No, that was fine."

"Then please, tell me what I did to upset you. I'll make it right, I promise."

She forced a little smile. "It's not you, Pierce. You're

perfect, I swear. I just…I need to talk to you about something. Could we go to our table?" He was less likely to make a scene when they were seated in the restaurant with other people around. But then Pierce didn't strike her as the type of man who'd make a scene at all. He was far too suave for that.

"Of course." He let go of her hands to speak to the maître d'.

Moments later, they were ushered in and seated at a quiet half-circle booth in the far corner. Easily one of the best tables in the place. Under different circumstances, Donna thought she would be looking forward to enjoying the evening immensely.

Right now, she had no idea how things were going to turn out, and that tension kept her from sinking into the experience.

Sad, because she couldn't remember when she'd been out like this with Joe. When they went out, it was always to the same nice, but local places where Joe could be assured the meal, or at least a bottle of wine, would be comped, and he'd be treated like royalty, which basically meant a lot of fake compliments and fawning service.

She'd grown to hate those meals.

No one here seemed to know who she was. Pierce, yes. But she might as well have been any other woman in Manhattan.

It was bliss.

Pierce took the wine list from the server, then politely dismissed the man and turned his attention to her. "What's going on? You seem distraught."

She nodded. "I am. I'm...in trouble. And I need your help."

"Anything." He put the wine list down. "Just tell me what I can do."

She took a breath and looked him straight in the eyes. "Defend me."

For a moment, he didn't say anything. Then he smiled. "Are you teasing me?"

"No, I'm dead serious. I want to hire you." She lowered her voice, the air in her lungs as thick as mud. She felt like she might suffocate before she got the words out. "I'm about to be put on trial before the vampire council. And if I'm not cleared, they will put me to death."

His face fell. "What? I cannot allow that. Of course I'll defend you. What are you accused of doing?"

She closed her eyes for a moment. This was it. The moment in which he'd either turn on her or be supportive. "Killing the first human I drank from."

"Breaking the tether with a sire is serious." She wasn't sure what surprised her more—that he knew the consequences of what she'd done or the degree of detachment with which he'd answered. "Did you do what you're being accused of?"

"Yes. But it wasn't intentional."

"The hunger took over?"

"That and self-defense." She was able to breathe again. His understanding of things was a welcome relief. "So you'll do it?"

He frowned like she was silly to think otherwise. "Not only will I do it, I'll win your case."

His bravado was kind, but she couldn't let herself be swept up in it. She had to be realistic about this. "Have you ever done anything like this before?"

"I once defended a vampire in human court, but that's as close as I've come."

"Then why do you seem so certain you can do this?"

He took her hands in his. "I realize you know very little about me, but I am undefeated as an attorney. The vampire council may have some different rules and regulations but arguing is arguing. We'll put a case together that they cannot deny. When is this trial?"

She frowned. "Tuesday."

His brows rose. "That doesn't give us much time."

"I know. Would you like to come stay with me until then?" The words were out of her mouth before she truly considered them. But it would make things easier. "If it's convenient for you, of course."

The light in his eyes was unmistakably joyous. "That would certainly give us more time together."

"Can you afford to put so much time into this case? I mean, you must already have cases you're working on that require your attention."

"I'll adjust things. This is more important. And with such a short deadline, giving it first priority is the only way to be sure I can present the best defense possible."

"Thank you." She squeezed his hand. "I do have a few people already willing to testify on my behalf."

"Excellent. We have a lot of work to do, but that will help."

She smiled, a real smile this time. "I cannot tell you

how much this means to me. There is one other thing I need legal help with, however."

"What's that?"

She held his hand, clinging to the connection as the reality of what she was about to ask sank in. "I need a will."

She expected him to argue. Instead, he nodded. "That's wise. It's not my area, but we can certainly draw something up that will do the trick." Then he leaned in, smiling. "You're not going to need it, though."

"Thank you. I hope you're right. I just want to be prepared."

"I understand. You must have been so worried about all of this."

"I was. Still am. Not as much now, though, thanks to you. I don't feel like I'm alone in it now, you know?"

"I understand." He brought her hand to his mouth and kissed her knuckles. "And I am honored you came to me."

"I owe Neo for taking me to Redline, or I never would have met you."

He smiled. "What do you say we get a great bottle of wine and celebrate our new partnership?"

She nodded. "A drink sounds wonderful."

He'd barely raised his hand when their server reappeared. Pierce ordered, then they were alone again. "We should start tonight on preparations."

"I'm all for that. We can work around the clock if need be."

"We might have to."

Whatever it took to keep her alive, she was in. "I

should have asked already, but how much do you need for a retainer?"

He shook his head. "I'm not charging you for this."

"Pierce." She tipped her head the same way she might when one of her children misbehaved. "You can't do this for free."

"With all due respect, I can do whatever I like. And I'm not charging you."

She studied him for a moment. "Is this because you want to become my assistant?"

His eyes twinkled. "I wouldn't turn down that offer."

"Would you really give up your career for that life?"

"I would. Does that surprise you?"

"Very much so. Have you ever been an assistant to a vampire?"

He hesitated, his expression taking on a wistful look that matched the faraway gaze in his eyes. "I was, yes."

"Why aren't you still? If I can ask that."

"It's a fair question. And...he chose a different path."

"He?" Donna's brows went up. "I wasn't expecting that. Not that it matters. So you're—"

"No. The 'he' in question was my brother."

That explained why Pierce knew so much about vampires. "Ah. Did you have a falling out, then, since you're not assisting him now?"

Pierce shook his head, his gaze shifting downward. "No. He was reckless. Wouldn't let me help him the way he should. He was out too late. Didn't make it home before sunrise and couldn't find shelter in time."

He looked away, but the pain in his eyes was clear.

"That was just his way. Always pushing things right to the edge. Vampires like that don't last long."

"Neither do people." She touched his hand. "I'm so sorry."

He smiled and met her eyes again. "What's past is past, right? Anyway, you gave up your life to become a vampire, so why shouldn't someone give up theirs to be your assistant?"

"Not on purpose, I didn't." She sighed. "Let me explain…"

Two hours later, they'd had a wonderful meal, two amazing bottles of wine, and some of the best conversation she'd ever had. Pierce not only listened to her, he was interested in what she had to say. That felt like a revelation of what could be.

She wanted more of it. More of him. More of this kind of life that was carefree and overflowing with peace and happiness. She dearly hoped the council would find her innocent. Life with a companion like Pierce would be a lot of fun.

He called the car service for her right before they left the table. Then he stood with her in the foyer, waiting for it to arrive. "I'll go to my place, pack a bag, and then come to your house. All right?"

"Perfect. Thank you. I can't say I'm looking forward to this, but I am so glad you're helping me. I'd be lost without you right now."

"This is going to be difficult, but it's nothing I can't handle." The car arrived. He gave her a quick smile and went to open the door for her. "Try not to worry, all right?"

She nodded. "I'll do my best. See you in an hour or so?" She'd already given him her address.

"Yes."

This time, she leaned in and kissed him on the cheek. "Thanks again, Pierce."

"My pleasure."

True to his word, he arrived at her home an hour later with his computer bag, a small suitcase, and a bottle of wine. He'd changed into jeans and a sweater. It was the first time she'd seen him looking casual, and she liked it. He handed her the bottle. "Thank you for this opportunity to be of service to you."

She took the wine. It was easily an eighty-dollar bottle, but then she realized Pierce was all about impressing her. It was sweet, really. "Please, I'm the one who needs to be thanking you. Come on, I'll show you to your room."

She took him to the first-floor guest room. "I hope this is all right."

"It's perfect. Your house is beautiful." He put his suitcase next to the bed, then pulled his laptop from his computer bag.

"Thank you." She glanced at the laptop. "I guess we should get to work."

He nodded, suddenly all business. "The sooner, the better."

CHAPTER 33

Hours later, when dawn approached and Donna's eyes were barely staying open, Pierce shook his head. "That's enough for now."

She straightened. She'd been sitting sideways on the couch, facing Pierce, who was one cushion away, but she'd slumped down a good bit. "No, I can keep going."

"No, you can't. You need to sleep." He glanced at his screen, the glow lighting up his face. "I have research and writing to do anyway."

Reluctantly, she nodded. She was pretty worn out. "All right. But I should feed you, shouldn't I?"

He shook his head without looking up. "I know where the kitchen is. I can make my own breakfast when I'm hungry. I want to work on this—"

"I didn't mean breakfast."

His head came up. "Oh."

When he didn't say anything more, she nudged him. "It would help, wouldn't it? Gives you strength and speed and stamina?"

He stayed very still. "It would, yes."

"All right, then." She called down her fangs and nipped her wrist, then offered it to him.

He took it and drank. He was gentle and ended it quickly, releasing her wrist and closing his eyes.

The small, twin punctures healed immediately. "Are you all right?"

He nodded, eyes still closed. "Just feeling the power go through me." Then he added, "Thank you."

"You're welcome." She stood. "I'll see you in a few hours."

He opened his eyes. They were brighter and clearer than she remembered, and he seemed suddenly younger. If that was her blood at work, it was amazing. But then, she'd seen how the change had affected her. "Sleep well."

"Thanks." She went upstairs and fell asleep almost instantly.

"Donna?"

She pulled the covers up higher against the voice in her dream.

"Donna, I'm sorry to wake you, but—"

"What?" She squinted, still not fully aware if she was dreaming or what. "Pierce?" He was standing a few feet from the bed, brows bent, mouth in a frustrated frown.

"There's a woman at the door who claims to be your sister, but she's dressed like a nun, so—"

Donna bolted upright. "Crap. Cammie. What time is it?"

"Going on eleven. Do you know her? Or should I send her away?"

"No, she's really my sister. I just didn't know she was coming." Donna grabbed her phone off the nightstand. A text from Cammie had come in at six a.m. to let Donna know she was going to stop by. "Let her in. I'll be down as soon as I can."

"All right."

As he left, Donna jumped out of bed. She'd thought Cammie would just call, but she must have had the time and decided to swing by instead. Obviously.

Donna ran a brush through her hair, then pulled on leggings and a big sweatshirt and went downstairs.

Cammie was sitting at the kitchen island with a cup of coffee. Donna already knew by the tilt of her sister's head that Cammie had questions.

She started with the first one as soon as Donna entered the room. "Why did a strange man answer your door?"

"He's not a strange man. He's a friend and an attorney." Donna really needed coffee. And blood. But that last one was going to have to wait. She took a cup out of the cabinet and went right to the Keurig.

"Okay, but then why was he awake while you're sleeping? Are you sick? He didn't say anything about you being sick. And you look fine. Amazing, actually. But a little sleepy."

"Cam, hit pause." Donna turned and smiled at her sister. "I have to tell you something before we go any further."

Cammie's brows went up, but she didn't say another word.

Donna took a breath. This was one of those rip-the-Band-Aid-off moments. Best to just jump in and get it over with. "The day after Joe's funeral, I went to the cemetery to have a few last words with him, and I was attacked. There's a lot more to it than that, but the upshot is, I was turned into a vampire that night."

Cammie was silent long enough that she blinked twice before speaking again. "The day after Joe's funeral?"

"The night after. But yes." Donna figured her sister was in shock if that's what she was focused on.

"But you went into the chapel the day you came to see me. Which was the next day." She shook her head. "That shouldn't have been possible. Forget the fact that you visited during the day, the chapel is holy ground. You didn't even smell like smoke."

Donna's mouth fell open. "I just told you I'm a vampire, and all you want to know is how I entered the chapel without bursting into flames?"

Cammie's head went into a full-on side tilt. "Belladonna, I work for the church. Do you really think we're blind to the truths of this world? Where do you think the best hunters come from?"

"What?"

Cammie sighed and shook her head. "I have to tell the mother superior. I'm not sure what she's going to say about this."

"Hold up a second. You know about vampires. And now you have to report me?"

"Not you, exactly, but that there's a vampire in my family. It's policy." She put her hand to her head. "I'm sorry. I haven't even asked you how you're doing with all this. You do look great, by the way. I'm sure that part of the change has been fun, huh?"

Donna shrugged slightly. "That part has been nice,

yes, but the rest of it...not so much. It's been hard. Not exactly the life I saw for myself, you know?"

"I'm sure."

"I can't believe you already knew about vampires." The Keurig sputtered as it finished brewing Donna's coffee. "Even so, there's more I need to tell you."

"Oh?" Cammie sipped her coffee.

"I did something I wasn't supposed to. It was an accident, but because of it, I'm being put on trial before the vampire council."

Cammie grimaced. "The Immortus Concilio? They're pretty tough, from what I hear."

Everyone knew more about being a vampire than Donna did. But really, all this time she'd needed to talk to Claudette and really, she'd just needed to talk to her sister. The nun. Life was crazy. "Yes. That's why Pierce is here."

"Is he going to be your assistant?" A brightness came into Cammie's eyes. "He certainly isn't hard to look at."

"Maybe. I don't know yet. If I don't win my case, it won't matter." Donna stared at her bare toes. Her pedicure still looked good. At least she'd die with nice-looking feet.

"Because?"

Donna lifted her head. "Because I won't be around anymore. If I'm found guilty, the punishment is death."

"What? No." Cammie got to her feet and charged out of the kitchen. "Hello? Mr. Attorney?"

Donna went after her and found her and Pierce in

the living room. He had his laptop open on the couch beside him.

Cammie stood in front of him. "You're my sister's lawyer? Representing her before the Immortus Concilio?"

"I am." He stood.

"How sure are you that you can keep her from being put to death?"

"Very." He glanced at Donna. "There are no guarantees, but I haven't lost a case yet."

"Would it help to have a nun as a character witness?"

Donna shook her head. "Cammie, that's sweet of you to offer, but it might not be a good idea. What would the mother superior say?"

Cammie looked at Donna. "They might kick me out anyway, just by having a vampire sister. Might as well get the most out of being a nun while I can."

Pierce cleared his throat. "You know the council has always had a tenuous relationship with the church."

"I'm aware," Cammie said as she folded her arms. "But a nun willing to testify on behalf of a vampire? That ought to carry some weight."

He hesitated. "Yes, it should. Although some of that weight is alleviated by you being related."

"Even so, if it will help, I'm in."

He nodded. "Good, good." He stuck his hand out. "I'm Pierce Harrison, by the way."

She shook his hand. "Sister Mary Lazarus Immaculata. But you can call me Cammie. I might be reverting to that anyway, depending on how things go."

"Cammie," Donna started.

Cammie turned. "Look, if the church doesn't want me because of you, then I don't want them. If they're good with it, then I'm that much happier to stay. It's all up to them."

Donna took her sister's hand. "I love you, you know."

"I know. And I love you too."

Pierce sat down and took up his laptop. "We might as well work on your statement, Cammie. Donna has a few other people who are willing to give character references, but since you're here, we can get this done now."

Cammie took a seat across from him. "Absolutely. When's the trial, by the way? You're acting like it's any day now."

"Because it is." Pierce put his hand on the top of the laptop. "Tuesday evening."

"That's two days from now." Cammie looked at Donna. "Why didn't you call me sooner?"

"I just found out." Donna put her hands up. "I need my coffee."

"You need sleep," Pierce said. "You've only had a few hours. You're too young a vampire to survive on so little sleep. Trust me, it won't be enough to see you through the day. Go back to bed. Your sister and I can get our work done while you catch up."

Donna glanced at Cammie.

She nodded. "Go. There's no point in you getting run-down."

"Okay. But don't leave without saying goodbye. Even if that means waking me."

"Promise." Cammie gave her a soft smile, her sisterly gaze shifting. "I like that you're still wearing the crucifix I gave you. You know I got that when I was in Rome. Even had it blessed by the Holy Father."

"Did you?" Was that why it gave Donna such protection? Her hand went to it. "I have no intention of taking it off. Ever. You have no idea how important it is to me."

CHAPTER 34

The next two days passed in a whirlwind of work, work, legal forms, and more work. Pierce assured Donna that they were as prepared as possible, given the short time frame. She clung to that, because doubt had settled over her like a dark cloud.

The Immortus Concilio was no joke. The very fact that they existed and wielded enough power to condemn her to death meant she might have little chance of proving her innocence. After all, it was her word against Claudette's. Who were they going to believe? A newly turned vampire, or one who was three hundred years old and the child of the Queen of North America?

At least her will was done, and Cammie was prepared to act as executor. Donna had told her about the safe-deposit box too. But the injustice of it all weighed on Donna. For Pierce's sake, and for Cammie's, Donna kept her spirits up.

Rico had given them his time, too, going over his testimony and providing a copy of Yuri's file, which he'd graciously turned over to Pierce.

During the day, Pierce worked tirelessly on the

case, organizing testimonies and preparing everything necessary for Donna's defense.

During the evening, he kept her company, and they worked on the case together, but by midnight, she made him go to bed. He was human after all, and she needed him sharp.

Once she was left alone, however, the doubt circled her like a hungry vulture. She spent hours trying to numb herself by watching television or getting lost in a book, but the metaphorical sound of time ticking down made concentrating on anything but the trial impossible.

The hours were both dreadfully long and woefully short. And yet, somehow, they passed until, a few minutes after sundown on Tuesday evening, a sleek black sedan pulled up outside Donna's house.

Artemis had returned. This was real. There was no turning back. No escaping the inevitable.

Donna let her in and introduced her to Pierce, Cammie, and Rico. Willpower alone kept Donna going. If she stopped for a moment and focused on what was about to happen, she thought she might run off into the night and never look back.

Even if the darkness beyond her property line was filled with fae.

Artemis greeted Pierce, Cammie, and Rico with a nod and a smile, never once saying a word about there being a nun in Donna's house. Instead, she moved into preparation mode, turning to her two assistants, who'd come into the house with her this time. "Florian, Heath, set up the equipment."

SUCKS TO BE ME

They went to work, opening the two aluminum cases they'd brought in.

Donna was about to ask if they needed an extension cord or anything, when her doorbell rang. Pierce looked at her, but she shook her head. "I'll get it."

She didn't bother looking through the peephole, just opened the door, expecting to see Claudette.

Neo, Francine, and Bunni stood on the porch, smiling at her. Neo gave her a wink. "Your character-reference team, ready and willing."

Donna put a hand to her heart, caught off guard by the unexpected support. "Wow. You all came."

Francine hitched her purse up higher on her shoulder. "Honey, we aren't about to let you go through this alone."

"Yeah," Bunni said. "Plus, I was dying to see a real Mafia house."

Neo rolled her eyes. "Don't be so low-rent."

"Girls," Francine warned. "We're here for Donna."

"Please," Donna said. "Come in. And thank you."

Artemis caught her eye as the First Fangs Club trooped in. "Quite a group of friends you have there."

"I know, right?" Donna grinned. The presence of her new friends had given her spirits an unexpected boost. "And the word is 'squad.'"

"Squad?" Artemis frowned.

"That's what the kids say these days." Donna walked over to her. "By the way, after you left the other night, a fae showed up. Told me he—or she—isn't interested in me. They wanted 'the old one.' Which I assume is you."

Artemis nodded. "I'm sure they meant me. The

more powerful the vampire, the more sustenance they gain. You would provide them with very little. Not to worry, I have three of my personal guards outside patrolling."

"Hold on. Sustenance? As in food source?"

"In a way. What vampire blood does for a human, it does tenfold for the fae. There are fae known as harvesters, like the one you met, who do nothing but hunt our kind and sell our blood to the highest bidder."

Donna stared, aghast. "Holy communion. You're just telling me this now?"

The sparks in her eyes flared brighter. "You should know all this already. That is Claudette's job."

"Oh. Speaking of Claudette, she's supposed to be here, right?"

"Yes. The hearing begins at midnight. She still has time."

"So do we, then." She looked for Pierce. He was talking to Neo, who seemed to be introducing him to Bunni and Francine. "I should let my attorney know that. I wasn't sure of the start time."

"Do what you need to. You don't need to babysit me. I have to make sure everything is ready for the trial on my end anyway."

"Okay. Thank you. There's blood in the fridge if you want it. A fresh order arrived yesterday."

"I do, thank you." Artemis headed for the kitchen.

Donna went over to Pierce, touching his arm to interrupt. "We have until midnight, so if you want to work with Neo, Bunni, and Francine, there's time."

He nodded. "Perfect. Ladies, why don't you follow me into the dining room?"

As the four of them disappeared, Rico came up to her. "How are you doing?"

She smiled, but let it go immediately. "I feel a little better that my new friends showed up, but..." She sighed and shook her head. "This is the hardest thing I've ever faced."

"You spent twenty-seven years surviving marriage to one of the most notorious criminals I've ever gone after. I'd say that was pretty hard."

"But this is life and death."

"And being married to Joe wasn't?"

She blew out a breath. "I get what you're saying, but this feels so much more immediate."

"I understand that. Listen, I've testified in court many times. My best advice is tell the truth, stay calm, and never answer in absolutes."

"Thank you. I'll do my best. Pierce has gone over every possible question we could come up with, so I feel pretty prepared. I just don't know if I really have a chance."

"I think you have more of a chance than you realize."

"Why's that?"

He shrugged, a little smile playing on his lips. "I don't want to make myself sound more important than I am, but I don't think the council would want it getting back to pack leaders that they run their trials in a manner that's less than aboveboard."

Donna let that sink in. "Wow. I hadn't thought

about that. But it makes sense." She grabbed his arm. "I am so glad you're here. Not that I wasn't already, but that really makes me feel better."

Impulsively, she leaned in and kissed his cheek. He turned his head at the same time, and her mouth landed on his.

The spark of desire went through her the second she made contact. She pulled back, a little breathless. "Sorry, I didn't mean—"

Rico's smile was slow and easy. He pressed his mouth to hers. This time, she was too stunned to react, and it was over quickly. "I know what you meant to do. I wish things could be different, but until the Villachi case is closed, you're off-limits to me. You know that, right?"

She nodded, still dumbstruck.

"Good." He glanced at the front of the house. "Car."

She heard it then, too, the soft squeak of rubber on asphalt, the hum of a motor. She turned toward the door, glad for the distraction, because kissing Rico wasn't something she needed to be thinking about right now. "I hope that's Claudette."

"No, you don't."

She looked at him. "I don't?"

"Think about it. Her failing to show up helps your case."

"I guess that's true. But it means she'd be a fugitive."

"Not your problem. She decides to ghost the council, that's on her."

Knocking brought Donna's head around again. "I think she'll show."

"We'll see."

She answered the door. "Hello, Claudette."

The woman had the nerve to look put out. "Donna."

A man stood behind her, another vampire. Looked like he'd been around thirty-five or forty when he'd been turned. It was hard to tell with the effects the change had on people.

Donna looked at him. "Are you her assistant?"

"Deputy." Which meant his job was on the line, too, Donna imagined. "Marcus. Nice to meet you. Governor, I'll be out here if you need me."

Claudette lifted her hand to dismiss him.

Donna didn't have much else to say to him. She just moved out of the way to let Claudette in. "Artemis is in the kitchen."

Claudette stiffened a little. "I saw her car. And her security. Trouble with the fae?"

"Not yet." Donna closed the door after her, but not before taking one quick peek outside. A woman with short black hair and a sword strapped to her back stood at the end of the driveway.

The neighbors would think that was perfectly normal.

With a shake of her head, Donna went back to the living room. Claudette had gone to the kitchen. Maybe to check in with Artemis.

Florian and Heath were testing the system they'd set up. She'd never seen technology like it before. A slim black cylinder projected a video image roughly the size of a big flat-screen television. At the moment, it showed a beach scene with gently rolling waves and swaying palms.

Unfortunately, that peaceful scene would be replaced with the council in a few hours.

A few hours later, she was proven right.

She'd dressed for the occasion in black trousers, a superbly cut jacket, and a silk blouse of burgundy silk. Diamond studs, but she wore no other jewelry beyond her ever-present crucifix, unless you counted the ornate gold broaches adorning the toes of her Dolce & Gabbana pumps.

The council was on the screen now. All seven members were in shadow, seated at a long table against a wall draped in dark fabric. They could have been anywhere. And been anyone. She could make out shapes, tell who was male, who was female, but that was it. She supposed some level of anonymity was necessary, but it felt desperately unfair not to see the faces of those who held her life in their hands.

One of the female members, seated in the middle, banged a gavel on the table. "This trial is now called to order. Are all parties present?"

Artemis stood beside Donna. "Yes, all parties are present."

"Thank you, Artemis."

Artemis nodded and sat down on one of the chairs near the fireplace, leaving Donna alone in front of the council, which was how Artemis had said things would begin.

The female council member continued. "You are Belladonna Barrone, the accused?"

"I am," Donna answered.

"Where is Claudette Martine?"

Claudette stepped forward. "Here, Your Honor."

"You reported this child of yours cut her tether with you by draining to death the first human she drank from?"

Claudette kept her eyes straight ahead. "I did, Your Honor."

"Do you, Belladonna, understand what you're being accused of?"

"I do, Your Honor."

"Then how do you plead?"

Donna took a breath, catching Pierce nodding out of the corner of her eye. "Not guilty, Your Honor, which my attorney will prove, but I also accuse my sire, Claudette Martine, of neglect, something else my attorney will prove."

"What?" Claudette screeched.

The councilwoman ignored Claudette. "You have an attorney?"

"I do, Your Honor."

The council members spoke amongst themselves for a moment, then the leader spoke again. "We will allow it, as well as the counter suit. The trial shall proceed."

353

CHAPTER 35

"You can't do that," Claudette growled.

The councilwoman banged the gavel. "Order. It is well within the accused's right to make a counterclaim. Belladonna, please present your attorney."

Pierce came to stand beside her. He looked every inch the professional in a dark suit and power tie.

Donna introduced him. "My attorney, Pierce Harrison."

Pierce nodded.

The councilwoman seemed unimpressed. "You are human?"

"I am, but I have known about vampires most of my adult life. My brother was a vampire."

"I see." Her tone changed slightly, but not enough to keep Donna from being worried. "Please present your argument."

"Thank you, Your Honor. I would first like to call Rico Medina as a character witness for Ms. Barrone."

"A character witness?" The councilwoman shook her head. "This is highly unusual."

"Your Honor," Pierce began, "Ms. Barrone's life is at stake. I see no reason not to make the council aware of her stellar character and upstanding nature."

The councilwoman seemed to frown. "I suppose we must allow it. After this witness, you will present your case?"

"After him and the other four character witnesses who have come to speak on Ms. Barrone's behalf. I also have a letter from a respected physician attesting to Ms. Barrone's outstanding character."

The councilwoman hesitated. "You have five witnesses and a letter."

It wasn't a question, but Pierce answered anyway. "Yes, Your Honor. Three vampires, one werewolf—Mr. Medina, who is also a special agent in the United States Federal Bureau of Investigation—and Sister Mary Lazarus Immaculata of the Sisters of the Holy Rosary."

The councilwoman seemed flummoxed. "The accused has a *nun* as a character witness."

Again, not a question. But again, Pierce answered. "Yes, Your Honor."

"One moment." The councilwoman conferred with the rest of the council, and Donna realized they'd put themselves on mute. Minutes ticked by.

Claudette scowled at no one in particular. Maybe at all of them. "I was just doing my duty as sire when I reported what you did. You told me you killed that man. What was I supposed to do?"

Artemis answered before Donna could say a word. "We are allowed to make our own judgments based on the circumstances. A lost tether is a serious matter. As is the gaining of unusual or extraordinary powers, but I don't find Donna to be a danger, nor do I think she will become one. Things I believe you would have known if you had taken a more active role as her sire."

Claudette frowned, but was prevented from responding by the return of the council.

The female spoke again. "We have determined that you shall present your case. Once we've heard it, we will decide if the character witnesses are necessary."

That wasn't exactly fair, but at least it meant the positive things Donna's friends had to say would be the last things the council heard about her before deciding her fate. That actually didn't seem so bad.

Pierce nodded. "Then let me begin."

Twenty minutes later, Pierce concluded. He'd perfectly mapped out Donna's human life and how she feared the dangerous men her husband had dealt with, how she'd been abandoned by Claudette, how she'd struggled to learn the elementary steps of becoming a vampire, and how the lack of support from her sire had led her unwittingly down a dark path.

Donna wished she could have clapped. He was brilliant, and she understood perfectly why he'd never been defeated. He'd somehow made the fact that they were even gathered for this trial seem foolish.

The councilwoman spoke again. "And now the secondary accused may speak. Claudette?"

She stood again, coming to face the council. She shook her head. "I didn't mean to leave Donna alone for so long. She really didn't seem to want me around, and my last child had gone rogue, so—"

"Then you admit there was neglect."

Claudette's entire body slumped. She looked beaten. Donna felt for her. "Yes."

Soft whispering filtered through from the council side, then the councilwoman spoke. "We find Belladonna Barrone not guilty. We find Claudette Martine guilty. The trial is over. Belladonna is free to go. Claudette is sentenced to death."

Claudette fell to her knees, a desperate cry ripping out of her.

Donna's mouth came open as the gavel banged the table. "Wait."

"Yes?" The councilwoman paused.

"Do I now take over Claudette's position as governor?"

"Yes, but Artemis will swear you in."

"I want it done now. In front of the council and before Claudette's sentence is carried out."

"That is highly unusual."

Donna's heart was pounding. "Please, Your Honor."

"Fine. We will grant it."

Artemis joined them. "Raise your right hand."

Donna lifted her hand. Claudette was sobbing softly where she lay on the floor.

"Do you swear to abide by the laws of the Immortus Concilio, to uphold them as ordered, and to obey the edicts of your queen?"

"I do."

"Then I hereby pronounce you vampire governor of the state of New Jersey."

Donna put her hand down. "Is that it?"

"That's it," Artemis said. "You're governor."

"Perfect, thanks." Donna turned to face the council. "As my first act as governor, I pardon Claudette Martine."

Claudette gasped and looked at Donna. "You would do that for me?"

Donna nodded but said nothing. The council members had muted themselves again.

All she could see were heads bent in conversation. After a moment, the councilwoman came back to them. "Such mercy is unusual in our world. Perhaps it is merely a holdover from your human life, but we hope it is a sign of the kind of governor you will be. We will grant the pardon, but a second leniency will not be allowed."

Donna smiled. "Thank you. I'm sure Claudette understands that."

"I do," Claudette called out.

"Be well, Governor Barrone."

"And you, councilwoman."

The image of the rolling waves returned, and a collective sigh filled the room as if everyone had just released the breath they'd been holding.

Florian and Heath started packing up the equipment.

"That was freaking amazing," Neo said. "I can't believe I'm friends with the governor."

Donna laughed, but a few tears fell as well. "Crazy, right?"

"Congratulations." Pierce looked as if he wanted to hug her.

Donna shook her head. "You were the amazing one,

Pierce."

"You really were," Francine said.

He smiled. "Thank you. Just doing what I was hired to do."

Artemis approached Claudette, who was still sitting on the floor, apparently in shock. "Let this be a reckoning for you, child."

"Yes, sire." Claudette nodded hard. "It definitely is."

Artemis glanced back at Donna. "I will be back tomorrow at sundown to show you the governor's residence and turn over the keys. We'll set everything else up then too."

"Everything else?" Also, a residence?

"Your salary, for one. Plus, you'll need to meet your assistants, your secretary, and your driver."

"I...okay." It was a lot to take in. Almost too much. "Tomorrow night."

"Until then." Artemis left, Florian and Heath following behind with their aluminum cases.

Cammie got up and hugged Donna and whispered in her ear, "I'm so glad I don't have to be the executor of your will."

"Me too." Donna laughed softly even as she sniffed back a sob. "Thank you for being here."

Cammie let go and smoothed her habit. "I might be here a lot more, depending on what the church decides. They're supposed to tell me tomorrow."

"You always have a home here."

"Well, for now I need to get a taxi back to the convent. Love you, Sis."

"Love you, Sis."

KRISTEN PAINTER

Rico had his keys in his hand. "Would you like a ride? I go right by there."

"That would be kind of you. Thank you."

Rico nodded. "Happy to do it." He waved to Donna. "Glad it all worked out. I'll be in touch."

She waved back. "Thank you for coming and for all your help."

As he and Cammie left, Claudette approached Donna. "I owe you my life."

Donna wasn't going to casually brush that off. "Yes, you do. But in a way, I owe you mine as well. You saved me in the cemetery and your help with Big Tony was huge. I appreciate both of those things. Just please, don't mistake my mercy now for weakness. You didn't deserve to die for being a bad sire but coming after me in an attempt to get your position back will not end well. Do you understand me?"

She nodded. "I do. And I'm not going to try to take it back. I wasn't very good at being governor. I really think I'm going to get out of here. Maybe go to Europe for a bit. I don't know. But I promise I'm not going to cause you any more trouble. I owe you too much to do that."

"Yes, you do."

Claudette nodded. "Thank you again. If you ever need anything from me, you have my number."

"I do. Be well."

She went outside, reminding Donna very much of a scolded dog.

Francine, who'd been sitting on the couch with Neo and Bunni, raised her eyebrows. "Boy, you sure came

360

out on top." She got up and walked over. "Tell you what. Next week, I'm throwing you a big party at my place to celebrate."

"You don't have to go to all that trouble," Donna said.

"Trouble? Honey, I'm about to show off to all my friends that I'm besties with the governor." She laughed. "You just show up and look pretty." She patted Pierce's arm. "And bring this tall drink of water."

Donna snorted and looked at Pierce. "Would you like to go?"

"I would love to."

Donna nodded at Francine. "We'll be there." Then she glanced at Bunni and Neo. "Thank you all for coming. Really means a lot to me that you were so ready to stand up for me."

Neo shrugged. "We newbies gotta stick together."

She and Bunni joined Francine. "Yeah," Bunni said. "Plus, if Sergio knew I was in Joe Barrone's house, he'd lose it. In fact, I might even text him. Not that he'll believe me."

"Why don't you go down that hall and into Joe's office and take a selfie to send to Sergio?"

Bunni's eyes widened. "For real?"

"For real."

As Bunni tottered off on her stilettos, Donna took a long, deep breath and looked at Pierce. "I can't believe I'm governor."

He smiled. "You're going to be great. You are going to need an assistant, however."

"I thought I already had one."

His smile widened. "You do."

Neo nudged Francine. "Come on, we can't let Bunni be the only one with a selfie in the Mafia guy's office, or we'll never hear the end of it."

"You're right," Francine said.

The two took off down the hall.

Donna slipped her hand into Pierce's. "You saved my life tonight. There's no way to repay you for that."

"I meant it when I said I was doing my job."

"Well, you did it extraordinarily. Thank you."

He kissed the back of her hand. "You're welcome, my queen."

"You're really going to make space in your career to be my assistant?"

He nodded. "I am. But I have to ask you something. And I want an honest answer."

"Okay." She owed him that much.

"Could you see me as more than your assistant? I'm talking someday in the future. Not tomorrow."

The question gave her a moment of pause. She liked Pierce a lot. But she also liked Rico. Or was that just some kind of cross-species attraction? She didn't know. And she was done trying to figure things out, at least for a day or two. "I think I could. Someday in the future. But right now? You need to know that my life is beyond complicated. I'm not ready to add a romantic relationship to the chaos I'm dealing with. But I do like you. A lot. Not just because you saved my life either. I think being friends would be perfect for me right now."

His smile remained. "I'm okay with that. I'm okay with anything that involves getting to spend more time with you. Even if it's because of the chaos in your life, some of which I have a feeling might require a lawyer."

She laughed. "You're not wrong there."

He tugged on her hand. "Well, Madam Governor, how about I draw you a hot bath and pour you a big glass of whatever you'd like? Then make sure your friends are safely on their way home? I'll even get Lucky his dinner."

"A bath...just for me, right?"

He laughed. "Just for you."

Her grin felt permanent, a nice change after the couple of weeks she'd had. She nodded and let him lead her toward the stairs. "I think I could get used to this."

"Being governor? Or being a vampire?"

"Both." As well as having a man around who genuinely wanted to look after her, but she'd keep that to herself for now. Although she might tell him to tone down the goddess stuff. Eventually.

"Good, because it's nice to see you smile."

"It's nice to be able to smile." She meant it too. Despite everything going on, she was somehow happy. Her problems still existed, but she'd worry about them tomorrow.

Tonight, she was just going to enjoy her life. Because, for once in a long time, it didn't suck to be her.

THANKS FOR READING!

WANT TO BE UP TO DATE ON NEW BOOKS, NEW AUDIOBOOKS & OTHER FUN STUFF FROM ME?

Sign-up for my NEWSLETTER (http://bit.ly/1kkLgHi). **No spam, just news (sales, freebies, releases, you know, all that jazz.)**

If you loved the book and want to help the series grow, tell a friend about the book and take time to leave a review!

ABOUT THE AUTHOR

USA Today Best Selling Author Kristen Painter is a little obsessed with cats, books, chocolate, and shoes. It's a healthy mix. She loves to entertain her readers with interesting twists and unforgettable characters. She currently writes the best-selling paranormal romance series, Nocturne Falls, and award-winning urban fantasy. The former college English teacher can often be found all over social media where she loves to interact with readers.

For more information go to www.kristenpainter.com

For More Paranormal Women's Fiction Visit:
www.paranormalwomensfiction.net

OTHER BOOKS BY KRISTEN PAINTER

PARANORMAL WOMEN'S FICTION

First Fangs Club Series:

Sucks To Be Me

Suck It Up Buttercup

Sucker Punch

The Suck Stops Here

Embrace The Suck

COZY MYSTERY:

Jayne Frost Series:

Miss Frost Solves A Cold Case: A Nocturne Falls Mystery

Miss Frost Ices The Imp: A Nocturne Falls Mystery

Miss Frost Saves The Sandman: A Nocturne Falls Mystery

Miss Frost Cracks A Caper: A Nocturne Falls Mystery

When Birdie Babysat Spider: A Jayne Frost Short

Miss Frost Braves The Blizzard: A Nocturne Falls Mystery

Miss Frost Says I Do: A Nocturne Falls Mystery

HappilyEverlasting Series:

Witchful Thinking

PARANORMAL ROMANCE

Nocturne Falls Series:

The Vampire's Mail Order Bride

The Werewolf Meets His Match

The Gargoyle Gets His Girl

The Professor Woos The Witch

The Witch's Halloween Hero – short story

The Werewolf's Christmas Wish – short story

The Vampire's Fake Fiancée

The Vampire's Valentine Surprise – short story

The Shifter Romances The Writer

The Vampire's True Love Trials – short story

The Vampire's Accidental Wife

The Reaper Rescues The Genie

The Detective Wins The Witch

The Vampire's Priceless Treasure

The Werewolf Dates The Deputy

The Siren Saves The Billionaire

Shadowvale Series:

The Trouble With Witches

The Vampire's Cursed Kiss

The Forgettable Miss French

Moody And The Beast

Her First Taste Of Fire

Sin City Collectors Series

Queen Of Hearts

Dead Man's Hand

Double or Nothing

Standalone Paranormal Romance:

Dark Kiss of the Reaper

Heart of Fire

Recipe for Magic

Miss Bramble and the Leviathan

All Fired Up

URBAN FANTASY

The House of Comarré series:

Forbidden Blood

Blood Rights

Flesh and Blood

Bad Blood

Out For Blood

Last Blood

The Crescent City series:

House of the Rising Sun

City of Eternal Night

Garden of Dreams and Desires

Nothing is completed without an amazing team.

Many thanks to:

Cover design: Janet Holmes
Interior Formating: Gem Promotions
Editor: Joyce Lamb
Copyedits/proofs: Chris Kridler

Made in United States
North Haven, CT
02 May 2022

18823035R00212